THE VOICE ON THE PHONE

"Eddie, someone is after me," Rachel said.

"What do you mean?"

"Someone keeps calling and saying things. Horrible things."

Eddie stared at her wet cheeks, tangled hair, and trembling fingers.

"What does he say?"

"He says he's coming for me," she replied. "He says he's coming to finish what he started."

"What the hell? What does that mean?"

She didn't respond.

"Who's calling you?" he asked. "Do you have any idea?"

"That's why I wanted to talk to you." Rachel appeared sad, yet angry. "I thought you should know. That you deserved to know."

"Who is it, Rachel? Please tell me."

There was another long silence. Then: "Eddie, he sounds like your father. I think it *is* your father."

Eddie's eyes widened in horror. "You're kidding, right?"

"No. I wish I were."

"But he's dead. We saw him die!"

"I know. Trust me, I know."

JAMES KIDMAN

BLACK FIRE

LEISURE BOOKS NEW YORK CITY

LEISURE BOOKS ®

May 2004

Published by

Dorchester Publishing Co., Inc.
200 Madison Avenue
New York, NY 10016

ISBN 0-8439-5327-6

Printed in the United States of America.

BLACK FIRE

ACKNOWLEDGMENTS

For my mother and father . . . This book has traveled many roads, and although the destination was often unknown, you told me to never look back.

And for Kathryn . . . Your fire is the purest color of all, and not a day goes by that I don't wonder why it took me so many years to truly understand what that means. Thank you, with all my heart.

With special thanks to: the Freemans, the Hockers, the Chizmars, Douglas Clegg, Matt Schwartz, Mindy Jarusek, the Laymon family, Tom and Elizabeth Monteleone, Rick Hautala, Christopher Golden, Al Sarrantonio, Gary Braunbeck, Gerard Houarner, Simon Clark, Tom Piccirilli, Del James, Tim Lebbon, Holly Newstein, Brian Keene, Geoff Cooper, Garrett Peck, Rick Smith, Megan Klein, Adam Gonsman, Jeff Miller, Roger Range, Bev Vincent, Austin Dagen, MJ Rose, Kristian Turner, the good people at Waldenbooks in Central Pennsylvania, and everyone at Cemetery Dance Publications and Dorchester Publishing, particularly Richard Chizmar and Don D'Auria, who were willing to take a chance. Without you, none of this would have been possible.

Prologue

Two Weeks After The Showdown
From the Handwritten Account

My Mental Reconstruction of Events Past
by Eddie Farris

The doctors say this will help me heal.

In the days since I awoke from the white haze, the world has been a blur of blinding lights and muffled noises and distorted memories fading in and out of reality, in and out of my dreams and nightmares. Machines beep and hum. Voices carry down the hallway. Somewhere, someone screams for reasons I can only begin to imagine.

I'm trapped in my own little hell.

A personal inferno.

The lights are bright during the day. At night they dim so I can sleep. That's never a problem, although my dreams are haunted by visions of the recent past. Nothing solid. Every moment is like gazing into a broken mirror. Echoes of confusion. Flashes of movement. But those echoes grow louder and the flashes become brighter with each passing night.

I'm eighteen years old, and the doctors say I'll recover from my wounds.

Right now my side aches, as if the bullet is still in there. I feel the burning, like a white-hot knife is being jabbed into my flesh.

The drugs create a fog in my head, but I can't imagine the pain without them. The pain comes in waves, blinding me, branding my mind.

I can't remember much. Not yet.

But I know a way to recover the memories, to rebuild what I once had.

I told the doctors how I can remember what happened, with a little help from them.

I told the doctors I used to write every day.

The act of putting words on paper has helped me through a lot of difficult times. My fears and dreams, spoken through other people's mouths. My fears and dreams, acted through other people's bodies. Nothing real, all fake, all make-believe, yet all reflections of reality.

After some discussion, the doctors have decided it's what I need to do now: I need to write.

My memories are distant and disjointed, but I'll try to make this as coherent as I can.

The doctors tell me to write, so that's what I'll do.

I'll write about the day my life changed forever.

I'll try to explain The Showdown, if I can discover what that really means.

I'll write this down like any other story I've ever dreamed up.

Like any work of fiction that has ever lived inside my mind, and inside my mind only.

What I can't remember, I'll piece together along the way.

I'll pretend it's all make-believe.

But . . .

This is real.

This is what happened.

This is why we had to run.

Why my flesh was torn open.

Why I'm here now.

It's why I'm alive and others are not.

I've lost everything that ever mattered to me.

But I'm going to get it back.

Chapter One

Seven Years After The Showdown

Now: Present Day

At times the fog moved like it was alive.

Or maybe that was just the poet inside of Eddie Farris going a little overboard. But if Eddie could claim to love anything these days, it would probably be the way the fog flowed through the small town of Black Hills some nights like a quiet stream in the woods, gentle and peaceful. There was something so natural and perfect about the movement of the white mist. Many nights he sat by the bedroom window of his apartment watching the world below for hours.

This evening there was no fog, at least not yet.

Eddie raised his gloved hand to block the blinding glare of the setting winter sun. The fat, squashed ball of fire was creeping down behind the low mountains of western Pennsylvania, its orange and red glow painting the valley, making everything blush. The few clouds in the sky were not gray or black, but shades of purple with scarlet hints. The wooded mountains running parallel to the small town were blanketed in snow, and the river to the north was a long, curvy mirror reflecting the vivid colors of the sun, as if the thin layer of ice coating the water were on fire.

Better get going, it's almost show time, Eddie thought, as if the show would begin without him. He looked both ways and quickly crossed Main Street, heading straight for the movie theater that loomed in front of him like a dilapidated tomb.

The Black Hills Theater no longer showed first-run movies, and the building had grown decrepit over the years. Faded paint was flaking off the theater's exterior. The half-dozen display cases where the posters of coming attractions had been exhibited were shattered and empty. Rows of dead fluorescent bulbs were visible through the smashed marquee, a remnant from a bygone era. Most of the flashing lights that bordered the marquee, the doors, and the ticket booth were burned out, although a few still flickered on and off, steadfastly maintaining their duties even though their brethren had perished long ago.

Gene Varley sat on a tall three-legged stool inside the ticket booth. The windows were cleaned whenever his arthritis allowed him the luxury of moving his fingers without lightning bolts of pain, but grime was hardening on the glass as the years claimed their due on both the old man and his building.

"How's life treating ya, Eddie?" Gene waved a wrinkled, liver-spotted hand as his best customer approached the glass partition that isolated the theater owner from the rest of mankind. Gene was dressed in a dark red usher's uniform, the same one he had worn in the 1940s when he was a teenager working in the theater for his father. He wore the uniform every day, from when he awoke in the morning until he went to bed at night. Some people said Gene wasn't quite right in the head. They said the way he dressed and lived in the past was particularly sad, but Eddie liked the uniform. The red pants and jacket helped complete the dreamlike quality of the old-fashioned theater, even if the clothes were tattered and smelled of mildew.

"Same as it always does, Mr. Varley," Eddie replied, his breath turning to fog. The wind gusted, snapping and channeling the freezing air straight into him. The cold stung his lips in a series of sharp blows. Before Gene had even begun to speak, Eddie knew what was going to be said. He came here every Sunday, and they had the same discussion every week.

"Still writing those crazy stories?"

"Please don't call them crazy," Eddie said, right on cue. "But yeah, I'm still writing. Always writing. Is the place hopping tonight?"

Eddie would have known the answer to the question even if he didn't ask it every week. There was no one to be seen in either direction on Main Street, but that didn't surprise him much. Most shops in Black Hills didn't open on Sunday, including the bookstore where he worked. Many businesses had closed permanently over the years as people left to search for a better future and the community dwindled in size. Eddie considered himself fortunate to even have a job, given his reputation and what had happened his senior year of high school, but tonight none of that mattered. He just wanted to get out of his tiny apartment for the evening.

"Nope, looks like you're gonna have the joint all to yourself."

"So, what's showing?"

"Well, I have a real treat for you." He had broken the weekly routine, and a sly smile spread across the old man's wrinkled face. Two yellowed and crooked teeth protruded from gray, decayed gums.

"Oh?" Eddie asked. "What kind of treat?"

"A certain little seventies movie called *Alien* I thought you might be keen on."

"Mr. Varley, I've seen it a billion times." Still, Eddie's smile grew a little wider. "Practically worn out my VCR. You know that."

"Yep, I figured as much," Gene said, nodding. Then he looked pained, as if someone had sucker punched him. He pulled a tattered, red handkerchief from his shirt pocket and coughed violently into the cloth, his face wrinkling and shriveling. The old man's tar-covered lungs were trying to climb into his throat, kicking and screaming. Slowly the attack subsided. Gene wiped some dark phlegm off his lips and put the handkerchief back into his pocket. His dull eyes glimmered. He asked, "But have you ever seen it on the big screen?"

Eddie looked surprised. No, he hadn't seen *Alien* in the theater. He hadn't even been alive when the movie was first released. For a brief instant, a wave of happiness flooded through Eddie, making him want to run into the street proclaiming that it was great to be alive, that the world was an amazing place, that love and God and true happiness were just a heartbeat away. This was the same kind of rush he had experienced on Friday afternoons when he was in high school—a surge of instant and total love borne from the realization that only forty-five minutes stood between him and a weekend-long pardon from teachers and boring class work. Those afternoons had made him believe anything was possible.

"Well, I guess I can cancel my busy social agenda tonight, but just this once." Eddie laughed at his own self-mocking sarcasm. He pulled the black, faux-leather wallet out of the back pocket of his blue jeans. He opened the battered wallet, frowned, and grabbed his last five-dollar bill. It was stuck in between dozens of slightly tattered, torn photographs. Some of the photos were folded, others had been wallet-sized to begin with. They were all of Rachel. Other than the memories, this was all he had left.

"What's wrong?" Gene asked.

"I thought I had more cash than this. Not a big deal." Eddie handed the bill through the opening in the bottom of the window, but Gene pushed the tattered green money back out.

"This one's on the house, kid."

"No, I can't let you do that." Eddie tried to slide the money through the slot again, but the old man's bony hands refused it a second time.

"Eddie Farris," Gene said. "Go on and enjoy the movie and don't make me feel bad for being kind."

"Okay. Thank you," Eddie said reluctantly. He knew he shouldn't be vain, and he tried not to show his embarrassment. Still, he was accepting handouts. No matter how bad life had been the last few years, he hadn't taken anything from anyone. Never.

"Give me a holler if you want something to eat or drink. I'm gonna wait and see if anyone else comes, but

I'll start the movie in a couple of minutes," Gene said, his voice suddenly cheerful. He laughed. "Remember, in my theater no one can hear you scream!"

Eddie thanked the old man again, opened the door to the left of the ticket booth, and stepped into the lobby. The carpet was dark red, spotted here and there with silver stars, and the high ceiling was like a photographic negative: silver with red stars. Velvet ropes weaved a path in front of the concession stand, as if demand were so great that Gene had to force his customers to form an orderly line. The ropes reminded Eddie of his visit to the Pittsburgh International Airport when he was a little kid.

The glass case in the center of the concession counter was sparsely stocked with boxes of candy, and a river of buttery popcorn flowed from the cooker behind the register. Eddie wondered why Gene even bothered. Although the popcorn smelled incredibly delicious, most Sunday nights he had the theater all to himself. Friday and Saturday could get pretty busy, at least with the high school kids who couldn't hitch a ride to Slade City, but Sunday nights were almost always dead.

As he walked, Eddie found himself staring directly into the curvy fun house mirror propped next to the concession stand. According to local legend, Gene had bought the mirror from a traveling carnival in the 1960s. The dirty and distorted reflection made Eddie's head balloon to gigantic proportions while his waist shrank to the size of a grapefruit and his legs stretched in length, like he had spent the last seven years strapped to a rack.

Eddie hurried up the frayed stairs and out onto the balcony. The red curtains at the front of the theater were shabby around the edges, and the seats were stained with the rigid remains of soft drinks and melted candies. An exit sign glowed next to a door by the left side of the screen, although now all it said was EX. The other bulbs behind the plastic facade were dead.

Eddie took a seat in the front row of the balcony where he and his friends had spent their Saturday afternoons when they were kids, just like their fathers had before them.

Giggling and whispering drifted up from the lobby, and for a brief instant Eddie thought the sounds were only in his mind, a splinter of the past. They weren't. A teenage couple appeared on the steps behind him, hanging onto each other like a pair of drunks staggering home at two in the morning when the bars closed.

The tall young man had a buzz cut and wide shoulders. A white bandage was draped across the bridge of his nose, and he was wearing a blue jacket with BLACK HILLS COMMUNITY SCHOOL WRESTLING TEAM imprinted over his heart. He held a bucket of popcorn and a large soda in his giant hands. The girl holding on to his bulky arm was a pretty brunette with the thin and perky body of a cheerleader. Her hair was littered with small, colorful plastic clips and her skin was dusted with glittery makeup. Although it was cold enough outside to snow, her jacket was open to show off the tight yellow T-shirt clinging to her breasts and ending at her navel. Her equally tight blue jeans hung low on her hips. Her pale abdomen caught Eddie's attention, and he couldn't stop himself from staring at the bare flesh.

The wrestler and the cheerleader sat in the back row of the balcony as darkness descended upon the theater.

Eddie stared into the dark and listened to the rustle of curtains pulling to the side. The screen ignited in a burst of white light. Numbers flashed on the screen, starting at eight and counting down. The theater was dusty, and Eddie could see the particles floating in the light streaming above his head. He sniffled, fighting the urge to sneeze.

There were no previews, and the credits rolled as the camera began its slow, smooth sweep through space. Eddie watched intently. It didn't matter that he had seen the movie many times before. In his opinion, Sigourney Weaver had never looked more natural than she did in her role of Ellen Ripley, and he thought the alien was amazingly realistic and haunting. He was always suffocated with a sense of dread as the suspense grew.

But before the entire title had even formed on the screen, Eddie heard the young man behind him whisper, "That's Eddie Farris. You know what he did, right?" Only he hadn't whispered. He had spoken loud enough to be heard over the movie.

The cheerleader replied, "Stop kidding around. That's not funny."

"He is Eddie Farris. I'm serious. He killed his family."

"Stop that, Johnny. It's not funny." But still, the girl giggled.

Just ignore them, Eddie thought. People usually did stop bothering him if he didn't react, if he just stayed calm and didn't try to correct their misconceptions about him. *Ignore them and they'll leave you alone. They'll go away.*

* * *

After the movie, Eddie began the long walk home, sucking in the night air. Yet the cold did little to soothe the warmth in his chest. His pulse raced. Despair flooded him.

Eddie couldn't stop thinking about the whispering teens. He couldn't forget what had happened seven years before. The night his father tried to kill him. Eddie wanted to stop walking. He wanted to fall into the drifts of snow and die. Death couldn't be any worse than the life he was living. The isolation. The fear. The yearning.

The one person he had ever really loved was gone. Rachel had left him forever, and it was all his fault.

Chapter Two

Two Weeks After The Showdown
From the Handwritten Account

My Mental Reconstruction of Events Past
by Eddie Farris

I may only be eighteen years old, but I feel like I'm eighty.

My eyes are heavy. So is the rest of my face, as if weights have been tied to my skin. Invisible weights, but heavy ones. I can barely lift my head.

My right hand is bandaged from where the pieces of glass sliced me open.

I shouldn't even be here. This is not where I belong.

I should be in some boring class at school, not in a hospital.

I should be with my girlfriend.

I should be enjoying life.

But instead I'm in this place, probably still bleeding internally for all I know. The doctors don't tell me much, or if they do, by the next day I can't remember what they said.

The painkillers mess with my head.

So here I am, secluded from the real world, all alone in the hospital.

Where will I be in five years?

In seven? Ten?

Doesn't matter. Not today. I have to get started on this little project of mine.

My goal is simple: to figure out what went wrong.

I can't remember much of what happened between me and my father, and the doctors refuse to tell me.

They say those details will return eventually.

They say I need to heal.

Maybe writing will jog my memory. Get my mental engine kick-started.

I do know this: I'll probably never see the house on the hill again. I don't think I could go back, even if I wanted to.

This is where I grew up: beyond Black Hills, where the valley is a hodgepodge of farms and isolated homes scattered along Rural Route #324, the lone road into town.

In the winter, the valley smells earthy, like your face has been shoved into fresh dirt.

In the summer, there are wildflowers and corn and grass clippings and the river and the odd composite smell created by all of the above being almost overwhelmed by the cow shit from the farms.

In the winter, there is the dirt, and occasionally the stench of wet cattle.

This is where I've lived all my life.

The valley can be defined by one major landmark at each end of Black Hills.

Toward Slade City, past our shared community school, is the Black Rock State Penitentiary.

The facility is at least a hundred years old.

There are two dozen buildings inside the thirty-eight-foot-high stone wall. There are cell blocks, a workshop, a laundry, a chapel, and even a garage for doing maintenance work on the prison's vehicles.

Jeep Cherokees patrol the area. They're white with red-and-blue lights on top and the Pennsylvania Department of Corrections logo on the doors.

Orange NO TRESPASSING signs are posted on the trees near the prison. There are guard towers every forty yards or so along the wall.

This is where my father went to work after he dropped out of high school.

The other major landmark of Black Hills cannot be seen, but it's there.

In the opposite direction, on the other side of town, the gloomy complex sits at the end of a windy road known as Darden Lane.

The road is barely wide enough for the trucks that carry shipments of supplies to the locked doors.

It's in the mountains.

It can't be seen from RR #324.

It was constructed during one hot summer in the 1880s.

Originally there were ten separate buildings, but additions have been constructed over the years, connecting every section to another, creating a single, giant, slithering structure.

This is a state-run mental hospital with some long, fancy name posted on a small, wooden sign.

But everyone just calls it the Asylum.

The Asylum is one of the hidden worlds along RR #324. There are many others, many more I probably don't even know about.

Every now and then a gravel or dirt driveway cuts through the fields or the woods to meet with RR #324. Some of the driveways are no larger than a small path and most get little traffic, if any at all. They lead to the homes and shacks of outcasts and isolationists alike, for whom Black Hills is a place to visit as little as possible.

I wouldn't be surprised if there are some old kooks sitting dead on their front porches at this very minute, rocking in the breeze, the runners on their rocking chairs creaking, their loaded shotguns laying on their laps, their bodies slowly being devoured by eternity and Mother Nature.

This part of the valley could be a small slice of Idaho.

Everyone has his or her reasons for avoiding civilization.

Some of those reasons are a little more off the wall than others.

At the top of one particular gravel driveway is a brick ranch-style home sitting in a small clearing, an image from a modern-day, blue-collared fairy tale.

This is where my story begins.

The house was built by Kurt Farris, my grandfather. Father to my father.

He had a long history of problems.

I learned some details of his life from my mother, the rest from people in town. They enjoy talking.

Every now and then, in the halls at school, I hear someone whispering my sister's name.

Mary.

Poor, sweet Mary.

She died when she was four years old.

She had been a miracle, the doctors said.

My birth had complications. They said my mother would never have another child.

And then, seven years later, she began to show.

Her belly grew large and our family grew closer.

My father couldn't express his happiness. He and my mother had always wanted another child.

We loved Mary.

But something happened a week after her fourth birthday.

I was eleven when the accident tore our family apart.

If it really was an accident.

Mary will be four years old until the end of eternity.

But I've grown up.

I have a semester left and then I'm done with high school.

Unlike many of the kids I went to kindergarten with way back when, I will graduate.

I live with my mom and dad in this house on the hill.

I spend most mornings alone in my room, working on my short stories or some last-minute homework.

Not today.

Today my life will change forever.

Chapter Three

Then: Seven Years Ago
The Day of The Showdown

On a cool, fall morning like any other in the history of Black Hills, there was something very wrong within the walls of the Farris home. Yet, down in the valley, there was nothing to set the day apart from every other day that came before it. A brisk wind shook the trees, clapping their branches together. The leaves were changing color, dropping free of the trees and drifting to the ground, more and more with each passing day. The fields were barren and frozen, crisscrossed with rock-hard furrows of dark earth. Cattle huddled inside barns and people in town bundled themselves in heavy layers, readying for the approaching winter.

The Farris home sat alone in a small clearing high on a hill. The small, brick structure had no neighbors, but a rutted gravel driveway connected the property to RR #324. The garage attached to the left side of the house was large enough for a single car, and one of the small, square windows in the garage door was broken. A child's swing was secured to the branch of an enormous weeping willow in the front yard. The wooden seat blew in the wind, twisting and falling back to the ground after every gust. The branches of the weeping willow whispered in the breeze.

From the front porch there was an amazing view of the town and the rest of the valley, including some bends in the Slade River, but the picturesque scenery wasn't why the original owner had built the house there. He didn't care to be one with nature. It wasn't meant to be his Walden without the pond. Kurt Farris had been motivated by his desire to escape Black Hills. To escape his past.

Inside the dining room, at the circular wooden table decorated with a white tablecloth and a centerpiece of plastic flowers, three people were gathered for breakfast. In the kitchen behind them pots and pans sat in the sink, waiting to be washed. There was the hollow sound of water dripping from the leaky faucet and tapping on a metal pot, again and again. The morning sun blazed through the large picture window at the front of the house, causing the rooms to radiate with an odd, orange light. The colors were surreal, like an expressionist painting in some museum, or possibly a work by Salvador Dali. The three people sat together in the odd, bright light for the first time in ages.

"So, how are your classes, Eddie? I hope everything is A-OK," Michael Farris said as he adjusted his seat and reached for a plate of scrambled eggs. He sat tall, a bear of a man with broad shoulders and a bulging chest. He was dressed for work, his blue pants pressed and creased, his unbuttoned blue uniform shirt showing off the white T-shirt underneath. Attached to his belt was a metal key ring, the type for which janitors are famous, along with a black pouch holding a can of Mace.

"I'm doing fine," Eddie replied. He had to leave for school in another half hour, and he was more than ready to go. His brown hair was carefully parted and, as was the ritual, he had spent nearly ten minutes trying to get it just right. He was an outsider in the Community School on the other side of Black Hills, but he still tried to keep his appearance as nice as possible. Every day he was taunted, poked, prodded, and laughed at while nasty stories and jokes were traded like baseball cards. He did his best to ignore the insults. He hadn't done anything to deserve them. Every school had its share of targets for the bullies, and in Black Hills he had a bull's-eye on his chest.

But no matter how bad school was, today Eddie would have preferred to be there. This morning was too strange. He sat patiently, but he wanted to stand and scream, just to break the tension. His mother sat across the table from him, and she hadn't spoken all morning. This was just too weird, this formal breakfast.

"Is school going well?" Michael asked. He shoveled a pile of scrambled eggs off the cheap metal serving platter and onto his plate. With each swift movement, his fork scraped the platter, sending a piercing screech through the room, like a chef sharpening his knives.

"Yeah, it is," Eddie replied, pouring himself a glass of milk from the rounded ivory pitcher. He filled his red-and-yellow cup to the brim. He stared at the wall across from him where a large family portrait was encircled by smaller pictures of the individual members of the Farris clan in various poses. The pictures had been taken in the portrait studio at the old K-Mart in Slade City when Eddie was a little boy. Even though he was only a teenager, the pictures made him long for the past.

"You have any tests or homework due?" Michael asked, his huge hands picking up his knife and reaching for the butter. He methodically buttered three slices of toast. When he finished, he passed the breadbasket to his son.

"An English test on Shakespeare next week." Eddie grabbed two pieces of toast. They were warm. He handed the basket to his mother. Laura took it with trembling fingers. She was barely in her late thirties, but her hair was already graying and her eyes were masked by dark bags the color of bruises—the result of long, sleepless nights. Her skin was pale, wrinkled, and her teeth were stained from a nicotine habit she had only recently abandoned.

"So what's the special occasion, Michael?" Laura finally asked, timidly picking two slices of wheat bread and placing them on her plate. Forcing a little laugh, and without ever making eye contact with her husband, she added, "Did I forget our anniversary? It's been a while since we ate together."

Michael shoved the toast and eggs into his mouth. He chewed the food, his mouth open wide, reminding Eddie of a gross joke he had learned at lunch in first grade: There was a train wreck last night, want to see the passengers? Michael took a swig directly from the carton of orange juice, his heavy gulping filling the eerily silent room.

"The special occasion is the promotion I'm gonna get

today," Michael said, grabbing a handful of bacon from the plate in the middle of the table, next to the plastic flowers. Laura had made the bacon extra crispy, just the way her husband liked it. He nodded his approval and crushed the red strips in the palm of his hand, sprinkling the remains onto his eggs.

He continued, "That old bastard Gorman is finally retiring and I'm gonna get his job. The Warden owes me. I'm the best man he has, and I don't take shit from no one."

Michael took another bite of his eggs and bacon. His big shit-eating grin remained in place, and that was when Eddie finally realized why his father had called for this special family breakfast. He was gloating. He was bragging in the same way you might if someone told you a feat was impossible yet you accomplished it anyway.

"Well, that's great," Laura replied, a note of feigned pride in her voice. Her eyes stayed dead.

"Damn straight it is! Come on people, eat some breakfast," Michael said, waving at the food on his wife and son's plates. His grin grew even wider. He was an animal baring his teeth, yet he rubbed the day's worth of fuzz on his chin as if he was some great intellectual deep in thought. Two long white scars dashed across the flesh directly below his lips. They formed a slightly crooked cross. Michael wore the mark with pride. The wounds were the result of the last time an inmate had given him trouble. There had been a discipline issue, but it didn't last long. The inmate spent a month in the hospital as a result of the "attitude adjustment" Michael administered after the situation was under control.

"Eat it all," Michael added. "This stuff ain't getting any warmer and I paid for it so it better not go to waste."

Eddie took a bite of his eggs and then, still fixated on the snide happiness chiseled on his father's face, he reached for his glass of milk. Suddenly Eddie's throat cramped and his entire body spasmed, like part of him already knew what was going to happen. The premonition was not supernatural or psychic; it was just some primitive instinct kicking in. But the warning came too late to save him from the consequences of his actions.

Through the odd orange morning sunlight, Eddie watched his hand strike the top of the red-and-yellow plastic cup, toppling it. He sat in frozen panic as the milk spilled across the table in a tiny tidal wave, moving faster than he could think. The smooth, white liquid splashed across his father's plate and onto his immaculate uniform. The cloth of Michael's T-shirt grew dark, absorbing the milk, and he jerked backward as if someone had thrown acid at him.

No one moved, no one said anything for a long moment. Then Michael stood, his knee striking the table leg and sending an earthquake from one side of the table to the other. Without saying a word he left the dining room. His footsteps echoed after him, and the door to the largest of the three bedrooms opened and closed with a bang.

"I didn't mean to," Eddie said, glancing at his mother. His stomach had knotted and sweat trickled down his brow. His heart hammered against his rib cage, as if he had just run a country mile. "It was an accident."

"Eddie . . ." Laura hesitated, and for a moment Eddie thought she wasn't going to say what he knew she wanted to say. Then she quietly finished the statement, "You've got to be more careful."

His mother stood and moved into the kitchen to grab some paper towels from the kitchen counter, but Eddie's attention was drawn to the carpet in the living room and the thought of what his father might be doing. The carpet was spotted with bleach marks, the permanent results of his mother's frequent attempts to clean up the beer and whiskey spilled when Michael held his late-night drinking binges. He cringed. He pictured his mother's hands and how her fingers sometimes bled when she scrubbed the carpet too long. Her fingers were bones dripped in anemic flesh, brittle and on the verge of snapping.

Eddie took the paper towels from his mother. "Let me do that."

Laura didn't argue with her son, but she replied, "If he comes back angry, get out of here if you can. Any way you can."

"Mom, I can't leave you with him," Eddie said as the dimpled paper towels slowly soaked in the mess.

"Do what I say, Eddie." She paused. "Anyway, maybe he won't be too angry, what with him getting promoted and all."

Eddie looked at his mother with a slight twinge of sadness and disbelief. They both knew better. That wasn't likely. Not anymore. Not now. Not even if this was going to be the best day of his father's life.

Laura sighed, and they waited in silence for Michael to return.

Chapter Four

Now

There was no one else on Main Street as Eddie walked home from the theater, and he thought that was probably for the best. Although he didn't want to be seen, he refused to stray to any of the side roads. The sidewalk was dimly illuminated by globed lights sitting atop ornate posts. The posts had once been green, but they now showed slivers of the original metal under the flaking paint. The lights ran along Main Street from one end of town to the other, and the artificial glow comforted Eddie. Not a lot, but it was something.

A few stray memories surfaced to the front of his mind: *Rachel's hand on my cheek, stroking my skin, the glimmer in her eyes, the taste of her lips, the smell of her breath, the talk of Pittsburgh, the dreams and plans, sitting in the window, looking at the mountains, dreaming and planning . . . our plans to leave the town together.*

An odd warmth filled Eddie, starting from deep inside and spreading to his limbs. He thought he might be getting sick, might be running a temperature, but then he realized what was really happening. The warmth was knowledge. Enlightenment. If he hurried, he might actually have a chance to break the chains binding him to Black Hills. Escape wasn't a dream. Escape was possible. It was merely a matter of running while he could summon the energy, running before the darkness of the town and his family sapped the will from his body. The weird experience in the theater had been his brain telling him he had to leave. He couldn't wait for the end of the film—his window of opportunity would vanish if he delayed for even an hour.

"I'm going to make it," Eddie said, his body tingling, a surge of euphoria flooding him. He hadn't felt this alive since high school. Back then there had been moments when he truly believed he would eventually break free of the small town he had grown up in, the town that smothered him more and more with each passing day. There had been those hot summer nights when he dreamed of taking the people he loved and driving them out of the one-stoplight hellhole they had been sentenced to die in. Those dreams had kept him alive.

"If I go, if I don't stop, I can make it!" The feverish excitement drove Eddie forward. The wind kicked up again like an angry, ancient god, the cold air snapping at his flesh. Small clouds of breath escaped his mouth. A thin layer of ice and snow crunched beneath his feet. The sidewalks were slick and the roads were lined by mounds of plowed snow spotted with stones, cinders, and streaks of mud. Fog was rolling off the Slade River to the north of town, blocking the moon above, hugging the snow-covered fields below, transforming the land into one large, endless white wall.

Eddie was nearly sprinting, and as he ran he recalled

an earlier attempt to flee Black Hills, a memory he had tried to forget with all his might, a memory that gave him nightmares: *The car shakes and rattles, veering off onto the sidewalk, barely missing a row of trees and streetlights by inches. The police cruiser is too heavy and too fast! Our car's engine growls, angry and tired. The rain pounds us from side to side, the wind gusts wailing. The headlights grow larger like an oncoming freight train . . .*

When he reached the edge of town, Eddie slowed to a stop, although he desperately wanted to keep moving. There were no more buildings, no street signs, nothing but snow-covered fields and trees. The road was flanked by telephone poles and forested hills until it vanished into the fog. Eddie had arrived at the mud-and-snow splattered curb where the sidewalk ended. To his left was the hand-carved wooden sign that welcomed people to town. The streetlights glowed behind him like the brightest stars peeking through a thin veil of clouds.

Eddie's chest grew tight and a shrill panic swelled from deep inside of him. The voice of doubt was brewing a storm in the darkest corners of his mind. He knew he should have gone straight home to his apartment instead of making this journey. Eyes watering, he peered into the darkness of the valley where Black Hills lay hidden from the rest of humanity. Where the small town slept.

A dense layer of fog enveloped the land. The sight had always fascinated Eddie. Sometimes he would sit by his bedroom window and watch the fog until he grew weary and stumbled to bed for a few hours of restless sleep. The ghostly white shroud engulfing the town had been prominently featured in his stories. The light and the shadows dancing within its vaporous grip almost hypnotized him. Sometimes he thought the fog moved like it was alive.

Keep going, keep going, keep going! a voice in the back of Eddie's mind demanded, and he wanted to obey. He wanted to take another step so badly he could feel his stomach aching with greed. But he couldn't make himself move. The past surged up and overwhelmed him.

This is useless, he realized, a wave of defeat crashing down on him. This was how the attempts to flee his destiny always ended: with a broken heart and a fatigued body. *I'll never escape. Never. Why did I think this time would be any different?*

He turned. The wisps of fog danced around the globes of the streetlights.

He was still alone. He shivered.

If it hadn't been for the fog and the lights on Main Street, Eddie would have been blinded by the nothingness of the night. Sometimes he wondered if this was how the astronauts had felt when their capsules glided behind the dark side of the moon: alone and scared and chilled to the bone, like ice had been shoved inside their veins.

A shiver shook his spine, but the sensation wasn't from the cold. His mind blistered with an almost blinding montage of memories as he began to walk. He was a prisoner of an emotional war as he returned to the apartment building where he lived, and his brain twisted and distorted like his image in the fun house mirror at the theater. The town was a blur of fog and streetlights. He moved in a daze, but he understood where he was headed.

"Home, of course. Where else can I go?" Eddie asked without comprehending what he was saying. He silently added, *But I can't ever go home again. Someone said that. Who? My mom, maybe? She can't say anything now. She's dust and bones and ashes. Home for Mom is a cheap plywood casket in the ground.*

He shuddered, tried to push the imagery away.

"What's happening to me?" Eddie asked. He received no reply from the night, and he didn't notice the massive man headed in his direction until it was too late. The man was limping, but he moved quickly and in a straight line. They bumped into each other, the force of the collision almost knocking Eddie off his feet.

As the two of them briefly touched, a string of bizarre, but fascinating phrases popped into Eddie's head: *A man's heart and soul are filled with a fire that burns in his words and his actions and in his love. Some men are consumed by a white fire and they do good for the world and they love life with a passion that burns to and from everyone they meet. Other men are consumed by a black fire and they can be nothing but evil. They burn everyone they love; they burn their spirit and their mind. A man is his own fire. That is all he can be. He has no say in what he becomes; it is decided long before he ever steps forth onto the earth. A man cannot change the color of his fire.*

Eddie tripped over his own two feet, his mind spinning. The words had appeared in the blink of an eye, like they had been lying dormant inside of him, simply waiting for the right occasion to awaken within his mind. Or had the man who bumped into him actually spoken the phrase? Either way, Eddie couldn't make the echoing madness stop, no matter how hard he clenched his fists or gritted his teeth. He pounded on his chest and bent over, breathed in the freezing night air, and counted to ten. Slowly everything came into focus.

Oh shit, that's insane, Eddie thought.

As he regained his balance, another thought jumped into his mind, a thought more deranged than the confusing phrases. The man had been wearing a blue guard uniform from the Black Rock State Penitentiary. The uniform didn't mean anything in particular, of course—there were lots of guards at the prison—but the man's uniform had been old and tattered and spotted with blood. There had been crossed scars under the man's lips . . . was that even possible? And had he been wearing an eye patch? That couldn't be right! Eddie had only ever seen one person in town with a piece of rounded cloth strapped over an eye, and that was Mattie St. Claire. The wound was seven years old, and there hadn't been any doubt after The Showdown that Mattie would always be blind in her right eye.

But what about the guard? Had Eddie *ever* seen a guard with an eye patch? No, definitely not. A person couldn't work in the prison with only one eye. So did the man really work there? Was he some kind of impostor? If so, why? In his frenzied emotional state Eddie could only think of one answer: After what he had done to his father on the day of The Showdown, Michael Farris certainly would have required an eye patch to conceal the disfigurement. And the limp. His father would probably have a bum leg, too.

But Michael Farris was dead.

"No, it can't be him," Eddie muttered, spinning and futilely searching for the guard who had disappeared into the fog. All he could see were the buildings along the street, the lights on the green poles, and the vast whiteness of infinity. The earth had been vaporized by the night and nothing remained.

Against his better judgment, Eddie moved in the direction the mysterious guard had been headed.

It is *him!* a nagging voice of paranoia shouted in his frazzled mind. The paranoid voice sounded like Eddie's, but it said things he didn't want to consider: conspiracy theories involving the townspeople and what they were planning to do to him, cries of prophecy that made him wonder whether he was losing his mind, and unnerving questions meant to keep him on his toes every moment, always distrusting the world around him. Although the voice was overly paranoid, the warnings it spoke were also often correct. There was a reason to fear the dark, to question what people were saying behind his back, to be aware of his surroundings. Eddie didn't know where the warnings came from, but he suspected everyone had the same kind of internal speaker. Some people could ignore what they heard, and he was willing to bet they didn't last very long in the real world.

It is your father! the voice shouted. *Who else would have an eye patch? And the scar? The scar! You won't escape this town alive! He's going to get you for what you did! He's—*

Eddie stopped abruptly, slipping on the slick sidewalk. He braced himself against the rounded top of a blue mailbox. His legs were ready to give out, and he wanted to scream. He wanted to scream so badly his lungs hurt.

There was a fire in the middle of the road up ahead,

near the corner of Main and Maple Street, by Dolores's General Store.

"No, no, no!" Eddie took a few steps toward the flames. They were growing larger, greedily feeding on gasoline. "This is all wrong!"

A pile of notebooks burned brightly at the edge of the street, next to the curb. The air was saturated with the harsh stench of gasoline, and the smoke and orange light sliced the fog, cutting a hole through the night. The sight knocked the wind out of Eddie. He could tell the notebooks had been green and spiral bound, although the metal was melting and the cardboard covers were being devoured. The pages were curling, turning black, and swirling into the fog where they were lost forever.

Out in the night a voice summoned Eddie. He heard the calling, both sweet and bitter, and it ripped through him like a rusty blade.

More people were going to die.

Chapter Five

Then

When Michael returned from changing his shirt, Eddie didn't feel any better. His father's cold expression when he entered the dining room could have frozen water on the hottest day of the year. He had tucked in his blue uniform shirt and buttoned it all the way to the top. His keys jingled on his belt. When he opened his mouth to speak—his chipped teeth showing from between his cracked lips—his voice was far too impassive and steady.

"Boy, come with me. We need to talk," Michael said.

Eddie shot a terrified glance at his mother. He didn't want to go anywhere with his father. Not right now. Something bad would happen if he did. But he couldn't run, even though his mother had told him to leave. Running was not an option. No way, no how.

Laura stood. "Eddie didn't mean to spill the milk."

"Sit down, Laura. Sit right back down." Michael paused slightly after every word, his voice not rising, but the threat loud and clear. His wife complied without questioning him. "This is between me and my boy. Now come with me, Eddie."

Eddie glanced at his mother, but she weakly shook her head. There was nothing she could do and they both knew it. Anything she did or said would only make Michael angrier.

Eddie put the wet paper towels on the table, careful not to spill anything else, and followed his father through the kitchen with its faded, curling linoleum floor and cheap wooden cabinets. They headed in the direction of the garage on the far side of the house. Michael ducked to pass through the doorway, his arms brushing against the frame. He flipped the switch on the other side of the door, and a fluorescent bulb flickered and burst to life. A long worktable was pushed against the back wall of the garage. From the smallest screwdriver to Michael's favorite buzz saw, the vast array of tools were held in their proper places.

When Eddie had been a small child, when life had been happier for the family, long before Mary's accident, he had spent entire weekends with his father. Eddie had played on the concrete floor of the garage with his toy trucks while Michael worked on some project or another: a birdhouse to put on the pole in the backyard, a new window frame to replace the one rotting in the kitchen, or maybe even the swing tied to the large weeping willow in the front lawn. After the work was done, they'd go and watch the Pirates game together or cook hot dogs on the grill or hike to one of the many ponds in the woods to skip stones all afternoon. There would be laughing and tickling and fun.

But today they weren't headed for the worktable or the charcoal grill stashed in the corner. Instead, Michael pointed to his Hechinger's store-brand lawn mower with its fading and flaking orange paint job and the dirty bagger attachment. The hardware and lumber chain had gone out of business many years before, but their equipment had been built to last. Michael often joked that a person could use the mower to get rid of a body or two, if he were so inclined.

"Get that." Michael gestured at the red container sitting behind the mower, nestled against the bags of salt he used on the front stoop after winter storms.

"But why?" The words left Eddie's mouth before he could stop them.

"Son, I'm teaching you a lesson."

Eddie nodded, just happy not to have been clobbered for asking the question. He moved slowly toward the mower. The garage was dripping with the scent of old grass, and with the smell came memories of Eddie's childhood summers, particularly the sweltering heat and the sun and the air so sticky, as if he were wearing a wet wool blanket. He picked up the red container, the liquid inside sloshing around, shifting the weight from left to right, right to left, until he held the can steady long enough for the gas to settle. The handle was cold against his hot flesh.

"Come on," Michael said, leading his son back into the kitchen and through the dining room. His head bumped the little faux chandelier, sending it swinging. He cursed, but didn't stop.

Laura nervously glanced at her son, asking him what the hell was going on without opening her mouth. The question was in her eyes. Eddie shrugged, unable to hide the dread creeping through him. Whatever his father intended for him, it couldn't be good.

Eddie entered the living room, and his heart dropped into his stomach. A flush of acid surged up his throat, the vile, burning taste potent in his mouth. The cold handle in his sweaty hand suddenly weighed a thousand pounds.

"Here is our problem," Michael said, a slight hint of irritation in his voice. He pointed at a pile of notebooks stacked neatly on the chipped coffee table. They sat in a spotlight of morning sunbeams blazing through the picture window. They were green and spiral bound, and the lined pages were filled with Eddie's stories, essays, and poems.

"How?" Eddie stuttered. When he was done writing his stories, he took special care to hide the notebooks behind the green bookcase in his bedroom, the one place he could safely store them. Everywhere else seemed far too obvious: under his bed, in his closet, in his dresser. So he stacked the notebooks horizontally, spine to spine. He had been certain his father wouldn't find his writings there.

"My job is to know how the cons hide their contraband. You thought you could fool me?" Michael laughed, but the sound was angry and completely void of warmth. His statement was a surgeon's knife, cutting into his son with precision, driving fear into him. "This is garbage, Eddie. Farris men are better than this. We don't hide away in our rooms and scribble nonsense about the flowers and the wind and symbols and shit. We act like men. It's time you grew up. I allowed this hobby of yours to go on too long. That was my mistake, but I'm fixing it now. Put your shit in the fireplace."

"No," Eddie whispered, closing his eyes and bracing

for the impact he was certain had to be coming. His lungs burned as he held his breath, and his bones ached from anticipating the beating that would follow if he didn't do what his father wanted, but he couldn't move. Nothing. When he wasn't hit or kicked or thrown to the floor, Eddie opened his eyes.

Michael had gone to the other side of the table, and now he was dragging Laura by the arm toward the living room. Eddie could see the white marks forming on his mother's flesh from where his father's huge hand squeezed into her. She winced, but said nothing.

"Eddie, don't make me ask you again. I'm doing this for your own good. It'll make you right," Michael said, easily forcing his wife along. Pain flashed in Laura's dull eyes. Her body twitched under the force exerted by her husband's hand, and Eddie knew he had no choice. He had one option and it was nonnegotiable. If he disobeyed his father, his mother would pay for the defiance. He understood how this game was played. He had chosen to take a risk and he had lost. Now he had to pay up, the loser in a big gamble.

Hands trembling, Eddie slowly picked up his notebooks. Three years of hard work filled their lined pages. Three years of dedication and devotion. Page after page contained the mental images he developed during the day and then composed on paper each night with a loving craftsmanship that only someone passionate for the written word could truly understand. His dreams were in his hands, and there wasn't anything he could do to save them. He walked to the fireplace, his legs heavy, as if they were coated with lead.

"Son, this is for the best," Michael said. "It really is. You'll understand eventually."

Eddie didn't respond. He opened the glass doors in front of the fireplace, but he held onto the notebooks as long as he could. Then, when he heard his father grunt and take another step toward him, he tossed the spiral-bound pages onto the pile of charred logs. They landed there, helpless and pitiful, a couple of them open to random stories he would never read again. He wanted to dive in and pull the notebooks out, but there really wasn't any reason to try. His father would beat him and his mother and then destroy the contraband himself. Or maybe he'd do something worse.

"Now the gas," Michael coaxed.

Eddie unscrewed the rusted cap. Acrid fumes drilled straight into his nose. He held his breath and fought the urge to run from the house. He splashed gasoline onto the notebooks. The paper soaked up the gas, the white pages growing dark, the darkness spreading to the edges, to the metal spiral binding, saturating the thin cardboard covers Eddie had carefully labeled with titles and dates when the works were created. When the container was empty, he put it on the floor.

Michael's callused fingers handed his son a single wooden match. Eddie took the tiny piece of wood. Tears dribbled from his eyes, and his entire body shuddered. For a moment he couldn't move, but then he felt his arm raising, as if some other entity had taken control of his motor skills. He swiped the red tip on the stone mantle. The match flared to life. The flame chewed down to his skin, the sulfur smell reaching his nose, burning his eyes. His flesh stung.

Eddie prayed for a reprieve, prayed for a miracle, but he knew none was coming. Breathing deeply, he tossed the match into the fireplace. The notebooks burst into flames, a loud whoosh engulfing the room, a plume of black smoke rising into the air. Foul vomit rushed into Eddie's throat, but he managed to choke it down again, the acid still burning in his mouth. He coughed. His chest hitched, like his heart was trying to break out through his ribs.

"Ashes to ashes, dust to dust, and all that jazz," Michael whispered into Eddie's ear. "Don't fuck with me, son. Don't ever break my rules or I'll break you."

Eddie remained motionless, his eyes locked on the fire and his notebooks.

"I'll be home at five tonight," Michael stated. "But you'd better be here right after school. Understand me, boy?"

Eddie nodded, but he didn't look away from the smoke and the flames.

Chapter Six

Now

Snow gently fell across the valley, and the streets of Black Hills were gritty with salt and cinders. The morning air was crisp. Flurries drifted from the heavens. The thin, wavy branches of the trees lining Main Street drooped with icicles that grew longer with each passing night chill, making the trees look even more limp and naked than they had in the fall when they surrendered their leaves. The valley appeared to be painted with dirty gray chalk, but somewhere to the east, beyond the dark clouds, the sun hung low in the sky.

Eddie's feet moved on their own and he didn't question where he was headed. His body led him without thought. He could travel this route in his sleep. It only made him think about his forbidden dreams of lost love, but all the same, he couldn't make himself stop.

Just like the night before, a series of memories flashed before his eyes, unrelenting, no matter how hard he tried to suppress them: *The body lies on the floor, on top of the glass. The storm is raging outside and wind-blown rain is propelled through the broken window. He stands there, star-*

ing in, looking like some horrible B-movie monster. Large, wide, ugly as hell. He grins and growls and I know he's coming in to kill us. I have to do something, but I can't move. Screams pierce the night and—

Eddie stopped, ripping himself free of the memory. A seven-story apartment building rose before him. The ominous structure stood alone, like a prehistoric tomb in the corner of some abandoned and forgotten cemetery. Most of the windows were dark, with the exception of one on the fifth floor. He could almost hear the demons of his past calling to him from within the barren walls.

"If I could just find a way to go back," Eddie said. "To make things right."

He hadn't been inside the Richard Street Apartments since Rachel had apologized, whispered her good-bye, and gently touched his face one last time, but not a day went by that he didn't wish there was some way he could fix what had happened there. Apartment fifty-seven was a monument to everything wrong in his life. He didn't dare go any closer to the building. Someone might see him, and they would almost certainly tell *her*. Although he often considered trying to make some form of atonement, to try to heal the wounds of the past, he understood he would never again be welcomed into her life.

"Ashes to ashes," Eddie idly whispered, unaware he was speaking aloud as he pulled his gaze from the building. It didn't do him any good to get worked up about the dire acts he had committed. The people he had killed. The Showdown. He had simply done what he needed to do. What he had been forced to do. Otherwise, he wouldn't have lived to see his nineteenth birthday. That knowledge didn't restrain the regret he felt. The despair. A long dead voice finished the phrase for Eddie: *dust to dust . . .*

He hurried back to Main Street, wiping the melting snowflakes from his skin, not slowing his pace until he reached the blue-trimmed bay window that jutted out from the front of the Black Hills Books and News. Much of the paint was chipping and flaking into specks of dust. The orange YES! WE'RE OPEN! sign hung from a suction cup on the window in the door. Sometimes the stone ledge next to the door was used to display four different newspapers: the *Black Hills Herald,* the *Pittsburgh Post-Gazette,* the *Harrisburg Patriot-News,* and the *Philadelphia Inquirer.* Patrons could browse the news and take a paper inside to purchase if they were so inclined, but not now. Until the days got longer and the weather warmer, the papers were kept inside, next to the register.

"Another few months, they'll be here, like the flowers blooming, a sign of spring," Eddie said, writing some unrhymed poetry on the fly.

Although the store was his destination, he didn't enter through the front door. He continued beyond the building, around the corner, and down the back alley. When he was working, he wasn't supposed to use the customer entrance. That was one of the rules. It was one of *his* rules, although he didn't really understand why anymore. The decision had just seemed to make sense in the grand scheme of his life.

The alley was long and narrow, with a dozen service doors to a dozen different stores, although most of the businesses had closed up shop years ago. Eddie hurried past an old, stinking dumpster. Rotting cardboard and food lay next to the large, green container, and it smelled like death. The buildings were only two or three stories tall, but they seemed to tower over him. The sky above was dark and more snow was beginning to fall.

"Dammit," Eddie muttered as he tried to open the bookstore's back door, failing and banging his leg with a hard thump. He swore again under his breath. The door was slightly wedged into the frame, sticking there. He pushed a little harder. The door popped open. He stepped inside.

As he put his jacket on the coatrack, Eddie over-extended himself, and his lower right side ached. The jab of pain was short, but powerful, like someone was tugging on his ribs. The doctors had said nothing could be done to help him. There was no physical explanation for the pain. There were plenty of psychological reasons, though, none of which Eddie wanted to contemplate today.

"Mattie, I'm here!" he called, searching for a bottle of aspirin. He checked the desk piled high with paperwork, finally finding the half-empty bottle hidden behind a stack of accounting books. "Sorry I'm late. What do you want me to do today?"

"Anything you want," Mattie St. Claire answered from the sales floor. Her voice was rough and uneven, but Eddie was used to that by now. "It's not like we ever get busy."

And Eddie's day went on from there. He cleaned the racks, swept the floor, and shelved books for most of the morning. When he finished with his work, he browsed for something new he might want to read. Nothing caught his eye. He had once believed there were millions of great books just waiting to be discovered, but lately it seemed like he had already read all the good ones and there was nothing new to find. That was okay. Most of the books he enjoyed had hidden meanings, making them even more fun to read a second or third time.

Pausing from his work, Eddie watched Mattie tuck a strand of graying hair behind her ear with trembling fingers. Deep lines circled her face, and her hands were twisted. Her vision was so poor she could no longer drive. She had committed an incredibly brave act once, and it had most likely saved Eddie's life. He couldn't repay her for her sacrifices, but every day he wished he could do more for her, to make her life as happy as it had been before The Showdown.

"Mattie, you have a minute?" Eddie asked. "I have a question for you."

"Ask away," Mattie replied. She opened a box of magazines and checked a shipment number on one of the yellow invoices attached to her clipboard. She stopped to retie her gray hair into a bun the best she could with her twisted and shaking fingers. She also adjusted the cloth patch covering her right eye—it was the most obvious physical injury from The Showdown—and then she began pulling bundles of magazines out of the box.

"You knew what people would say when you hired me, didn't you?" Eddie was certain Mattie had understood exactly what would happen when he came to work for her, but he had never mentioned it before. Today, though, curiosity got the best of him. He didn't know why they hadn't discussed this earlier, but he quickly decided the answer was simple: the strange experience in the movie theater, the weird run-in with the prison guard, and the burning notebooks had left him shaken. If any of those events had even really occurred. Eddie remembered everything with the fragmented consistency of a bad dream. Everything with the exception of the weird words that had flooded his brain. They were still crystal clear.

"Well, of course I did. I ain't stupid." She continued placing bundles of magazines wrapped in plastic next to the box. "I knew people would make angry phone calls and some of them would vow never to buy from me if I lived to be a million years old, but I also realized they would get tired and leave you alone sooner or later, which they did, didn't they?"

Most nights Eddie couldn't get the memories of the chants and phone calls to go away, but Mattie was right. Most of the trouble had ended eventually. Almost everyone had found other fish to fry, although there was still one person who went out of his way to remind Eddie of what he had done. And the dirty looks and the muttering behind his back hadn't stopped, of course, but the most blatant attacks had ended.

Mattie continued, "They generally quit sooner or later. Most of them, at least. They chant and rant until they find something else to attack. This month they're working on a plan to close the adult video store in Slade City, from what I understand. All things pass."

What she didn't say, but what Eddie knew she had to be thinking, was a simple, but chilling statement: *That doesn't mean people forget. They never forget.* The tyranny of tradition was always there. Most everyone in town hated his family, they didn't trust him, and that would never change. But at least the verbal assaults had, for the most part, ended.

"I've lived in this town too long to care what any of those old buzzards say," Mattie added. "And anyway, where else would you get a job?"

"I could probably head to Pittsburgh and find work there. Maybe write reviews for the *Post.*"

"So why don't you go?"

"Well . . ." Eddie stopped. He didn't want to say he was scared. He didn't want to discuss how he became paralyzed when he reached the city limits, how he couldn't go any farther because he feared the real world would devour him. No, not the world, but the night. The night would eat him alive.

Eddie thought about standing at the edge of town, staring into the distance and desperately trying to inspire the courage he needed to keep going. He had considered hitching a ride or buying a one-way ticket for the lone Greyhound Bus that still came to town each week, but what if he got to the edge of Black Hills and freaked like he did when he was on foot? What would everyone say then? People were already discussing his treks, and the talk made him nervous. Some said he was staring at the prison in the distance, while others—these were mostly the old-timers—said he heard voices in the night calling to him, telling him to do things. Horrible things.

Finally Eddie admitted, "I guess I really don't have anywhere else to go."

"Well," Mattie said, "you can count on me for anything you need."

"I know. Thank you, Mattie."

"You feeling okay? Aren't you sleeping well? You look tired."

"I keep having the nightmare."

"Do you think you should talk to one of the doctors at the free clinic? They might be able to help you."

"No." Eddie stared into Mattie's good eye, ignoring the patch of colorful fabric held to the right side of her head by an elastic band. He could see the sadness in her quiet gaze. The sorrow haunted him. "They'll say it's survivor's guilt. That's what they always say."

"Eddie, we've discussed this too often for my poor old heart." She was stern, yet sympathetic. "It wasn't your fault. You can't blame yourself. You did what you had to do."

"I know," he replied, thinking that Mattie had read his mind. "But that doesn't stop the dreams."

"We were both there, Eddie. You can't feel guilty. You can't. It ain't right."

Eddie stared at Mattie's eye patch and twisted fingertips like he had never seen them before. They made him sick. He knew he had every reason to feel guilty. He said, "You saved our lives. Not me."

"No, I did what I had to do. Just like you. Those nightmares will pass and we'll get through this together, like we always have." She sighed and put her clipboard on top of the brown box. "But for now, I gotta use the bathroom. Be right back, kiddo."

"I'll be here," Eddie said as Mattie pulled open the curtain hanging in the doorway at the rear of the store. She limped into the office area, the curtain falling shut behind her as she started up the wooden stairs to her apartment. Eddie could hear her bum leg stomping every couple of seconds, and he imagined her using both hands to help bend the knee. He watched the swaying curtain in the doorway. The burgundy-colored piece of cloth made him think of *The Wizard of Oz*, and his mind traveled to a faraway place.

Don't look behind the curtain, his overactive imagination cried, but instead of seeing a man pretending to be a great wizard there, Eddie pictured a group of fantastic monsters waiting for him in the other room.

A daydream had begun, taking over his mind and focusing all his energy on the creation of the extraordinary story. The mental images grew in complexity and depth with each passing moment.

Before Eddie's eyes, zombies appeared. Hordes of them. Their clothes were rotting and stinking; their flesh had been ravaged by worms. Sunken, disgusting eye sockets gazed at the room. The creatures pushed the book racks, and the books and shelving tumbled to the wooden planks of the floor. The zombies homed in on their target. They wanted human flesh, and they had found some.

A pretty teenage girl was trapped behind the sales counter, with nowhere left to go. Eddie could picture every little detail, right down to how she had tied her tennis shoes. There was blood splattered on her arms and legs and clothes. A lot of blood. She had the build of an athlete—tall, with long legs, a thin waist. Her blond hair was tangled and dirty and her blue eyes were wide with fright. She screamed.

The front door exploded inward as pyrotechnics shattered the air—a high-budget Hollywood special effect.

The story's hero, who could have been Eddie if he

were a body builder, charged into the phalanx of zombies. He carried a grease-covered machine gun and a belt of ammunition draped over his shoulder. Yelling a fierce battle cry, he shredded the zombies with white-hot bullets. A smell of gunpowder—whether there was such a smell Eddie had never bothered to research, but he had read about it often enough in cheap, paperback novels to believe it must exist—and raw flesh saturated the room. The resourceful hero leapt from aisle to aisle, never slowing for an instant as he shot off limbs and pierced soft brains with lead. The zombies fell backward like dominoes as spent shell casings flew out of the hero's machine gun like confetti, landing on the floor in a rapid, cascading pattern. Rotting bodies covered the bookstore floor with bloody limbs and brains and bodily fluids.

In the end, the dirty and buff executioner of the already dead saved the girl, and she instantly fell in love with him. In the end, the hero always got the girl.

"That's good," Eddie said, laughing gleefully as the bookstore returned before his eyes. He'd have to write the story in one of his notebooks tonight. In fact, he might—

Eddie's hand froze in midair. He had been reaching for a book sitting by itself on an empty shelf, but then he saw the title. That alone was enough to paralyze him. He studied the yellow spine of the small hardcover. He read the title again and again, thinking it might change upon closer inspection. No such luck. Forcing down his fear, he grabbed the book.

Kahlil Gibran's *A Tear and a Smile* the front cover proclaimed above a pencil drawing of an angel with his arms extended like Jesus being crucified. The angel was surrounded by some kind of smoke morphing from nude bodies. Something like vines encircled his legs.

"What are the odds?" Eddie asked, running his fingers across the title. "It can't be the same one."

As he opened the cover and listened to the crackle of the spine, his heart stopped. There, on the front page, was the proof he needed. Written on the faded paper was a note in his own distinctive script. But how was it possible? How could the book have gotten here?

As Eddie stared wide-eyed at the four sentences he had composed seven years earlier, his mind came alive with memories of Rachel Matthews. He saw her as clearly as he had seen the imaginary zombies moments earlier. Her blond hair and blue eyes were etched into his memory. He remembered how wonderful her hair smelled when he held her tight and kissed her neck, how soft her lips felt on his whenever they could sneak a few minutes alone. Those kisses had been long and sweet. He often daydreamed of their walks in the park or their dates to the movies. Sometimes they had stopped at the Black Hills Diner and he had gazed into her eyes and smiled and seen how truly happy she was simply because she was with him. Eddie had often joked that he couldn't really afford such luxuries as eating at the diner, and that made Rachel laugh. He loved her laugh and her smile.

Eddie saw himself as a teenager again, sitting with Rachel where the forest stopped at the edge of his family's property, right above RR #324. Parked nearby on the shoulder of the road was Rachel's battered and dented green Honda Civic. She had to leave soon, but there was still some daylight remaining on this warm, spring evening, and Eddie planned to put the time to good use. He took Rachel's hands into his own. The scorching sun was a blaze of orange and red above her shoulder, but its light and heat were nowhere as radiant as her smile.

Eddie found himself uttering, "So, do you want to, maybe, you know, go out officially sometime?"

He tensed, expecting the worst and praying for the best. Rachel tossed her hair the way she often did when she was feeling playful, and said: "Of course, silly, what took you so long to ask?"

The book slipped from Eddie's hand, striking the floor by his feet, kicking up a dust bunny he had missed when sweeping. His eyes moved to follow it, but he wasn't really seeing the book. All he could see was Rachel. She stood before him, young and gorgeous in a simple kind of way. He could see in her smile and her shining eyes the love she had for him and him alone.

But the passion that had once filled her was gone.

As the images of beauty and love faded away, they were replaced by a snapshot memory of Rachel with blood on her hands.

Chapter Seven

From the Handwritten Account

My Mental Reconstruction of Events Past
by Eddie Farris

Before I go on, I need to make something clear.

Yes, my father is the infamous Michael Farris, a man with a bad temper and an even worse reputation.

The temper is in his blood—the reputation he earned.

But he wasn't always like that. He didn't always act this way.

These days his arms are thick and heavily veined, his chest is broad.

He wears shirts displaying a wide range of colorful sentiments: YOUR MOTHER IS FUCKING UGLY TOO! YOU AND THE BITCH YOU RODE IN ON! THE GOVERNMENT CAN KISS MY BIG WHITE AMERICAN ASS!

He spends two hours every day lifting weights in the prison weight room.

When he's pressing the iron, listening to heavy metal on the old boom box, coating his hands in gritty chalk, and pushing his body to the max, I think he feels alive.

He began this weight-lifting mania years ago.

I think it helps him accept the part of him that's dead now.

Perhaps.

Alcohol also makes him feel alive. Or at least it helps him forget.

The last few years of heavy drinking and a piss-poor diet—fast food, junk food, beer, and more beer, and whiskey and vodka—are showing on his body.

His gut grows larger, and no amount of daily crunches will keep the muscles tight.

His eyes are bloodshot most mornings, but he long ago reached the point where his body forgot how to puke, no matter how much he drinks.

Just like his father.

But that's not how *my* father used to be.

He's gone through a lot.

I think of poor Mary.

Before her arrival into our lives, my father was a good man. He worked hard and believed in honor and trust and noble creeds.

Since Mary's death, he's decayed.

Disintegrated.

Soured.

But there are still days when he tries to be his former self. When he tries to be human.

Three months ago he and I went to see a movie at the big megaplex in Slade City, the one at the far end of the Wal-Mart parking lot.

I didn't want to go anywhere with him, but he asked and I couldn't say no. Pissing him off is a bad idea.

So I went and we discussed how the Pirates were doing (they had been mathematically eliminated from the play-offs already, of course, even though it wasn't a week into August) and how the Steelers might fare this year and whether the Penguins should trade some of their veterans for young blood before the season started.

We got syrupy sodas in huge cups and a bucket of popcorn. They cost far too much but the buttery popcorn had free refills.

We saw an action flick. We laughed at the one-liners, cringed when the hero took a bullet in the leg, and we even cheered together when the bad guy got what he deserved during the final shoot-out.

The whole experience was strange, like a slice out of history, like an afternoon from when I was much younger. Somehow a day from my youth had been pulled into the present.

You have to understand, my father was a good man.

You must understand that.

Do you?

I don't. Not always.

Sometimes I can't remember.

I keep telling myself he used to be ethical and decent.

I think it's important, but I don't know why. Not yet.

After my father makes me promise to be home when school is done, he walks out the front door and across the mist-covered lawn to his pickup truck.

The truck's engine roars to life, and then he's speeding down the gravel driveway to RR #324, the wide tires sending gravel flying.

"Oh, Eddie, I'm so sorry," my mother cries as she wraps her thin, bony arms around me. I can feel how much weight she has lost during these past few years.

"We can get you some new notebooks at the store, okay?" she says. "We'll hide them somewhere else. He won't find them. I promise."

The same woman who just ten minutes ago warned me to be careful so I didn't upset my father is now suggesting we break one of his all-important rules.

"Yeah, Mom," I whisper, not sure if I'm really speaking or merely thinking.

My eyes feel like they're bursting as I watch my notebooks burn, the image searing onto my brain.

I've heard most of the stories regarding my family's past.

I've memorized all the jokes. The dumb, sick jokes.

I shake my head.

I say, "Everyone's right. Dad's crazy, isn't he? Just like Grandpa was."

"People say dumb stuff. That's all. It don't mean nothing."

A horn honks on RR #324.

I think: *What the hell is he going to do to us? Why doesn't he leave us alone?*

But then I see the clock on the dining room wall. I was supposed to be waiting for Rachel at the bottom of the hill five minutes ago.

How time flies when you're destroying what you love, I think, although I'm not sure why.

Rachel is sitting in her car by the side of the road. I'm sure she's wondering where I could be.

I hurry to my room at the end of the hall. My bookcase has been overturned and all the novels are scattered across the floor. No time to worry about that now.

I grab my book bag. It's black, battered, tattered, and torn. The straps are fraying, but the bag is holding together well enough.

When I return to the living room, my mother is holding my Pittsburgh Steelers jacket—her birthday gift to me from two years ago. She bought the jacket even though it meant siphoning money from the food budget.

"We'll be all right," she says.

She's trying to comfort me in the one way she can, with promises she can't keep. I love her for it, but something is gnawing at me. Something bad.

She says, "Really, we will."

"I gotta go."

I want to find something I can say to make her feel a little better, but I'm grasping at straws.

There isn't much to be said.

My gut is full of acid. Fire. It hurts so bad I want to die.

My eyes are drenched with tears, but I can't let them go.

My lungs spasm.

My head is throbbing.

My hands are shaking.

I hate my father so much. I almost savor the venom I feel flowing in my veins.

A copper taste fills my mouth from biting my lips, from trying to hold the rage in.

Except those aren't the only reasons I can't find a reply to comfort my mother.

For the first time in my life, a little voice deep inside my mind has spoken up, telling me a fact I don't want to admit.

I don't like what it says.

I don't know why I feel the way I do.

But the voice is right.

It says, "You're pissed at her! She could have stopped this! She's as guilty as he is! She never even tried to stop him!"

I try to shove the insane thoughts away, they're making me more confused, but I can't deny my feelings.

I *am* pissed.

I'm pissed at my father and humanity and, yes, maybe my mother, too.

I hate everyone who has ever walked on the earth.

The anger threatens to become uncontrollable.

I want to destroy everything. Everyone. I hate the entire planet.

Then I drive the emotions down the best I can.

My entire body hurts.

I was thinking like my father, and that frightens me.

My mother is on my side.

She has always stood up for me whenever she could.

"You're right, Mom. We can go to Mattie's store and get some notebooks," I say quietly, forcing the statement even though I still want to scream and cry and punch the wall as hard as I can. I want to throw a lamp through the front window. Break a table. Instead I say, "You're right. It will be okay."

My mother manages to smile, although the expression appears as forced as my words.

She gives me one more hug and then I'm out the door.

The screen door closes behind me, slamming shut with a crash.

The grass is wet with morning dew.

My shoelaces get soaked first.

The grass paints my sneakers as I cross the lawn.

I suspect this image will return to me for the rest of my life when I think of my thousands of trips to and from school. The way wet grass clippings soak your shoes and change their color to a uniform green and how your feet get wet.

In the house, my mother very calmly moves to the end table next to the couch in the living room. She reaches underneath and retrieves a white photo album.

I can't see this, but somehow, later on, I know it to be true.

I'm running down the hill.

My mother sits on the couch.

She opens the album and studies a faded picture of her and my father on the steps of the old stone church in town.

The smiles stretch on their faces like caricatures.

On the next page there is a large photo of the two of them kissing next to my father's first pickup truck.

They radiate happiness.

The truck is decorated with streamers. Tin cans are tied to the bumper.

The picture has yellowed with age.

My mother flips through the rest of the pages, carefully examining each image from her past.

She quietly closes the photo album.

She stands and heads to the fire.

My notebooks burn.

She says a prayer, although she hasn't been to church in years.

She tosses the photo album into the flames.

My legs are shaking under me as I run to where Rachel is waiting.

My mother is burning all the photos of her and my father.

My heart is pounding.

My mom is torching her memories.

My lungs burn.

My mom burns the pictures.

I see Rachel, and she's worried and beautiful as she leans out the driver's side window.

My mother sees her own past going up in flames. She is scared and relieved as she prepares herself to let go.

Letting go of the past is the true beginning of the future.

I want to hold Rachel and I want to scream and I want to cry. Tears demand to be let out.

I need to scream and cry and hold her tight.

Because letting go of the past is the true beginning of a happier life.

I run faster.

Chapter Eight

Then

Eddie slowed as he neared the green Civic waiting for him on the gravel shoulder of RR #324. The car was old and dented, but it ran and Eddie knew that meant a lot to Rachel. Her father had been the only full-time janitor for several of the apartment complexes in town, and Roger Matthews had just finished paying off the car when he died of pancreatic cancer. Rachel had been very young then, but she often said her father lived on through the vehicle. She told Eddie she hoped the Civic never stopped working. Somehow, she said, it would be like losing her father for good.

Rachel leaned out the window, waved, then stopped, as if she felt the rage coming toward her. She was both beautiful and plain, and her blue eyes sparkled in the morning sunlight. Eddie barely looked at her as he hurried around the car and opened the door. His eyes were focused on his hands. They had curled into fists.

"You okay?" Rachel asked as Eddie got in, tossing his book bag with more force than necessary. It hit the backseat and bounced onto the floor. "Eddie, what's wrong?"

"My dad," he said, and then the tears flowed. His eyes were red, his hands clenched into fists.

"Christ, what did he do?" Rachel unbuckled her seat belt and took Eddie into her arms like a mother cradling her child. Her blond hair fell past her shoulders, covering his head. His chest contracted as he sobbed against her. "It's okay, Eddie. I'm here for you. I love you."

"I love you, too." His eyes stung from the gasoline fumes enmeshed in his clothing and hair.

"Now tell me what the hell the son of a bitch did." Rachel sounded colder and more hostile than Eddie had ever heard her before. It shocked him. He could taste the angry current running through her, as if the pain and agony overpowering him were flooding into her, too. Then he understood. She *was* feeling the same emotions that were surging through him. That was part of being in love, wasn't it?

Eddie began to speak, and when he finished, the words were flowing like tears, but he was no longer crying.

Chapter Nine

Now

Eddie didn't say much the rest of the day, although part of him desperately wanted to talk to Mattie about the book he had found. She was in the office taking care of some paperwork, and he was alone on the sales floor. Every now and then he stopped working to stare into the round mirror set in the corner of the store. It was angled so the person at the register could see what was happening by the magazine rack. Mattie had added the security mirror when she noticed large quantities of comic books disappearing. She had quickly discovered a group of kids who sat on the floor and stuffed loot into their bags when she was busy at the register with her customers. The kids didn't try to steal from the bookstore anymore. Getting caught once by Mattie was enough to set even the worst of kids on the right path for the rest of their lives. Hell hath no fury as a Mattie St. Claire pissed off, as Mattie herself often said.

But Eddie wasn't searching for shoplifters. There hadn't been a customer all afternoon. Instead, he was standing below the mirror, where he could just barely see his own reflection. The dirty and deformed image made him look flat and distorted. He shuddered. His hair had been touched by a hint of gray, a pretty horrible development for someone who was only twenty-five.

"Hey mister," a small voice said from directly behind Eddie. He hadn't heard the bell above the door ring, and he nearly jumped in surprise. A small hand tugged on his sleeve. He turned and found a young boy with dirty brown hair and big brown eyes. The boy's cheeks were bright red, and he wore navy blue overalls, a heavy winter jacket dusted with snow, and boots covered in ice and mud. It was obvious he had been playing out in the cold, maybe throwing snowballs, maybe making a snowman, maybe tunneling through his front yard. Eddie remembered those days fondly, and he often wished he could be young again. Young and innocent.

"Can I help you, little guy?" Eddie asked with a smile as he squatted down like a catcher so he'd be the same height as the kid. The smile faded a bit. His right side was aching, and he didn't have any aspirin left. He had to go see the doctor soon. This kind of reoccurring pain couldn't be normal. Perhaps a rib was broken and they had somehow managed to miss it during all the examinations. He hated doctors and their tests, but sometimes the alternative was worse.

"My name isn't 'little guy'! It's Adam."

"Okay, Adam, what can I help you find?" Eddie tried to sound all man-to-man. He liked little kids, but many of the town's children feared him. Or at least his name. They had heard the horror stories and the clever rhymes.

Eddie Farris sitting in a tree: K-I-L-L-I-N-G.

To make life even more unpleasant, there were always

those parents who used him the same way some people used the bogeyman.

Eddie Farris is gonna get you if you don't behave! He'll sneak into your room in the middle of the night and snatch you in your sleep and kill you dead!

"I need to find a book my grandma doesn't have for her birthday," Adam answered, a big, goofy grin spreading across his face. "And it's gotta be a fat book!"

Eddie nodded. "Does she read mysteries? Romances?"

"She likes big books with God and Jesus and miracles."

"Well, we have lots of books like that." Eddie wasn't a fire-and-brimstone believer (although there were plenty of those in town), but he could navigate the religious section of the bookstore well enough. He retrieved a relatively new copy of a thick trade paperback called *On The Day He Rises: The Resurrection of Jesus.* Given the condition of the book, Eddie guessed the previous owner hadn't read much further than the jacket copy. Perhaps this had been an unwanted gift, returned for credit or as a trade-in on two mass-market paperbacks. The previous year Eddie had borrowed dozens of reference books about almost every religion from the town library, including this one, when he was going through a phase where he was fascinated by the concept of a spiritual center to the universe, a supernatural yet religious core tying all life together. But in the end, he just couldn't believe much of what he had read. It was all too preachy for his liking. He handed the book to the boy.

"Is this big enough?" Eddie asked. Adam's eyes widened in surprise. There was something about the kid that made Eddie think of himself as a child. A sense of longing filled him. Wouldn't it be wonderful to never have to worry about paying the rent or dodging nasty looks in town?

"It's huge!" Adam cried.

The bell above the front door rang. Eddie turned. His heart skipped a beat. A goddess had entered the store, her body bathed in the light of the winter sun. And Eddie knew her name: *Rachel.* She had been gone for years, but now here she was, appearing out of nowhere like a divine vision sent by God to a man lost in the desert. Only this vision was troubling. Dark circles masked Rachel's eyes and her fingernails were chewed to the quick. Her body was emaciated and her sweater was too big. To Eddie she would always be the lovely teenager with perky breasts, soft skin, and a midriff perfect for cutoff shirts, but now she looked tired and old beyond her years.

"Adam, are you in here?" Rachel Matthews asked. She shivered from the bitter cold. The warmth of the store obviously wasn't enough to break the chill. Then Eddie realized the bookstore probably wasn't much warmer than the air outside. Mattie was keeping the thermostat set far too low in the name of saving money.

"Over here," the little boy called and waved, holding the book up on top of his head like a trophy. "I found a huge one!"

Rachel took a step, saw Eddie, and continued without missing a beat. If she was angry or upset, which Eddie well expected her to be, she didn't show it. She didn't smile either and that made his heart sink. Whenever he fantasized about her, about making life normal again for the two of them, even about the next time he might speak with her, she was smiling. That was how he wanted to see her now. He loved the way she glowed when she was excited, but he hadn't seen her happy in so long.

"Adam, I told you to go slow so I could keep up," Rachel gently reminded the child. She took the book from his hands and examined the cover. The title was printed in bright red letters above an illustration of a boulder at the mouth of a cave. The shadow of a twisted cross was etched into its rock. She flipped the book over and read the flowery jacket copy, which included a raving endorsement from TV evangelist preacher Matthew Moses himself.

Rachel shook her head and asked, "So, how much is it?"

"This is our only copy, and although it's used, the pages don't show any wear and tear, so ten dollars with the tax," Eddie forced himself to say, although his vocal cords didn't want to work. His mouth was dry and sweat was forming on his palms.

"Adam, are you sure this is the one you want to get her?" Rachel's hand was already in her pocket, pulling out a ten-dollar bill. "This is your spending money for the month."

"Yeppers! It's perfect!"

"I guess we'll take it," Rachel said softly. She handed the book to Eddie, along with the money. He nonchalantly wiped his sweaty hands on his pants as he walked to the sales counter. He tried to enter the transaction into the register, but it wasn't working. The register was the old-fashioned kind that didn't need electricity, just someone to push the buttons, but sometimes those buttons stuck and locked up the gears. Eddie sharply slapped the side, the little bell on the top rang, and the tray slid open. He put the bill into the appropriate slot and noted they were running low on change. Actually, they were pretty much out of bills and coins alike. It didn't matter right now. He had more important matters to confront.

Eddie slipped the paperback into a medium-sized brown bag with BLACK HILLS BOOKS AND NEWS printed on the sides in a blue newspaper-style font. He handed it to Rachel. As she took the bag, Eddie frantically tried to think of some excuse to keep her in the store. He couldn't stand the thought of her leaving. This might be their only chance to talk. He hadn't been this close to Rachel in years, and he desperately wanted to convince her that he was worth her attention. He needed to discuss what he had done so she'd understand how sorry he was for the pain he had caused.

Rachel, there are zombies in the store! Eddie shook his head, almost raising his hand to slap himself, to knock some sense into himself. *Fuck! Get it together! Zombies aren't real! Don't scare her! Don't!*

"Eddie," Rachel whispered, leaning across the sales counter and breaking into his train of thought. She obviously didn't want Adam to hear what she was saying, but the boy was off picking through the large comic book rack by the magazines. Eddie saw him in the security mirror. "We need to talk."

"What's up?" Eddie stammered. Rachel's lips were so close he could smell the cinnamon-flavored gum on her breath. God, how he wanted to kiss her. It had been so long. But instead he controlled his urges and kept his gaze on her blue eyes. They seemed empty compared to how he remembered them. So weary.

"I just need to talk to someone," she said.

"Is this about the kid?" Eddie had assumed Rachel was babysitting the boy—that was the only logical answer, right?

"Well, we should discuss Adam, too." Rachel laughed a sad little laugh, but her expression didn't change. She checked the mirror to see where the boy was. Eddie waited for her to speak. He couldn't imagine what she was thinking, but it was driving him crazy. He wanted to grab her and hold her and kiss her and never let her leave again.

Taking a deep breath, Rachel said, "He's yours."

A hot, dense ball of tension formed in Eddie's throat, winding itself smaller and smaller until it slipped into his stomach, like a burst of acid. He opened his mouth. Nothing came out.

"I found out I was pregnant after I left," Rachel explained without prompting. "I couldn't bring myself to tell you. Not then. I just came home a few months ago to help my mom. She's been sick. I'm not going to make a fuss. I don't want money or anything. You don't have to worry."

"But . . ." Eddie said, then stopped. What could he say?

Rachel continued, "Meet me at the apartment tonight after dark. I'm living with my mother. We'll talk."

"But . . ." Eddie said again, still unable to find anything else to follow.

"We'll talk. And Eddie, do me a favor. Don't tell Mattie. Go and see if she noticed I was here. See whether she's in the office, okay?"

Eddie did as Rachel told him, not questioning why. He hurried to the rear of the store and peeked behind the red curtain. There was no one in the back room. The light on the desk was dark and paperwork was piled in neat stacks. Mattie must have gone upstairs. Maybe she needed to use the bathroom again or maybe she had seen Rachel and decided to give them some privacy. Eddie didn't know which was more likely. He was going to tell Rachel they were in the clear, but he was too late. The bell rang faintly and the front door slammed shut. He spun around. The red-and-white sign that proclaimed the store's hours was swinging in the window. Eddie ran to the bay window and watched Rachel and Adam cross the road.

Adam. His son.

Rachel glanced over her shoulder. She was holding the little boy's hand. Eddie managed to wave, but Rachel didn't acknowledge him. Maybe she hadn't seen the gesture. Eddie prayed that was the explanation for her lack of a response. He was already beginning to wish for dreams he had given up on long ago. Dreams of getting Rachel back into his life. But how could he have a son? The idea of being a father was too strange to be true.

"My son," he whispered, the words foreign on his lips. He put his hand on his right side, where the dull ache from his old battle wound throbbed.

Ashes to ashes, dust to dust.

Then Rachel and Adam were gone as quickly as they had appeared.

Chapter Ten

From the Handwritten Account

My Mental Reconstruction of Events Past
by Eddie Farris

The drugs knock me out for days.

I wonder if I was in surgery. The doctors don't tell me, or if they do, I can't remember.

The last couple of weeks have been a big, white blur.

Am I even in the same hospital?

I can't tell.

I awoke from a nightmare this morning, and I was hollering for my father.

Calling to Daddy like a little kid.

I often wonder what changed my father.

He was a decent man when I was young.

I remember going to baseball games and watching cartoons and making snacks when he got home from work.

Sure, he had his moments, but who doesn't?

So what made him change after Mary was born?

I don't have any answers, but I think my mom was searching for them.

She went to the free clinic to talk sometimes.

The free clinic is part of the mental hospital.

Their no-charge outpatient counseling program might be the one thing that keeps people in Black Hills from rising up in opposition to the complex.

No one really enjoys having a bunch of crazy mental patients so close to the town, but the free clinic gets a lot of traffic, and anything said there is confidential.

Don't go to the old stone church to talk with Reverend David Smith if you're worried about your privacy.

No one you speak to at the clinic will tell his wife your most intimate secrets.

Reverend Smith often does that.

And Mrs. Smith gossips everywhere.

You'd be better off buying an advertisement in the *Black Hills Herald* instead of confiding to the Reverend. At least then everyone would get the story straight.

As rumors spread, people have to add their own little observations and bits of imagination.

You say, "I've been coveting my neighbor's wife."

When you hear your words repeated, they've become: "I'm sleeping with the neighbor's wife." And maybe sister and daughter and niece, too.

If you're lucky, it won't get much worse.

It does get worse.

Trust me.

You normally don't get to talk to a real doctor at the free clinic. Just some sort of counselor.

He can't give you pills, although he can send you to the people who have the pills.

He isn't a real doctor, but most people don't care.

They need to talk.

I need to write.

I should warn you: This is all a mixed-up and jumbled collection of hazy memories for me.

I'm trying to remember the chain of events the best I can, but there are a lot of blanks.

The doctors tell me it's shock.

I have to figure out what I'm missing.

This is the only way.

This is what happens after school: The classes empty quickly as the students hurry home or to social engagements that are far more important than their public education could ever be.

Most of them will end up as housewives, truck drivers, retail employees, waiters and waitresses, gas station attendants, fry cooks, janitors at the asylum, guards at the prison, or unemployed and living off the government, depositing most of their money at Buddy's Tavern. Some will spend the rest of their lives working the family farm that never makes a profit. Others will leave town forever, never to return.

A few will end up as inmates at the prison or permanent residents at the asylum.

Those are the options we have. People in this valley live lives of quiet desperation.

The coal mines have been dead for decades, since the late 1950s. We have anthracite coal, the clean stuff, the stuff that's better for the environment, but it costs more, so no one wants it.

Then the factories, which boomed during World War

II, began to shut down as the jobs were transferred south.

In the early 1960s, the state legislature in Harrisburg decided we didn't need an exit off the big highway they were building on the other side of the hills from which our town got its name.

But Slade City was given an exit.

So they grow larger.

We wither.

Soon Black Hills will be a ghost town, I think. Maybe not.

After all, the prison and the mental hospital remained after the mining companies and factories closed up shop and we didn't get that exit ramp.

They are the modern-day industries keeping the town alive. They pump blood through our veins, like the mines once did.

And there is the school, I guess.

Right now I'm late meeting Rachel at her locker.

I had to stay after biology class.

Mr. Henderson wanted to discuss my grade. It's pretty bad.

I haven't been scoring too well on the weekly quizzes, and I didn't do the extra credit project. Big mistake. I needed those points.

When I finally meet up with Rachel, I explain why I'm late, and she says, "What if your father finds out?"

"He won't," I reply, completely confident. "I'll ace the next couple of tests. No problem."

Rachel obviously isn't as optimistic.

"Well, just to be safe, maybe I should help you study so you won't be grounded."

"You mean put in lockdown?" I ask, using the same phrase my father loves so much. He constantly uses his work terminology at home.

"Yeah." Rachel frowns.

"It's all good," I say. "I can handle the class."

We leave the school together, barely speaking, mostly making small talk.

I've been quiet since this morning, since we spoke in the car.

I feel like a truck has crushed my chest, like my life is being ripped apart, over and over again, all day long. I want to scream and cry. I hate this place!

But for Rachel's sake I try not to act too depressed. I don't want her worrying.

As we exit the school and cross the patched and cracked parking lot, a strong wind cuts through the air, biting into us.

Low black clouds flow swiftly to the east.

It's not cold enough to snow, but sleet, hail, and heavy downpours are in the forecast.

There'll be a hard rain in the valley tonight.

Rachel tells me her mom is working a double shift at the diner today. She asks if I want to go home with her for a while, and I tell her I do.

We have some time until my father gets off work, so we'll make the best of it. I have a surprise for Rachel.

So we drive.

The school is located between Black Hills and Slade City, but closer to Black Hills, so our trip to her place is a short one.

The Richard Street Apartments stand seven stories tall, oddly narrow and deep, with rickety and rusted fire escapes on the rear and sides of the building. It was built in a different age, when thousands of men and their families inhabited the area and needed somewhere cheap to live.

Now, without the mines and factories, there are two developments of deserted homes on the north side of Black Hills. Ghost towns. And there are several other apartment complexes like this one. They're deteriorating around the people who still live in them.

The red brick walls of the Richard Street Apartments are dirty from years of coal dust settling into the valley.

The windows are small and grimy.

The lobby is empty, devoid of life, and often the front door remains unlocked day and night.

There is a single stairwell.

The steps creak and groan.

There are a few smoke alarms in strategic places so the building can pass the occasional state fire inspection.

This place reeks of abandonment.

I notice these details for what feels like the first time as we walk down the hallway past the uniform-looking doors, until we reach the one marked FIFTY-SEVEN.

Chapter Eleven

Then

Eddie stood in the living room of the apartment where Rachel lived with her mother. He gazed out the dirty window overlooking the rear fire escape. The abandoned lot behind the building was littered with rubble, trash, piles of cracked bricks from various construction projects, broken TV sets, dented and busted microwaves, numerous kinds of exercise equipment (most of which had been used once or twice before being ditched in favor of bigger clothes), the wooden frames of old couches, and the rusting shells of a couple of ancient cars that weren't worth what it would cost to tow them to the dump. Past the abandoned lot was Copper Street, one of the roads that ran parallel to Main Street.

"I love you," Rachel said, turning Eddie's head gently with her hand, pulling him back to more urgent matters. She kissed him and ran her hands through his hair, closing her eyes as they got lost in the moment. Eddie's body came alive, and the thought of the two of them in Rachel's bed jumped to the front of his mind. He saw them naked and doing the things he had read about, seen in movies, and fantasized about to no end, but never actually done. His pulse raced, pushing the horror of the morning even farther into the depths of his mind, at least temporarily. Then he gently broke off the passionate embrace.

"Hey, I have a surprise for you." Eddie opened his book bag and retrieved a wrapped package. It was too big for jewelry, but too small to hold just a card or some little trinket—not that he thought Rachel expected to receive any kind of gift today. Their gifts usually involved letting the other decide what movie they would see at the three-dollar matinee. There were rare exceptions, of course. The Stetson cologne she had given him last year or the copy of *Charlotte and Emily Brontë: The Complete Novels* he had bought her when they started going out. But those were special occasions. Today didn't mean anything, did it?

"What did you do?" Rachel asked, tearing at the red paper. Underneath she found another layer of wrapping paper. This was blue and white and declared *Happy Birthday* in cute, scripted letters. It wasn't her birthday. Not even close. "What is all this?"

"Well, you have to keep going," Eddie explained, laughing, smiling. The smile felt terrific, like he could actually be happy for a little while, like the events of that morning had never happened.

"I meant, why am I getting this?" She pulled off the next layer—this one was red with white hearts.

"Because I couldn't get you anything real for your birthday or Valentine's Day this year and I wanted to give you something special."

"Oh, silly." Rachel held the last shred of wrapping

paper in her right hand and the book in her left. Kahlil Gibran's *A Tear and a Smile* the cover proclaimed.

"Check inside," Eddie said.

Rachel opened the book to the front page where her boyfriend had written: *I love you with all my heart! No matter what, I will be with you until the end of time. That is a promise I could never break. Love is the blood of life and I'll always love you. Yours, Eddie.*

"Oh, Eddie, it's wonderful!" Rachel pulled him tight so they could kiss again. Her lips were soft and wonderful against his own, and he breathed her in. Something sparked inside of Eddie. He didn't want the moment to end, but a noise caught his attention: an alarm clock buzzing in one of the two bedrooms. But they were supposed to be alone. He opened his eyes as the door to their left, the one to the larger bedroom, swung open. Tabitha Matthews walked into the living room.

"Oh hello, Eddie," Rachel's mother said cheerfully. She was dressed for work—black pants, a white top embroidered with BLACK HILLS DINER on the breast, and a little gold pin stuck through her blouse. Written on the pin was the name TABBY in thick, bold letters. She was a large woman and the rolls of her skin filled the uniform like Silly Putty. Tabitha asked, "Is Rachel going to help you with your homework?"

"Um, yeah." Eddie tried to smile, to seem carefree, without a worry in the world. Technically, he and Rachel hadn't disobeyed any rules—they weren't in the apartment alone since Tabby had been there the entire time—so they might be okay. Maybe they weren't in trouble.

Then again, Eddie knew better than to push his luck in life.

"What's this?" Tabby asked, taking *A Tear and a Smile* from her daughter's hand.

"Eddie bought it as a surprise," Rachel said. She didn't sound the least bit worried. "Isn't it great?"

"That was very sweet of him." Tabby opened the book and read the handwritten inscription on the front page. Eddie felt his face flush red as Tabby's eyes scanned his jagged scrawl in the book. She chuckled, said nothing, and leafed through the pages.

"I really like it," Rachel said.

"I hope you thanked him," Tabby replied, glancing at Eddie. He nodded to say she had. "I'm glad you kids remember your manners these days. You could learn a lot from us old folks."

"Oh, Mom, you're not old."

"I sure feel it." She checked her watch, sighed, and crossed the room, grabbing her yellow raincoat from where it hung on a wooden peg by the door. As she slipped the yellow plastic jacket on, she reached for her purse. It sat on the kitchen counter. There was a pack of cigarettes nearby, and she pulled out two of the white-and-brown coffin nails. She left the rest of the pack sitting there, as if this was her method of suppressing the nasty habit.

Rachel asked, "You running late?"

"Yeah, I took a nap and set the alarm for the wrong time again. You've gotta help me learn how to get it set right," Tabby said, opening the door. "I'm the closer tonight, and I'm working a double tomorrow, so I'll probably collapse when I get home. But Rachel, if you need any help with your schoolwork, we'll do what we can tomorrow morning, okay?"

"That's cool," Rachel said, giving her mother a quick hug. "But I don't think I'll need any help."

"Okay, then you kids be good while I'm gone! Don't do anything I wouldn't do. In fact, pretend I'm still here, if need be." Tabby chuckled again and waved to Eddie. She stepped into the hallway and pulled the door shut. The room instantly felt empty, like a giant wind had swept through the apartment, a warm storm centralized to a limited space. All of Tabby's energy and exuberance disappeared, leaving the place barren without her.

Rachel breathed a sigh of relief. "I must have read her schedule wrong! I could have sworn she worked a double shift today. I'm sorry, Eddie!"

"Baby, it's not a big deal. She didn't seem to care, did she?"

"I don't think so, but we'll see what she says when she gets home tonight. Of course, she didn't kick you out. Could be she realizes her little girl is growing up." Rachel smiled and added, "Thank you for the book! I can't believe you bought it for me!"

"Yeah, well, I had to make sure you never listen to anyone who says a pretty gal like you shouldn't date a badass like me," Eddie replied in a poor John Wayne cowboy accent. He was joking and serious. Although he had always understood that Rachel didn't care what everyone said behind their backs, the stories did make life harder on them. He hoped they would eventually escape the town and his family's past. Deep down he knew every young couple dreamed of running away (or any of the other ridiculous teenage notions), but sometimes those dreams were all Eddie had.

"Silly boy," Rachel said.

Eddie opened his mouth to reply, but Rachel gently put her index finger across his lips. There was a flash of excitement in her eyes. She leaned closer, pressing her mouth against his lower neck, kissing her way to his ear. Eddie's body tingled as Rachel softly moved her lips to his, not kissing, but gently sucking, her mouth hot and wet on his cool flesh. He pulled her tighter, enjoying the sudden warmth of her body pressed against his.

She whispered into his ear, "I want to make love to you."

"Are you sure?" His voice shook a little as Rachel's hand found his zipper, tugging it down. They had never slept together, even though there had been several good opportunities when Rachel's mother was at work and they had the apartment to themselves. Sometimes they fooled around a little, and sometimes they fooled around a lot, but the fear of pregnancy or her mother coming home early had stopped them from going any further. Today, though, they'd be alone for a couple of hours. And as for pregnancy, well, what were the odds, right?

"Yes, I'm sure, you silly boy," Rachel replied, running her hand up to Eddie's chest. He grinned like a fool. He could see the desire burning inside of Rachel. She had never been so aggressive before and this new development thrilled him. He pulled her even closer and his heart throbbed from the wild fantasies and emotions overwhelming his mind.

"I love you, Rachel."

"I love you too. Now let's go to my room," she whispered as she moved to kiss his neck again.

Chapter Twelve

Now

The stairwell on the west side of the Richard Street Apartments was darker than normal, and Eddie immediately saw why. Several of the lights in the landings above him were burned out and there was no janitor to replace them. He began the long trek to the fifth floor, the stairs creaking with every slow step. The sound was so familiar. It reminded him of the last time he had ever really played with his friends, back when he was ten years old.

"At the Godwin Estate," Eddie said, and for an instant he was a child again, soon to be trapped in an honest-to-God haunted house. It had been years since he thought about that day, but now he was there, hanging out near the public campground by Black Rock Lake with a bunch of his friends. These guys really had been his friends, although their mothers discouraged them from playing with him. On this particular day they were debating whether to visit the old Godwin Estate, a real-life haunted house, and Eddie pushed for it. Pushed a little too hard, maybe. He just loved the idea of exploring the place. The crumbling Victorian mansion in the mountains was massive—it overlooked the town like a watchful guardian, too—but no one had lived there in eighty years, not since a fire partially destroyed the west wing during a dinner party. Ten guests hadn't escaped the flames, although no one in town ever discovered how or why the group became trapped. The owners—a spooky old couple who, according to rumors, practiced the dark arts—hanged themselves in the wine cellar while the fire still burned.

Eddie and his friends didn't last two hours in the dilapidated mansion. They arrived at sundown, carrying lanterns and flashlights they had stolen from the campground. Even with the lights, the house seemed too dark. The strange noises—like ropes rubbing against the wooden eaves—and the cobwebs and the rats overwhelmed their young imaginations. They thought they saw objects moving, heard voices. Then three of the boys disappeared into the basement. Their bloodcurdling shrieks of terror had sent Eddie and his other friends fleeing the abandoned house, knocking over small statues in the long overgrown garden and nearly breaking the front gate off its hinges. Eddie never forgot the frantic run through the thick woods surrounding the property or the tremendous sense of relief he had experienced when they reached town unscathed. Yet their missing friends were never found. Search parties covered every acre of the valley, scoured the mansion twice, and found nothing. Most people blamed Eddie, and after that no one at school was eager to play with him.

"Don't think about that," Eddie scolded himself as he

continued up the steps, pushing the memory away. Another took its place. Being in the apartment building on Richard Street made the painful reality of the last seven years return in one high-powered blow, stunning Eddie, twisting his stomach. The chants of the protesters rattled around his mind. Sometimes he still heard kids jumping rope and crying bizarre rhymes about him and his family.

Down by the river, down by the sea,
Eddie killed his family and blamed it on me.
I told Ma, Ma told Pa,
Eddie had the gun so ha ha ha.
How many people did he kill?
One, two . . .

When he finished the ascent to the fifth floor, Eddie's chest had tightened and his breathing had quickened. His legs trembled.

"What does she want to talk about?" he asked quietly. He put his hand on the scratched brass doorknob. Something had to be wrong. Given how long it had been since they had spoken, that was the only explanation for her unexpected contact with him.

Eddie opened the door. Hanging in the middle of the hallway were two light fixtures. They looked utterly out of place. The clear plastic icicles that dangled from the lights had darkened with age, and no one had bothered to dust them recently, making the hallway feel abandoned. The beige carpet was dirty, faded, and torn in places. Sections of the red-and-gray striped wallpaper had peeled, showing plaster and lines of paste. A cracked mirror with a thick, ornately carved frame was leaning against the wall across from the doorway. The mirror fractalized the light of the full moon blazing in through the window, and the result was a sparkling reflection of Eddie, making him radiate like a ghost.

"Hey stranger, how are you?" Rachel asked from the window ledge at the end of the hall. Eddie spun, startled.

Rachel sat on an alcove in the window, the full moon rising above her shoulder, a thin veil of cigarette smoke swirling around her. She limply held the cigarette, an addiction Eddie hadn't known about. It surprised him, but he didn't say anything.

"I'm holding on, I guess."

"It's been too long." Rachel patted the window seat. They could both fit there comfortably, if they wanted to. They had done so many times as teenagers. The ledge was a peaceful place to relax and talk. They could observe most of the town from the window, and sometimes, when they had been dating, Eddie and Rachel had pretended they could also see the glow of Pittsburgh in the distance over the mountains. They had often discussed running away to the city.

"Yeah, it has been," Eddie said, joining her. He tried his best not to show his nearly uncontrollable disbelief at the mere idea of Rachel sitting next to him after so many years. This was how he had imagined them reuniting. *Now that it's really happening—*

He abandoned the thought. It was best not to dwell on what was or what might be. Wasting the effort only made him hurt more when the nightmares came.

"I'm sorry I didn't contact you."

"You could have called," Eddie replied, just to say

something. None of the day's events seemed real. Being in the apartment building, sitting with Rachel, being a father, none of it. Having a son seemed about as possible as being an astronaut or a secret agent or the president of the United States.

"I'm sorry, but after . . ." She stopped. "I had to leave. I couldn't tell you."

"Where'd you go? I was worried. I missed you."

Rachel's reply came slowly, as if she had rehearsed this conversation a thousand times but now she had forgotten her lines. She said, "Life is strange. I don't think where I went really matters. But I'm sorry I didn't tell you about Adam."

"Where is he?"

"In there, sleeping in Mom's room," she said, nodding at the door. "She's become really religious the last few years, Eddie. You wouldn't believe it."

"Then she'll enjoy the book Adam got her."

A long, eerie silence stretched between them. Eddie focused on the row of streetlights and the fog creeping into the town. There was a shimmer to the moonlight as it burned through the white mist that he found to be absolutely beautiful. It was Mother Nature personified, alive and moving among the people of Black Hills.

Eddie shifted his gaze from the fog to take in every inch of Rachel. She looked tired, but she was still beautiful, and Eddie was slowly realizing he didn't mind being a father, especially if their son was the catalyst for the renewal of their relationship. He didn't care about the added responsibilities. He could work more hours. Find a second job. Whatever it took. He just needed to be with Rachel again, to make up for what they had lost.

But right now she was distant, as if she was on some other planet meditating in a secret language he'd never understand.

He asked, "So, what's this all about? Is Adam all right?"

"He's fine," Rachel said, her voice low. "It's just . . ." She paused again. "I'm really sorry I didn't try harder to fix our problems. I should have tried harder."

"It was my fault." Eddie grimaced, remembering the confused expression on Rachel's face and the blood on her hands and the ringing of the phone that could have changed everything for the two of them.

"You can't help it. Sometimes you . . . Sometimes you get pushed too far."

"Like my dad." Eddie hated saying it. He hated admitting he was anything like his father.

"Yeah, your dad." Rachel's frown deepened.

"Are you okay?"

"I don't know." Again, a long silence. Finally Rachel said, "I've been getting professional help, Eddie. I've been seeing a shrink. A counselor."

"Where? Who?"

"The free clinic," she replied.

Eddie tried not to show his surprise, but his mind spun. He asked, "What did the counselor tell you?"

"First, I told him everything," Rachel said. "And he made me realize I wasn't responsible for what came between you and me. That it was your fault, not mine."

Eddie didn't reply. Instead he imagined Rachel and the counselor sitting on ugly plastic chairs in a drab conference room. The room was lit by the bright fluorescent bulbs overhead, yet the corners were filled with shadows. The curtains were pulled tight. He saw the young counselor with his thin-framed glasses and his sweater and casual pants, and what the man was telling Rachel wasn't pleasant.

He's a beast! the counselor in Eddie's imagination declared in the tone of voice often associated with preachers on the television late at night who lectured their virtual flock to beware the tricks of the devil. *Eddie Farris is the cause of all your problems! He would have killed you someday!*

A blistering surge of jealousy and anger rushed through Eddie, as if he had discovered Rachel was sleeping with the counselor. He didn't understand where the emotions came from, but they were devastating. A sense of betrayal without rationality swelled within him.

"Eddie?" Rachel asked.

"Yeah? I'm sorry." He hadn't heard anything she had said. "I was thinking about the free clinic."

Rachel opened her mouth to say more, but then the dam broke. Her eyes welled up with tears. The liquid diamonds sparkled in the moonlight. She sobbed. Eddie reached to hold her, the feeling of betrayal melting into a cold, dead ball inside his gut. Rachel jerked to her left, out of his reach. She wheezed and coughed. Eddie wanted to hold her, but instead he dropped his hands into his lap. He didn't want to scare her.

Rachel said, "Eddie, someone is after me."

"What do you mean?"

"Someone keeps calling and saying things. Horrible things." Rachel lethargically lit another cigarette. She didn't ask if it was all right, and Eddie didn't ask when she had taken to the habit. He stared at her wet checks, tangled hair, and trembling fingers.

"What does he say?" Eddie's mind was running rampant. Rachel was in trouble so she had contacted him for help. That gave him more hope than he had ever believed existed in the long nights when he lay alone in his bed drinking beer, writing stories, and fantasizing about the two of them being together again.

"He says he's coming for me," she replied, taking a drag on the cigarette. "He says he's coming to finish what he started."

"What the hell? What does that mean?"

She didn't respond. In the maddening lull that followed, Eddie forced himself to concentrate on the problem of Rachel's mysterious caller instead of his hopes and fantasies for the future. If he was able to help her with the creep who was bothering her, then maybe, just maybe, she would see the good side of him, the side of him she had fallen in love with in high school. Then they could be together. And with Adam, they'd be a family.

"Who's calling you?" he asked. "Do you have any idea?"

"That's why I wanted to talk to you." Rachel appeared sad, yet angry, and the forgotten cigarette in her right hand sent a few red embers to the floor. "I thought you should know. That you deserved to know."

"Who is it, Rachel? Please tell me."

There was another long silence before she spoke. "Eddie, he sounds like your father. I think it *is* your father."

Eddie's eyes widened in horror. "You're kidding, right?"

"No. I wish I were."

"But he's dead. We saw him die!"

"I know. Trust me, I know."

Another long, unbearable silence. Eventually Eddie collected himself enough to ask, "Did you tell your mother? What did she say?"

"I haven't told her. She sleeps a lot. Your father . . . it was so difficult for her. She—" Rachel stopped abruptly. "I can't tell Mom. It would worry her and she's already been through too much as it is."

Rachel hopped off the ledge and walked to her apartment. She stopped by the door. Eddie hadn't moved. He couldn't stop thinking about the prison guard in the fog. The strange phrase—*a man's heart and soul are filled with a fire that burns in his words and his actions and in his love*—still didn't make any sense, but he remembered it with complete clarity. The babbled nonsense resembled the poems he sometimes wrote when he drank too much of the cheap beer he kept stashed on the bottom shelf in his refrigerator—beautiful and confusing.

Eddie managed to ask, "How could it be?"

"I have no idea," Rachel replied. "Maybe we were wrong. Maybe everyone was wrong."

Chapter Thirteen

From the Handwritten Account

My Mental Reconstruction of Events Past
by Eddie Farris

Two days since I last wrote. I think.

The days and nights blur together as the medicine does its job.

The painkillers make life a strange and mysterious place, but my right side and hand don't hurt as much as they once did.

I have to keep going.

Things are coming back to me, little by little. If I can keep writing, I'll be able to see the full picture.

Then I'll be whole.

Soon the nurses will tell me I need to sleep.

It's kind of funny: When they dim the lights, when I'm passing out for the night, I can see shadows moving on my wall.

It's as if I'm chained to this bed, imprisoned in some kind of cave, and all I have for entertainment are these dancing bits of darkness.

The shadows move from left to right, as people pass by in the hallway and block the light.

The people appear to be carrying objects on their heads.

The shadows become my world.

They come and go.

I wonder what would happen if I broke free of these invisible chains and found the source of the shadows?

What would I find? How would my comprehension of the universe change?

I hope I can go home soon.

Well, not home, but somewhere other than here.

These walls are boring, even with my black-and-white imaginary theater, and the nurses give me funny looks when they bring my meds.

I think I'm talking in my sleep.

I wonder what I could be saying.

I mutter under my breath as I run up the hill to my family's property.

Drizzle falls from the sky, wetting my jacket, my book bag, my flesh.

The gravel crunches beneath my shoes.

Rachel dropped me off a few minutes ago, but she didn't dare drive me to the house.

Her presence would make the situation worse than it probably already is.

You see, we lost track of time while making love at the apartment.

It was amazing.

Better than any of the stories in the magazines Mattie keeps hidden under the sales counter at her bookstore, the ones she only sells to card-carrying adults over the age of eighteen. I've "borrowed" a couple, stuffing them into my jacket while she and my mother chatted in the romance section. I hope she doesn't mind, but I couldn't actually buy something like that from her.

Now I'm late getting home.

Fear chokes me, but I keep moving.

Rachel made me promise to call her as soon as I get a chance.

She said she won't be able to sleep if I don't call.

I promised her, crossed my heart, hoped to die.

Bad choice of words.

I top the hill, and find a wonderful sight: My father's pickup truck is nowhere to be seen.

I cautiously open the front door and step inside.

If the truck is gone, my father almost definitely isn't home.

The house smells of harsh cleaning supplies. The ashes and whatever else remained of my notebooks has been swept out of the fireplace.

I wish my mother would have left the work for me. I could have taken care of the mess.

But there is another smell in the air.

It's just as harsh. Possibly more so.

I see my mother waiting for me.

She's nervously pacing in the dining room.

Six smashed cigarettes lay in the crystal ashtray on the table, and a lit one is in her hand.

The ashtray is from a Best Western motel in Slade City she and my father stayed at on their mini-honeymoon.

They stole it as a souvenir.

But why is she smoking?

She doesn't smoke anymore.

She quit after too many of her friends got lung cancer at far too young an age.

The black lung of her generation.

Then I understand.

She probably found the pack while cleaning the house.

And although she threw the cigarettes out, waiting for me terrified her so much she rummaged through the trash and retrieved the cancer sticks.

I'm pushing her to the edge.

How much more can her nerves take?

"Eddie, where were you?" she cries as I enter the dining room.

Chapter Fourteen

Then

Although Laura sounded furious, Eddie could see the stark relief in her eyes. She looked like a woman who had just discovered the tumor in her brain had miraculously disappeared. She dropped into a chair, exhausted, while Eddie searched for an answer to her question. He couldn't tell her the whole truth, of course, but he understood from the single sentence how completely terrified his mother had been. He couldn't lie to her. Not more than necessary, at least.

"I'm sorry. Rachel and I went to her place and lost track of time."

Eddie thought about his father and the events of that morning. The memory filled him with dread and anger, pushing away the lingering happiness from what he and Rachel had been doing half an hour earlier. Blood rushed to his face.

Why didn't you stand up for yourself? a pesky little voice in the back of his mind asked. *Why were you such a coward? You didn't have to burn the notebooks!*

Yes, I did! Eddie replied. *He could have killed Mom and*

me! Hell, he probably would have. He's too big and mean and one of these days he will *kill me if I'm not careful!*

The questioning voice ceased.

Eddie asked, "Where's Dad?"

"He's still at work, thank God," Laura said. "I guess he had to pull some overtime. But don't count on always getting so lucky. You have to be more careful! After this morning, you should know better!"

"I do, Mom. I do." Eddie studied his mother, her pale sagging skin, her exhausted eyes, her delicate and scrawny fingers. Some days she resembled a skeleton dipped in flesh, and she moved slowly, like great weights were digging into her legs while she walked across a thin sheet of ice on a wide lake, desperately trying to make it to the other side without falling through. She wasn't even forty, but any stranger on the street would easily guess she was at least fifty.

"We have to be careful. We don't want to set him off." Laura smothered the last inch of the cigarette.

The cigarette smoke hanging in the air made Eddie's eyes water. He blinked, trying to dampen the stinging. He asked, "You doing okay?"

"I'm holding on, I guess," Laura said. "Mattie stopped by this afternoon and we talked. We discussed your vivid imagination again."

"You like that phrase, don't you?"

"I love it! She brought you a surprise, too. I asked her if she needs some help in the bookstore, so you could get out of the house a little more often. She said she does, if you're interested."

"Dad won't allow that."

"Maybe if you ask him on the right day. I think it

would be good for you to work with Mattie. She's more than willing to give you the job."

"I know." Eddie said nothing for a moment, then asked, "What's wrong with Dad? What happened to him?"

"Your father wasn't always like this, Eddie. Don't forget that, okay? He used to be a good man. But after Mary . . ."

She stopped, a tear dribbling down her cheek. Eddie looked away. Thinking about how his little sister had died tore him apart. Yet there had been a time when his mother and father really loved each other. Although he was eighteen, and his parents' marriage was barely five months older than him, Eddie understood he wasn't the only reason his mother and father got hitched. If the knowledge of his budding existence had been the driving force in the relationship, their wedlock probably wouldn't have lasted a year. Real love had to have been there, not just an unexpected child. And even with all the hell of the last few years, his mother had struggled to keep the family together. Once there had been real love within these walls. But now . . .

"Why did he change?" Eddie asked, his thoughts returning to the cold September day when he was eleven years old and Mary died. Had it really been an accident? An act of God? An unfortunate series of coincidences ending with a death? Bad luck? Bad karma? In the days after Mary's funeral at the Stone Creek Cemetery, Eddie had desperately needed to believe his little sister's death had been the result of a foolish blunder on her part. But then his father began the never-ending stream of violent outbursts and long drinking binges. Reality set in. The reality of the present and of the past.

"I don't know, Eddie. I honestly don't know."

Eddie's eyes narrowed as he remembered his little sister, her lifeless body, and his mother's screams. The memories blurred into the image of his burning notebooks. The pages curling, soaked in gasoline, the flames eating through his writings. Those images faded into a memory of the first time his father had beaten his mother—the night of Mary's funeral. Eddie had run into their room, scared out of his young mind, certain someone was attacking his parents. He was rewarded for his concern with a left hook to the side of the head after he screamed at his father to stop. From that day on, Eddie had hid in his room whenever his parents were fighting. He cowered and covered his ears and tried to imagine when he would be strong enough to defend his mother. Eddie secretly knew he would never be that strong. His father was too much of a beast to fight. But there was another option.

"Maybe we need to make a run for it," Eddie said. "We could make it, with Mattie's help. Dad wouldn't find us. We could go somewhere he'd never check!"

"We can't!" Laura sounded horrified. "He would find us and then things would get so much worse. He wouldn't stop until he found us! Don't you understand? He wouldn't let us leave!"

"But we could go to the city and find somewhere safe to live!"

"Edward Michael Farris," Laura cried, sharp and biting, her voice rising with every breath. "Don't talk like that! We can't!"

"I'm sorry." Eddie felt beaten, broken, and now he just wanted to go to his room and be alone. He regretted even starting the conversation.

His mother sighed. "I didn't mean to be harsh on you, boy. I just don't want you doing nothing foolish. And anyway, could you really leave Rachel behind?"

Eddie paused, feeling confused. For some reason he hadn't even thought of that. "Of course I couldn't. But is Dad hitting you again?"

"No, no, he isn't," Laura said, turning away from her son, the lie thinly veiled and unmistakable.

The heaviness in Eddie's chest crushed him. He wished he could fix their problems, but what could he really do? Call in a superhero? Pummel his dad and save the day? Then he and Rachel would ride off into the sunset, right? Of course not. Those things only happened in books and movies and his dreams. Not in real life.

Eddie ate his dinner quickly and excused himself from the table, moving quietly through the living room where an ancient, boxy television sat under the large picture window. He continued down the darkened hallway, past the bathroom, the tiny spare bedroom, and the master bedroom where his mother read her cheap romance novels, religious books, and the latest release from any of the self-proclaimed self-help experts. Mattie St. Claire gave her the books at a nice discount, and Laura loved reading too much to refuse her friend's charity, even though she hated accepting handouts. Eddie's room was directly at the end of the short hall. He stepped inside, closed the door and flipped on the light.

At some point during the day his mother had put his bookcase back in place and reshelved the books. She had also organized his nightstand, neatly arranging his pencils and pens, his wind-up alarm clock, and the bottle of Stetson cologne Rachel had given him.

Laying on his narrow bed was a green notebook. Eddie wasn't completely surprised, but the sight made him feel a little happier anyway. He opened the notebook to the front page where Mattie had written: *Get to work and write another crazy story about that outrageous picture for me! Love, Mattie.*

Eddie raised his head and studied the poster on the wall next to his bed. Without a doubt, the reproduction of *Persistence of Memory* by Salvador Dali was the most prominent object in the room. The painting intrigued Eddie. He had once written a short story inspired by a dream in which he was trapped inside the strange, melting world. Mattie had read the story and claimed it scared her so badly she had to sleep with the light on for a week. She was prone to exaggeration, but he appreciated the encouragement.

Gotta get started, Eddie thought as he selected a pencil and made himself comfortable on the bed. *I have a lot of work to do.*

He quickly decided what he wanted to work on, since he was starting from scratch. The loss of his notebooks tore him apart inside, pushing him between the urge to scream and the need to cry until his tear ducts dried up for good, but the thrill of the two hundred blank pages was enough to motivate him. Even though the basic elements of the narrative were already organized in his mind, he enjoyed the actual act of composition. Previously unexplored concepts would appear out of nowhere and change the course of the story. Sometimes the ending even surprised him. The awe of creation was part of the real excitement of writing fiction. With essays and papers for school there was no variation or imagination. His own writing, on the other hand, was an adventure. He couldn't predict where he might end up, what worlds he might create, or what people he might meet. Anything and everything could happen. All was fair when it came to make-believe.

Eddie began to write, and like most nights the story came flooding out. As the words poured onto the page, he managed to smile.

Chapter Fifteen

Now: The First Nightmare

Eddie tried to raise his head from the desk in the office of the bookstore, but the room was hazy and his body moved with the slow, lethargic manner of someone coming out of a deep sleep. Every shape was fuzzy at the edges. The light on the desk was far too bright, almost blinding. Shadows grew and mutated throughout the room. There were no longer any piles of invoices and bills on the desk, no boxes stacked in the corner, and no books sitting on the old metal cart, waiting to be shelved or returned to the publisher. Cobwebs draped the furniture. Everything gradually came into focus.

"I'm dreaming," Eddie said, his voice distorted, like a twisted audiotape on the verge of snapping. Under the desk was the black safe where Mattie kept her petty cash and a few other important items. Something stored inside the square, metal box called for Eddie. He wanted to see if he still remembered the combination, but then he thought better of it. He stood. The steps to the upstairs apartment were dusty, as were the wooden floorboards. The curtain hanging in the doorway was grubby with age. Eddie pushed it to the side. Dust showered onto his shoulder.

"So weird," he muttered. "What happened here?"

Row after row of bookshelves were empty and draped with hundreds of cobwebs and dust bunnies. There was a splintered hole in the floor near the cash register, and a rat scurried down through the opening to its lair. Pieces of glass littered the moldy carpet. The morning sun shimmered on the dirty bay window, sending a strange, sickly light across the room.

Eddie opened the front door, the bell above his head clamoring with a loud ring. He stepped down to the sidewalk. There were people standing on the sidewalk along Main Street, as if they were waiting for a parade to pass by—except they weren't watching for marching bands and floats and pretty girls standing on flatbeds pulled by old John Deere tractors.

"Oh, shit." Eddie stepped backward, colliding with the door. It had locked behind him. "Oh shit, this isn't right."

Two bodies lay in the street, and although someone had draped the corpses with long, white sheets to conceal their shredded flesh and mangled bones, that act alone did little to disguise the horror of what had taken place on this sultry summer morning. The bodies were growing rigid on the pavement, the humid air making the thin fabric cling to the bloody flesh like wet rags. They lay on the yellow lines of Main Street, and a lake of thick blood formed deep puddles at the base of the chipped concrete curb.

"This is too weird," Eddie said, stepping toward the crowd, his eyes never leaving the scene of the accident.

A white Chevrolet Caprice—BLACK HILLS SHERIFF'S OFFICE was painted in a circle around the logo of two crossed pickaxes on the side of its door—sat to the right of the bodies. A line of police tape had been strung up using the light posts along the road.

Pieces of a shattered windshield sparkled in the morning sunlight and the remains of a burned-out Chevy pickup truck lay on its roof a dozen yards from the bodies. Wild skid marks dissected the street up to where the pickup had hit the curb, flipped upside down, and slid across the sidewalk. The subsequent fire had destroyed every inch of fabric in the cab and melted most of the body of the truck.

"Hey, what happened?" Eddie asked as he reached the edge of the crowd. No one replied. "Hello?"

Eddie gagged. The warm summer breeze brought the biting smell of gasoline, smoke, and burnt rubber to his nose. Although he was only dreaming, his stomach twisted into knots. The humid air bathed his lungs. Beads of salty sweat formed on his brow as the rising sun burned a hole through the bleak clouds blanketing the lush valley in western Pennsylvania.

Eddie realized something other than the bizarre accident was wrong with Main Street. Little details were out of sync with his memories. He became fixated on the general store. It still had the front porch where the old-timers rocked in their rocking chairs and gathered to shoot the shit about the good old days, and there was the same sloped roof with gray slate shingles, but there wasn't a sign proclaiming DOLORES'S GENERAL STORE hanging to the left of the front steps.

"That's been her place since I was a kid," Eddie said,

confirming what he was thinking. "She's always had that sign, right?"

Farther down the street he could see the Black Hills Hotel and Restaurant. Above the main entrance there was a green canopy, and the ruffles fluttered in the wind. The front doors were propped open, as if the hotel were welcoming people to come inside. But a grease fire had destroyed most of the interior of the building when Eddie was a little kid. He could remember seeing the big black clouds of smoke from his house and hearing the sirens of the fire trucks roaring to the scene. The hotel and restaurant had never reopened.

"Is this the past?" Eddie asked, although he didn't expect an answer.

"Very good, Eddie," a rough, uneven voice whispered from somewhere across the street.

"Who is that? Where are you?"

No reply.

A headache throbbed at the base of Eddie's skull, but he tried to ignore the pain as he scanned the crowd pushing up to the police tape like groupies at a rock concert. The townspeople were whispering and pointing like tourists witnessing some barbaric African tribal custom. They seemed almost too fascinated by the death and destruction in the middle of their small town, as if they were savoring the tragedy.

Sheriff Breiner was examining the accident scene. The morning sunlight reflected off his mirrored aviator sunglasses. He stood tall, reminding Eddie of some marshall from a classic western movie. He jotted notes onto his official accident report form and then he knelt, carefully lifting the sheets to examine one of the bodies. The cloth was sticky with dried blood and it tore off the dead man's bloody skull with a heavy, slapping sound. The sheriff stopped lifting the sheet, letting it drop back onto the body. He walked to his car.

"Oh no," Eddie whispered. A heaviness sunk in his chest. Something terrible was about to happen. The stench of death drilled straight into his nose, and he choked it down. He lurched backward.

A limb under one of the sheets had twitched. Eddie couldn't believe what he was seeing. He didn't want to believe it. He couldn't even remember that he was only dreaming. It all felt too real.

The woman's dead body sat up, her bones creaking, cracking. The corpse struggled to her knees. She almost fell forward, like a tall tower swaying too far in a heavy wind, but then she managed to stand, the top of the white sheet hanging from where the congealed blood pinned it tightly to her matted hair. The cloth covering the woman's mouth moved in and out as she sucked air into her crushed lungs.

She took a hesitant step. There was a stomach-turning crack as her right ankle finished snapping in half. She stumbled, clumsily regaining her balance. She groaned. Only the noise was more primitive, as if it came from some beast in the jungle. Some savage, wounded beast.

No one in the crowd noticed what was happening. Eddie kept waiting for someone to scream in terror and for everyone to flee the area, but instead the crowd passively stepped to the side, like the Red Sea parting for Moses.

The corpse shuffled toward Eddie. An ice pick of fear slammed through his head. Every cell in his body told him to run, but his legs weighed a thousand pounds. They wouldn't move. He wanted to scream, but he couldn't. An invisible hangman's rope was digging into his neck, squeezing the life out of his body.

The corpse—still draped in the bloody sheet that resembled a homemade Halloween costume—gently broke through the police tape, although she moved with an awkward rocking motion. Both of her legs had been broken in the accident.

The sheet caught on the woman's crushed feet. The fabric tore off her body with a sick, gut-wrenching snap as the sticky blood pulled away from the cold flesh. Eddie's stomach knotted as the bloodied sheet drifted to the pavement like a forgotten parachute.

The woman's red high-heeled shoes had been lost during the accident; her feet were crushed and mangled. Bloody leg bones were pushed through her skin. Her hips were twisted and facing the wrong direction, as if God had been drunk when he put her together. Her right breast was exposed, bloody and torn wide open. Her cheekbones had been crushed. Her teeth were cracked into jagged points. Her right eye had burst like a grape. Her blond hair was a soaking mess of blood, white bone chips, and gray matter. She was nearly mangled beyond recognition, but Eddie could see what remained of the woman's face. Revulsion shook him to his core.

"Rachel! Oh Jesus!" Eddie screamed, his voice cracking as he recognized the disfigured body of his high school sweetheart. His legs became rubbery and he collapsed. Everything streamed past him in a slow, surreal manner, as if he was on some kind of mind-numbing drug. He landed on his knees, his weight carrying him forward until he smacked the sidewalk with a quiet thud.

The bloody, mangled feet stopped a few inches from where Eddie had landed. Rachel's toes were twisted to the sides or missing in the jumble of bone and blood and raw flesh. She bent over, her cracked leg bones pushing further through her skin, her flesh and muscles tearing apart. Hot, revolting liquid flooded up Eddie's throat. His eyes bulged as he vomited onto the concrete. He tried to turn to escape the foul, nauseating mess, but he couldn't move.

Rachel gently took Eddie by the shoulders and rolled him onto his back, as if she was flipping a stranded turtle. He screamed. Rachel's pulped head blocked the sky from horizon to horizon, and the sun burned behind her like a hot lamp. Her one remaining eye slid out of the socket in an ooze of blood and dropped off her face like a bubble of snot. It was left hanging by a few white, fleshy strains of tissue. Terror ripped through Eddie as a grin spread along Rachel's fractured mouth, revealing her cracked and chipped teeth.

She whispered, "I love you so much, but a man is his own fire, Eddie. That is all he can be. Ashes to ashes, dust to dust."

"No, Rachel!"

"That was my name in life. In death you may call me Lehcar!" she said, choking, her throat clogged with blood, bones, torn muscle, and shredded cartilage. Her voice had the rough rasp of someone who was gargling gravel. "You need to see the past, Eddie. You need to understand who started the fire."

Rachel's broken, bloody hand tenderly stroked Eddie's pale face. Her flesh was textured, cold, sticky rubber.

She sang a children's rhyme: "Down by the river, down by the sea, Eddie killed his family and blamed it on me. . . ."

Chapter Sixteen

Now

Eddie sat straight up, his mouth open wide with a scream he was too terrified to release. The nightmare had been terrible, the most terrible thing, and in his mind it wasn't yet finished. In one frantic motion he stumbled out of bed, crushing a pyramid of empty beer cans, landing on the worn carpet with a heavy thud. The shabby apartment was bitterly cold, as if winter had snapped the locks on the windows, claiming the floors and the walls, binding the room with an invisible layer of ice. Eddie barely noticed the night chill as he crawled blindly to the shadowy confines of the bathroom.

"No, Rachel, no, don't eat me!" he whimpered, not understanding what he was saying. He threw one trembling hand over his mouth and slid across the cold, chipped tiles of the bathroom floor. A burning sensation hung in his chest, his stomach and throat ablaze in a raging storm of acid. He dunked his head into the toilet, thanking God he had left the seat up, thanking God the building's water pipes had been working earlier in the night so he had been able to flush. His mouth smacked against the porcelain and a tooth chipped, a whirlwind of pain exploding through his head. He bit down hard on his lips, a spray of blood erupting into the toilet. The water soaked the ends of his brown hair and the splashing echoed like he was in a dark cave. He swallowed, gulping the water into his mouth, the coolness washing through him.

Eddie pulled his head out of the toilet and gasped for air. Drops of water dripped from his hair onto his face. He gazed into the darkness with wide, bloodshot eyes, searching for an evil that wasn't there, that wasn't real. He crawled to the cast iron tub and curled up against its frigid exterior, the white hot flashes of horror burned deep into his retinas. His heart raced faster and faster, like an engine revving to the point of self-destruction. Beads of hot sweat seeped from his pores. His teeth ached, as if someone had smashed them with a hammer, and he tasted blood on the tip of his tongue. He wrapped his arms around himself as he cowered there on the cold floor, the demon of the night still alive and attacking him.

"What the hell?" Eddie gasped. "Lehcar! She said her name was Lehcar!"

This was the first time in seven years he had dreamed of anything other than the day his father had tried to kill him. That nightmare always ended with a body lying on top of shattered glass scattered across a carpeted floor. The nightmare stopped there without fail every night, as if even Eddie's mind couldn't bear to make him live through the entire event all over again, as if that would drive him mad. Right now, his brain felt so fried he couldn't even remember coming home after his meeting with Rachel in the fifth-floor hallway of the Richard Street Apartments. Everything was a distant, white blur.

"Jesus Christ," he muttered. Then, as if a key had been entered into a lock within his mind, Eddie instantly understood what he had just witnessed. What the dream had really meant. Those events hadn't been mindless randomness. "That was the accident! My grandfather's . . ."

Eddie crawled back into the bedroom, sweeping the crushed beer cans under his bed. He didn't recall drinking the night before and the sight of the cans sickened him. They made him think of his father.

Eddie opened the bottom drawer of the dresser and rooted under his sweaters for the writing supplies he hid there. Further down were two hundred pages bound by a large butterfly clip and labeled quite specifically: *My Mental Reconstruction of Events Past.* They contained Eddie's handwritten account of the night his father had tried to kill him—including details he hadn't even witnessed. Using his imagination, he had recreated all the events starting with the strange breakfast and continuing until the climax of the storm, when he was left wounded and holding on to Rachel for dear life.

And although Eddie hadn't read the work in ages, writing was one of the ways he tried to get past the horror of that day. He began the journal in the hospital, before his wounds were completely healed, but he didn't know if he could ever read it again. Sometimes he wondered if the journal was the secret cause of his repeating nightmare of The Showdown. Reading the homemade journal had become the equivalent of opening Pandora's Box. By reading what he had written while in the hospital, Eddie knew he might set something loose into his dreams that he couldn't stop. So there it remained, untouched.

Also hidden in the dresser were a dozen green notebooks, the tomes where Eddie wrote his short stories, poems, novels, and screenplays. Now he would add a nightmare to the collection. But why was he dreaming of an accident that had occurred decades ago? And why had Rachel been there, battered and broken and bloody? Eddie didn't have any answers, but he hoped to find them through his writing. Writing opened doors within his mind. It allowed him to see the world in a new light. He selected one of the notebooks, checking to make sure it had plenty of blank paper left. Then he grabbed a pencil.

"Got to get working," Eddie whispered, pushing himself to his feet and sitting on the bed. Blood seeped from the jagged wound in his lip, trickling to the corner of his mouth, and he wiped it away. With his slightly bloody hand, he opened the notebook and studied the thin blue lines on the white pages. He finally realized how dark the apartment was. He turned on the lamp next to his bed, and there was a quiet pop as the light bulb died. Darkness reclaimed the room.

Although slivers of the morning sun radiated in around the faded brown curtains, it wasn't nearly enough light to work with. Eddie reached for the frayed drawstring to open the curtains, but his hand stopped a few inches short. In his excitement and terror, he had almost forgotten about what he would almost certainly find when he checked his window. He knew the accusations would be written on the glass, just like they always were. He hated to see those words, but he also couldn't stand the thought of them remaining there all day long, a billboard proclaiming his guilt to the town. Not cleaning the window would be tantamount to telling the citizens of Black Hills he was guilty of every crime he had ever been suspected of committing.

"Either they're there or they're not," Eddie said, trying to quell his emotions, trying to keep himself focused. "If they are, they won't go away on their own."

He yanked the curtains open with one heavy pull. Morning sunlight flooded the room, causing his eyes to blink and water.

As expected, Eddie's uninvited visitor had returned. Scrawled in red paint on the outside of the glass were INSANE and CRAZY and FREAK. The letters were wild and sloppy as if someone had worked quickly out of fear of being discovered. It was a justifiable concern. Eddie knew what he'd probably do if he ever caught the person in the act. Normally he was able to control his anger when people said things about him, but this was crossing the line and going way too far.

"Damn shit," Eddie muttered as he went to wet a towel in the bathroom. Every single night someone climbed the fire escape to the window of his apartment and painted those accusations. He suspected it was one of Rachel's friends, one who had never really liked him from the beginning, but how could he prove that? He had never been able to catch the vindictive painter in the act. Someday he would, though. He vowed that he would discover the identity of the person who was determined to make his life a living hell.

Eddie opened the window and leaned out to wash the

glass. The smell of the farms in the valley filled his nose as he worked. He heard a few cars on Main Street, but not many. The day was still young. The paint on the glass was fresh, so it came off easily enough. He cleaned the smudges near the edges of the window panes and then tossed the drenched towel back into the bathroom. It landed on the green tile floor with a quiet slap.

Eddie sat on the edge of his bed and flipped open the notebook. The pages looked waxy in the morning light. He took a pencil in hand, composed himself, and then got to work. A heavy frown dragged on his face as the words limped onto the page.

Chapter Seventeen

From the Handwritten Account

My Mental Reconstruction of Events Past
by Eddie Farris

Another day without writing.

The painkillers must be too strong. I need to tell the new doctor when I see him.

Nice guy, he is.

Soft voice.

Silver hair.

He held my hand this morning after I awoke from a nightmare. A single fragment of it still remains through the drug-induced haze.

My father attacking my mother.

And me.

That's what I'll write now.

Maybe this will set me free.

This is how I imagine my father's rampage beginning: Thunder rumbles through the valley.

This is how I will always believe it began.

My father has never shown the true extent of his evil nature. Not until tonight.

He jumps out of his pickup truck and into the pouring rain.

It's nearly ten o'clock at night, and he is pissed.

He slams the door shut.

In his right hand, he holds a fist full of mail he grabbed from the mailbox at the end of the lane. In his left hand, he holds an open case of beer. The cans were sweating in the cab of the truck. Now they're wet with cool rain.

He hurries across the water-logged lawn, through the downpour that pounds the house in rhythmic waves. The storm kicked off right as I arrived home, and it doesn't show any signs of stopping.

My father shoves the front door open with a harsh grunt, like a Neanderthal returning to the cave after a fruitless hunt.

Lightning splits the sky, followed quickly by rolling thunder.

The power flickers.

The lights dim.

It looks like the power is going for good, but then the lights surge back to life.

The front of my father's uniform is unbuttoned to show his massive chest.

The white undershirt is speckled with blood. The shirt bears this cheerful phrase: ALIENS ATE MY BOSS AND I DON'T GIVE A SHIT!

He loosens his heavy black belt and drops it next to the couch. Landing on the stained carpet are his metal ring of keys, a pouch holding a small can of Mace, and the radio he should have returned at the end of his shift.

The only thing missing is a gun, but that's because he isn't allowed to carry one inside the prison.

No one is permitted to take a weapon in there. It would be insane to do so. On the walls, yes. In the marked Jeeps traveling the single lane road outside the walls, of course. But inside? Where, in a sudden turn of events, a pissed-off murderer could get his hands on it?

Never.

My father tosses the case of beer onto the dining room table. The seasoned smell of Hamburger Helper cooking on the stove fills the house.

"God-fucking-dammit," he mutters as he approaches the kitchen.

My mother cringes and quietly concentrates on mixing everything together. The hamburger meat. The prepackaged ingredients. She mixes and mixes.

It's late for dinner, and she and I already ate, but this meal isn't for us. This is for my father.

He's usually somewhat aggravated after putting in a double shift, but tonight he's angrier than normal. I'm sure Mom can sense the rage.

Finally she asks, "Michael, what's wrong?"

His appearance changes.

I can see the old expression of pure, seething indignation melting away, only to be replaced by a new emotion, an even more hideous one.

My mother stands there in her ragged white nightgown, her right hand on the handle of the skillet, and her mouth shut tight. She doesn't say anything else.

My father states: "I didn't get the fucking promotion, I worked fourteen hours straight with barely two fucking breaks, and it was a living hell, that's what's wrong! Inmates were fuckin' around because of the goddamn storm and I had to kick some major ass. Fuckin' bastards! So after I do my job, what happens? Fuckin' Warden Smithers comes down from his fancy house on the hill to ream me out! The little prick! Son of a bitch!"

Then nothing.

Silence, broken briefly by the rain.

My mother is shocked, but she realizes she has to say something.

Anything.

The silence is too much.

It's too loud.

Yet she's unable to speak.

The mail my father holds clenched in a death grip is crumpled and wet. He had almost forgotten it, but now he remembers.

He examines each envelope, tossing the letters into the garbage one at a time.

"Bill, bill, junk, bill . . . What the hell is this?"

He rips open a small white envelope.

The return address is the community school on RR #324.

My school.

With his slightly blurred vision he reads the progress report from Mr. Henderson, my biology teacher.

His eyes scan the page so he can comprehend what is written there.

He crumples the paper, lets it fall to the floor.

"Goddamn punk. You try to fucking raise a kid right, and then he pulls this shit! Eddie's failing his biology class. Fucking punk! I warned him not to break my rules, but did he listen? I guess my rules aren't good enough for him! Maybe I need to make some new ones! Maybe he needs an attitude adjustment!"

My father's hands curl into fists, his knuckles slowly and methodically cracking.

His breathing grows louder. He is a bull preparing to charge.

With one swift movement he kicks the trash can to the other side of the kitchen. The lid flies off and the garbage inside spills onto the linoleum floor.

"Michael," my mother pleads, breaking her terrified silence. "You've been drinking. Please, let's talk about this."

My father doesn't reply.

At first he moves like a bear heavy with fat and ready for hibernation, but he picks up the pace when he enters the living room.

He storms down the hall, his feet striking the floor with heavy thuds, his arms pumping wildly.

His hands are clenched so tight his veins pulsate out of his skin. White stretch marks show where his flesh is threatening to tear itself apart.

My mother is running after him.

"Michael!" she yells, reaching for her husband, grabbing his arm and holding on to his biceps for a split second.

My father spins, growls, raises his fist, and then, with the brutality of a professional boxer, brings his clenched hand down to his wife's head.

My mother tries to avoid the blow, but she doesn't move fast enough. The blur of bone and muscle and flesh connects against her jaw with a sharp crack.

Her frail body twists violently as she falls to the floor, a ribbon of blood spraying out of her mouth.

She lands on the carpet with a cry of pain.

She curls up into a tight ball and cries a high, piercing wail.

My father continues down the hall, not even bothering to look at her.

My father kicks the door at the end of the hall. His foot connects next to the old-fashioned lock and the door flies open, striking the wall with such force that it slams shut again.

He swears and shoves the door open a second time.

I'm sitting on the bed, my chest rising and falling rapidly, the new green notebook on my lap.

I had been writing nonstop until my father arrived home. I was lost in a waking dream, the mysterious place I go where fiction is reality.

I was working on a screenplay, one I thought would make a great vehicle for an action star.

Normally I write poems or short stories, but I love the movies. I would give my right arm to travel to Hollywood someday and help make one. Movies are my next favorite love behind books.

I'm wearing my shoes on the bed, violating a rule I rarely break. I was planning to wash the sheets tomorrow anyway so I didn't think it would matter.

When I first heard my father's ranting and the footsteps pounding closer and closer to my room, I knew there was trouble.

Now I realize this is going to be worse than anything I have ever experienced.

Chapter Eighteen

Then

Lightning crashed and thunder rocked the house as Eddie's father slammed the bedroom door against the wall again, just for spite. His nostrils flared and his bloodshot eyes sparked with rage as he reached behind the oak dresser next to the door, wrapping his fingers onto the ornate trim. With a grunt Michael shoved the dresser. The drawers fell out and the clothes inside spilled onto the floor as the piece of heavy mahogany crashed down with a roar.

Eddie gasped as he tumbled off the bed, dropping his notebook and knocking over his nightstand, sending the alarm clock and the bottle of Stetson cologne flying. He staggered and crashed into his green bookcase. Pain ripped through his right side. A crooked stack of well-read paperbacks scattered across the room, and he was already searching for a weapon, any weapon, while his mind searched for an answer to the all-important question: *How do I leave this room alive?*

"Get the fuck off your ass and fight me like a real man!" Michael took a step forward and rolled up his sleeves, exposing arms packed with well-defined muscles.

"I don't want to fight you!" Eddie backed against the bookcase, knocking a few more books to the floor. "What did I do?"

"You know damn well what the fuck you did!"

"I didn't do anything!" Eddie yelled, although he was certain his father somehow knew that he had been late getting home. Only later would Eddie remember the progress reports that were due from his school.

"Fight me like a fuckin' man!"

Eddie jumped to his feet, not because he wanted to go head-to-head against his father, but because he knew he had no choice. He reached behind himself and frantically clutched at the items on the bookshelf. His fingers found a heavy paperback—*The Complete Edgar Allan Poe.* He immediately cocked his right arm and threw the book, putting all his strength into the motion. He held his breath as the Poe collection flew through the air at his father's head.

Michael barely had enough time to blink as the book hit dead on its target. The heavy corner slammed into his right eye. He shrieked and fell. His hands clutched at his face, like he was a rabid animal trying to claw away diseased flesh.

Eddie realized that nothing would stop his father from killing him and his mother. Not the legal consequences, not what life in jail would be like for a former prison guard, none of it. His father had snapped and Eddie knew there was only one chance to escape the room alive. If he failed, his worm-eaten corpse would be found rotting in a ditch somewhere, next to the battered body of his mother. If their bodies were ever found. Most likely his father would bury them in the woods and tell everyone they had taken off during the night. They would never be heard from again.

Eddie took two tentative steps past the snarling man writhing in agony on the floor. The stink of his father's beer and sweat saturated the room, coating Eddie's lungs. He thought if he opened his mouth too long, he might drown. Or suffocate. The insane fear didn't make any sense, but it was very real.

Eddie was almost to the door when Michael blindly groped through the air, grabbing his son's right leg, tugging at him. Eddie yelled as he flew backward, landing in the far corner of the room, smashing into the bookcase, sending books flying as the wooden supports that held the sides together snapped in half.

Get moving! Eddie thought. *Gotta get moving!*

He jumped to his feet again, picking up the bottle of Stetson lying next to his overturned nightstand in the same motion. He raised the glass bottle, his instincts taking control, and stepped toward his father's writhing body. Michael pushed himself to his knees. His eye was red, and tears streamed along the side of his nose. Eddie brought the cologne bottle down like a hammer. The heavy corner collided with his father's sloping forehead, cracking as it slammed into his thick skull. Michael's head snapped to the side. He grunted.

Don't let him move! Hit him again! a voice in the back of Eddie's mind cried. He didn't argue with it or wonder where the statement came from. He quickly brought his makeshift club down again, hitting his father on the right side of the face. The bottle shattered, sending shards of glass everywhere. There was a quiet pop as Michael's right eyeball split. He roared. His massive hands clutched his head, swiped at the fragments of glass piercing his bloody flesh. The burning liquid splashed into his exposed eye socket and he shrieked again.

Chapter Nineteen

Now

Eddie heard the phone ringing in the outside world. The rough clamor was coming from a place he ignored when he was writing, a place as distant as the planets in some science fiction movie. It had been so long since he received a call that he barely understood what the sound meant. Then everything came rushing back to him: the real world and the ringing phone.

Who could be calling me? Eddie thought as he dropped the notebook and ran to the living room. In his hurry, he kicked a large stack of hardcover novels he had left in the middle of the floor. Pain rippled through his bare foot. He hopped twice, lost his balance, and landed on the carpet next to the old brown couch and end table. He whimpered and stared at the coffee table piled high with books and the slapped-together bookcases lined with novels, works of nonfiction, and outdated textbooks on a variety of topics. Although the apartment resembled a small library, he realized a lot of his collection was missing. Where could the books have gone? Someone must have broken in and stolen them, but why? Why his books? Maybe because he loved them so much. Maybe because the books had never judged him, and they never would. He'd have to get a better lock for the door.

The ringing continued.

Arms straining, Eddie pushed his lanky body up off the floor. His ribs poked out through his pale skin, like he was a junkie who had existed on nothing but heroin for months, although he had never touched an illegal drug in his life. Beer was his brain cell killer of choice, and there were nights when he lay sprawled on the living room floor, praying to the red-and-white six packs. Seven years ago the very notion of drinking anything alcoholic would have made him shudder; now entire weeks would pass when the beer was the only way he could make the pain vanish, at least for a little while.

Eddie answered the phone.

"He called again." Rachel sounded exhausted, breathless.

"What did he say?" Eddie asked after the initial shock wore off. He couldn't believe Rachel was actually calling him. There was a long silence, and he repeated the question.

"I need to see you," she finally replied. "Can you meet me at the diner in an hour?"

"Yeah, I'll be there," Eddie said, thinking it was far too early for the restaurant to be open. He looked at the clock. He blinked and looked again. He had been writing for nearly four hours straight without a break.

"Thank you, Eddie," Rachel said.

"Are you okay? Is Adam okay?"

There was another long silence until she whispered, "We'll talk."

The line went dead. Eddie dropped the phone back into its cradle. He slowly walked to the bathroom, the heaviness in his gut telling him he was going to burst a kidney if he didn't take care of business soon. He flipped on the light. A slightly yellowed speck lay in the water at the bottom of the toilet. It was his tooth. A ribbon of blood lined the porcelain and the water was pink. He flushed it all into eternity, the pipes behind the walls groaning until they refilled the tank. Eddie's lips and chipped tooth hurt, but the need to urinate had disappeared.

He returned to his bedroom, trying to remember what he had wanted to write next.

Chapter Twenty

Then

The potent scent of the cologne made Eddie's eyes water and burn. He dropped what remained of the broken bottle. His hand was slimy with the silky liquid, and his mind reeled at what he had done. He stared at his father's convulsing, bloodied body. Michael rolled on the floor like a crazed animal trying to escape an invisible trap.

Move, move, move, or you're going to die! the voice in the back of Eddie's mind screamed. He jumped onto his bed, fear exploding through him. The mattress sagged under his weight as he neared the edge. He held his breath and leapt to the door. Out of the corner of his eye he saw his father's arm blindly swinging at him. Eddie was certain he was going to die. There was no escape. His corpse really was going to be found in some ditch or never found at all. He was going to be brutally and slowly killed, and he'd never see Rachel, never hear her say she loved him, never look into her eyes again.

Eddie landed in the doorway, slamming hard into the door frame. Behind him his father hit the floor like a lead weight, as if he had tried to stand only to discover his knees had been sawed off.

Laura knelt in the hallway, sobbing, her hands holding her stomach as tightly as she could. Eddie knelt next to her, said, "Mom, we've gotta go!"

Laura raised her head, and Eddie flinched when he saw her cheek. The flesh was already swelling. Her mouth hung open, showing her teeth. They were splashed bright red, as if she had eaten a whole bushel of strawberries. Blood trickled from her lips to her chin and onto the frayed nightgown.

"I'll be all right," she mumbled.

"We have to get out of here," Eddie urged. He put his hands under his mother's arms, easily lifting the thin woman to her feet. She wept and yelped in pain as her son led her by the arm to the living room.

Eddie opened the front door. Lightning cut through the sky nearby and thunder followed, Mother Nature's fury nearly knocking them off their feet. The cold rain was so heavy Eddie could barely see the pickup truck parked on the gravel driveway. The land seemed to be plastered with a gooey layer of tar, and the wind blew the rain from left to right, making it almost horizontal with each gust. In the distance, trees cracked and wailed, a few of the smaller limbs snapping and flying off into the storm.

"Mom, get to the truck!" Eddie shouted. "I'll be there as soon as I find the keys!"

Laura reluctantly nodded and started out into the night while her son began frantically ripping the living room apart. He prayed the keys were close by, but he had no idea if they would be. For all he knew, he was never going to escape the house with his life. Then his mother would freeze to death out in the night. He had to find the keys! His father often kept them on his belt and neither Eddie nor his mother had their own set. Eddie wasn't even allowed to drive the truck, and Laura only took it when she had to go to market on Saturday morning. At least Mattie had taught Eddie to drive. Not that his father knew. Michael would have gone berserk if he had discovered someone was playing the role of dad for him.

Eddie moved to his right, toward the dining room, and there he saw the old brass metal ring attached to his father's belt. His eyes widened, like he had discovered the Lost City of Gold, the Holy Grail, or something else equally mythical and wonderful. The phone in the kitchen began to ring, but Eddie didn't even notice it.

Michael staggered into the hallway, one bloody hand held to his right eye. Screaming with rage, he punched his fist through the glass globe encircling the light in the middle of the ceiling. It shattered, sending shards everywhere.

"You goddamned ungrateful son of a bitch! I'm gonna kill you!" Michael yelled as he stormed down the hallway with pieces of glass lodged in his knuckles. His arms moved like pistons in a revving engine and his slight beer belly bounced, making him look like a crazed Santa from Hell.

The power died for good as thunder rumbled through the valley. Except for the streaks of lightning cutting across the black sky, father and son had been thrown into total darkness.

Eddie groped at the floor. At first he found nothing

but the carpet, and his heart exploded inside his chest in a rush of panic. Then cold metal brushed against his hot, sweaty hands, and he grabbed the keys out of the black void.

Now go! the voice in the back of Eddie's mind ordered. *Run as fast as you can and get the hell out of here!*

Eddie spun around and sprinted for the front door. He dove off the porch and hit the ground running, the cold rain lashing at his exposed flesh like tiny knives. Lightning split the sky, momentarily blinding him as it struck a nearby tree. The hairs on the back of his neck stiffened and the intense thunder knocked him from his feet, as if someone had taken a swipe at both his legs with a baseball bat. He flew forward, landing on his chest and sliding on the wet lawn, his knees aching and his flesh tingling. He planted his freezing hands deep into the wet grass, and he was on his feet before he even understood how he had fallen. He pushed on, the cold keys swinging around the metal ring, smacking his hand. He shivered; his arms trembled. His flesh had gone numb and he couldn't feel anything other than the coldness attacking his body.

Eddie reached the truck, opened the driver's side door, and jumped inside. His mother was sitting on the passenger side, soaked to the bone, shaking and shivering and waiting for him, an expression of terror frozen on her face. He locked the door and flipped the keys around the ring, picking the one marked with the brand logo of the truck. It slid smoothly into the ignition.

"Go, Eddie, go," Laura cried, staring across the cab, out the driver's side window and into the storm. Dread rattled her voice. "Your father!"

"I'm going!" Eddie replied, snapping the truck into gear. He slammed his foot on the gas pedal, causing the wheels to peel out, sending wet stone and thick chunks of mud flying. But the truck didn't go anywhere. The tires kept spinning and spinning on the wet gravel, digging deeper into the ground. Eddie's foot pushed harder on the accelerator, his mind paralyzed by panic, his eyes wide.

"You son of a bitch!" Michael slammed into the door like an angry bull pummeling a matador. He wrapped his hands around the handle and tugged, his face locked into a grimace of pure hatred, his empty eye socket full of blood, the lightning illuminating him like a spotlight. "I'll rip your heart out!"

Then the tire's rubber treads grabbed on to solid earth. The truck rocketed down the gravel driveway, dragging Michael for a few feet before throwing him to the ground.

Chapter Twenty-one

Now

Eddie walked slowly, the bitter wind cutting through his Steelers jacket as he lowered his head to protect his face. He approached the old-fashioned phone booth with its chipped and peeling red paint. There he found a path through the large piles of snow that flanked the road. He crossed Main Street in front of the Black Hills Diner. The pavement was slick and dark clouds stalked the valley, but he barely noticed. He was preparing himself for where he was headed and for what might happen when he got there. The long, narrow building sat at the intersection of Main and Maple, and he could see through the wide plate-glass window in the front of the family-owned restaurant as he trudged across the street.

During the day the elderly ruled the diner, but after school the teenagers came in rowdy packs and claimed it for their own. Right now the over-fifty crowd were still the kings and queens of the restaurant, although among their ranks were some of the employees of the stores located along Main Street. And Rachel was there, of course. Eddie could see her moving from one table to the next, dressed in her black-and-white work outfit. A round tray with plates of food was braced on her shoulder.

As he pushed open the front door, Eddie reminded himself he had to be cool; he couldn't blow this. The glass door was squeegeed clean, the glass reflecting a ghost of his image. Eddie decided he didn't look too bad, at least considering recent events. He stepped by the rickety tripod holding a blackboard where the day's specials were listed. Chicken noodle and old-style Mexican chili were the soups of the day, and the lunch meal deal was a six-ounce steak with mushrooms and onions, a plate of fries, and a large Coke for $4.99. The room smelled of burgers and fries and those steaks and sizzling onions.

Keep moving, don't look at anyone, keep going, Eddie thought as he searched for a place to sit. Booths lined the wall in front of the long rectangle windows, and round stools sat along the counter by the kitchen. The walls were decorated with faded newspaper clippings and mementos from when the coal mines were the lifeblood of the town. A blunt pickaxe hung above the doorway. Mining hats were arranged in a zigzag pattern near the water-stained ceiling. The steel-framed opening where the cook dished out plates of food was overshadowed by a large, weathered sign that read: BLACK HILLS MINING COMPANY. Then, in smaller print: FOUNDED 1888. At some point after the company had gone under, someone had stolen the sign off the old headquarters located to the north of town and it had ended up in the diner. The complex of buildings, roads, and mines was still there, deteriorating in the elements. Someday it would all melt away and the earth would reclaim its land, but for now the property was there for anyone to explore, if they were so inclined.

Eddie caught the glances of contempt from a few of the regulars, but he ignored them. The men's dirty fingernails, weathered faces, and callused hands showed the unmistakable discoloration that told Eddie the soot had never really come out of their skin no matter how hard they tried to scrub it away. He knew where they had once worked, where they had toiled for poor wages that barely kept food on the table. During their prime these men had rarely seen the sun. They had labored in the dim light of kerosene lamps for fourteen or more hours a shift. The daylight was not their friend. But the coal mines had closed, and these men had nowhere else to go, so they waited in Black Hills until the reaper came calling. The town was all they had left. They sat at the diner's counter and drank their coffee black and talked about the good old days, just like their counterparts on the front porch of Dolores's General Store.

Eddie quickly took a seat in a corner booth, facing away from the prying eyes. The flimsy paper place mat under his hands advertised a new kind of honey bee supplement. The ad claimed the product helped anyone lose weight, but that wasn't what Eddie noticed first. What caught his eye was the writing in the margins. It was a children's rhyme, the same one he had heard in his head the previous day.

Down by the river, down by the sea,
Eddie killed his family and blamed it on me.
I told Ma, Ma told Pa,

Eddie had the gun so ha ha ha.
How many people did he kill?
One, two . . .

Someone sat across the table from Eddie. Not Rachel, as Eddie was expecting, but Gene Varley. The old man was dressed in his dark-red usher's uniform. He looked scared.

"Are you feeling all right?" Gene asked. He wheezed and took a deep breath, sucking snot back up his nose.

"Yeah, I'm fine," Eddie replied. "Why? What'd you hear?"

"You seemed pretty darned scared when you left the theater the other night. Didn't even finish the movie! I was worried 'bout you."

"Sorry, I remembered something important I had to take care of," Eddie said, thinking of a lie as he spoke. "Left the oven on."

"Oh, that's terrible trouble! Terrible! I left the gas on when I was a kid. Almost blew the whole house to kingdom come! Terrible!"

"I'll be more careful in the future, Mr. Varley."

"You sure you're feeling all right?"

"Right as rain." Eddie forced a smile.

"You sure?"

"Yep, sure as sure can be."

The old man leaned across the table and said, "Then I'd suggest you get the hell out of here. You're a nice kid. I don't want to see you hurt. If she sees you here, all hell is going to break loose!"

Gene didn't look threatening or mean, just afraid. He slid out of the booth, went to the counter, and dropped a five spot to pay his bill. He left the restaurant immediately, as if he didn't want to be nearby when the shit hit the fan. Eddie never even opened his mouth to reply. How could he explain that he was helping Rachel? It probably wasn't possible. Or believable.

Rachel joined Eddie a few minutes after Gene had left the diner. Her hair was messy, although she had tied it into a ponytail, and she looked more tired than Eddie had ever seen her. Her face was weathered with thin lines and dark circles surrounded her eyes. He wanted to hold her, but he knew better than to try that in public.

"You want anything?" Rachel asked.

"No, silly, you don't have to serve me." Then, thinking of all the times they had eaten here when they were teenagers, he added, "Anyway, I can't afford any of this luxurious living."

She laughed at the comfortable old joke, her lips curling into a small smile. It was the first time Eddie had seen Rachel smile in years. The urge to grab her and kiss her was so strong he had to fight himself. He forced himself to continue speaking.

"We used to come here a lot," he said. "We were always happy here."

"Eddie, I know what you're thinking," Rachel replied, her smile fading into a frown. She checked the front of the restaurant, like she was trying to see who had noticed them. Obviously she wasn't too worried about what people would say. After all, she was the one who had asked him to come to the diner in the first place. She said, "Let's not think about that. It might not happen if we think too much. Forget the past for now. Okay?"

"Okay, Rachel. I understand. Where's Adam? Is he safe?"

"Yeah, he's at school. A neighbor will get him for me this afternoon. She baby-sits Adam until I get home."

"I could watch him, if you wanted me to."

"But Eddie, he doesn't even know who you are."

Eddie was speechless. He had assumed Rachel had told their son who his father was. Yet, now that he thought about it, he could understand why Rachel had made the decision not to tell their boy the truth. Eddie hated himself for it, too. Rachel had every right not to tell Adam. Hell, it was probably for the kid's own good that he not know. That no one find out.

"What did the caller say?" Eddie asked, trying his best to concentrate on his goals, trying to ignore the strange sense of pain and disappointment ripping through him. *Help Rachel, take care of her problems, protect her, don't let anything hurt her; protect her, love her, win her back.* His mind repeated the phrase again and again, as if the silent words were an affirmation that would come true if he said them often enough. They were a mantra of hope.

"He said he's coming to give me a message in person," Rachel whispered. "Then he said, 'Ashes to ashes, dust to dust' and the line went dead."

Eddie stared at Rachel in disbelief and thought, *Ashes to ashes, dust to dust? Why would the person calling her say that?* The realization hit him like a punch below the belt. He quickly exhaled. *Goddamn! My dad . . .* Eddie couldn't bring himself to think about the last time he had heard that phrase leaving his father's lips. *What does it mean?*

"What's wrong?" Rachel asked.

"We have to do something," Eddie replied. This new development deeply troubled him. What if Rachel was really in danger? Real danger? They should bring in the big guns. The real deal. The police. Eddie knew that decision would probably push him out of the picture, but he wanted Rachel to be safe. Her safety was more important than anything else. He didn't want to see her hurt. Never again.

"We can't go to the cops." It was as if Rachel had read his mind. She removed a cigarette and a single match from her pocket, lighting the cancer stick without even looking at it. "Or anyone. Please don't tell anyone."

"Why?" Eddie asked, secretly relieved. She was depending on him. That meant she had to love him. She had to!

"They'll say I'm crazy." Rachel raised her trembling hand to her thin lips to wipe away a drop of moisture from the corner of her mouth. Her fingers were thin and emaciated. "It's your father calling. I know it. But we can't go to anyone until we can prove it."

"Okay," Eddie replied, unable to believe what Rachel was saying, but also understanding he couldn't tell her that without hurting her, without making her want to leave again.

She stared at him with sad eyes, the cigarette hanging from the corner of her mouth, a veil of smoke floating between them. She quietly asked, "Do you think I'm crazy?"

"No, I don't."

"That means a lot to me," Rachel said, sounding distant and unconvinced. She gazed out the window at

Main Street. Eddie wondered if she was reliving the same memories she had told him not to think about. She asked, "Remember how I told you I went to the free clinic?"

Eddie nodded, but didn't reply.

"Well, I didn't just go to the clinic. I spent some time there, in one of their special rooms . . . after what you did."

Rachel cautiously studied Eddie, as if she feared he might attack her. He didn't move, but he did wonder how he could have been so out of touch with everything that he never knew Rachel had been in the asylum. He couldn't believe he hadn't heard one word about it. The townspeople didn't go out of their way to converse with him, of course, but why hadn't Mattie told him? Surely she had known. Or maybe not. Maybe Rachel had somehow kept her confinement a secret.

"Sometimes I wonder if the hospital really did me any good," Rachel whispered. "I was pretty messed up. I couldn't get anything right inside my own head. The doctors tried to help me, but I keep having these horrible dreams. Every single night I relive what happened, over and over again. The nightmares are terrible. Sometimes I think they'll never end."

"They'll stop. I'm sure they will," Eddie said, knowing better than to mention his own nightmares.

Rachel smothered the cigarette, checked her watch, and sighed. Eddie realized she was still on the clock, still worried about work, even with everything else that was going on in her life. She had sneaked in a quick smoke break to talk with him, but work demanded she return. He wondered about her priorities, wondered if she should just go home and bolt her door and stay out of the open for a while. Maybe she should take the rest of the week off. Rachel stood, straightened her uniform, smoothing the apron with the palms of her hands.

"Please meet me at my place tonight, okay? I want you to watch for him."

"Why don't you and Adam stay with me instead?" Eddie didn't make the suggestion because of his overwhelming desire to be with her. It had just seemed like a good plan off the top of his head.

"I can't. Not now."

"What should I do if he . . . if someone does show up?" Eddie had asked the question a little too loudly. The restaurant was dead silent, as if everyone had left for the day. Except everyone was still there, of course. But now they were intently listening to Eddie. *Shit.* The spinsters in town would certainly have more gossip fodder this week.

"Whatever you can. I trust you, Eddie. You're the only one I can trust," Rachel said, moving swiftly to the kitchen.

"Wait," Eddie said. He got up and took a step to follow her, but a sharp pain shot through his right side. He nearly fell to the floor as he doubled over. He sucked in a deep breath and held it, counting to ten until the pain subsided. He steadied himself and shook his head.

"Who the hell let this mongrel in here?" a harsh voice demanded from Eddie's left. He turned and gazed into the burning eyes of Tabby Matthews. She had gained a good deal of weight since he last saw her, and large rolls of fat filled her uniform. Her hair was mangy and poorly kept. She had aged twenty years. Eddie saw the hatred in her eyes, and he wanted to curl up under one of the tables and die. Her angry stare said she would never forgive him for what he had done.

"I was just leaving," Eddie managed to mutter as he headed for the door.

"Damn straight you're getting your sorry ass out of here, mister!"

Eddie grimaced, but said nothing. He wished Tabby could be the happy-go-lucky person she had once been, back in the days when she had said, *You kids be good while I'm gone! Pretend I'm still here, if need be.* But that Tabby was never going to return.

"If I ever see you in here again, I'll break you in half! You should be in jail, you son of a bitch! You crazy son of a bitch!"

As Eddie hurried to the door, he saw an elderly couple staring at him. They lowered their heads in unison, but without much imagination he could hear what they were thinking: *There goes crazy Eddie Farris! He'll kill us if he gets the chance!*

He glared at the old couple, but his pace quickened. The customers at the counter gawked at him. He heard the murmuring begin as he opened the door. Drawing in a deep breath, Eddie stepped into the cold winter air. He hated the looks he got from everyone. He hated the whispering. It transformed his emotions into a frenzied rage. He couldn't concentrate on anything except for his longing to escape the town and leave the gossiping masses behind.

Perhaps that was why he didn't question what had motivated Rachel to ask him to meet her in the diner, where it would be nearly impossible for him to avoid her mother's scorn. Had Rachel wanted this public confrontation? Couldn't they have met at the rear of the restaurant, where the Dumpster was located, where no one would see him? But those thoughts never occurred to Eddie. At least, not yet.

He hurried home. He would be safe there. Safe with his books.

Chapter Twenty-two

Then

Eddie kept glancing nervously at the rearview mirror as he drove through the rain. His mother sat motionless next to him. She hadn't spoken since they fled the house. Eddie slowed the truck as he saw the sign announcing the city limits. They weren't very far from their destination, although he didn't have to tell his mother where they were headed. Mattie St. Claire would be able to help them.

"It's going to be okay," Eddie said, driving by the post office, the VFW, and Mitch's Music Mania without really seeing the buildings. His eyes were focused on the yellow line dividing the roadway, as if he had never seen it before. "We're going to take a little detour, Mom. It'll be okay."

Instead of heading straight for Mattie's bookstore where she lived in the apartment upstairs, Eddie turned off Main Street and onto Old Mill Road. The street was empty, save for a few cars parked by some weathered duplexes that should have been condemned long ago. The structures were eerie on even the best of days, and in this storm they looked like the kind of place a group of teenagers in a slasher movie would most definitely want to avoid if their car had engine problems. Eddie parked the truck in the parking lot of the old stone church where it couldn't be seen from the main strip. At some point his father would probably search for them, and Eddie didn't want to make it an easy pursuit.

"Hang on, Mom," Eddie said, opening his door and stepping into the storm. Rain and sleet pelted him as he helped his mother out of the truck. She was trembling uncontrollably, hardly able to stand on her own. He grabbed her by the wrist and guided her through the storm.

The wind threw freezing rain at them like the sharpest of knives as they hurried to Main Street. They reached the front step of the bookstore and cowered under the blue canopy, the plastic trim snapping in the gusting wind, making a strange, sharp noise like a whip. The large bay window was dark, but in the flashes of lightning Eddie could see the books lined up like good little soldiers on parade. A single light had once lit the display day and night without fail, but the fixture was difficult to reach and Mattie hadn't replaced the bulb after it burned out the last time.

"Mattie!" Eddie called, knocking on the glass of the door. He hesitated. Then he turned the wet brass knob, not expecting the door to be unlocked. But it was. Mattie had apparently forgotten to fasten the bolt. Black Hills was a small town, after all, and crime had never really been much of a concern, but in this day and age everyone had to be a little more cautious than they had been in years past. You never knew when a crazy person might wander into town. Eddie had told Mattie that a thousand times, so he was simultaneously surprised and thankful to discover the door unlocked.

The bell above the door rang. Eddie and his mother stepped onto the red carpet. He closed the door, the bell ringing again. The orange OPEN/CLOSED sign swung back and forth erratically. The bookstore was dark, but in the flashes of lightning, the spines and covers of the paperback novels lit up, showing Eddie a thousand different worlds as envisioned by hundreds of authors.

"Come on, Mom," he said, gently leading his mother toward the back of the store. As they moved past the magazine rack, Eddie glanced at the security mirror in the corner. He was surprised to see how hopeless the two of them looked. He was pale and drenched to the bone. His body felt far too heavy to move. His mother's white nightgown was soaked to her skin, and the eggplant colored bruise next to her mouth was growing larger. Her hair was wet and wild like she belonged to a clan of mountain folk who had never seen a comb in their lives.

Eddie reached to open the red curtain separating the sales floor from the office area, and he said, "Mattie?"

The curtain shifted as he spoke. The row of lights by the magazine rack flickered to life. Mattie St. Claire stepped out of the office area. She wore a blue dress that had obviously been thrown on in a hurry. Under her eyes and around her lips was a trace of makeup she hadn't removed yet. A mix of worry and confusion clouded her face.

"What happened?" Mattie cried, her hands flying to

her mouth as she gasped. She wrapped her arms around Laura, who was crying.

"It was Dad," Eddie started to reply, but he couldn't find an answer to her question. His voice trailed off.

"You're safe now, you're going to be okay," Mattie said. Then she was gone, slipping behind the curtain. A moment later she returned with two big, white towels from her upstairs apartment. She handed one to Eddie. He hadn't truly realized how extremely cold he was until the warmth of the soft cloth draped his skin. He had been chilled clear to the bone, as one of his favorite novelists might have written.

"Eddie, you can dry off here. I'm going to take your mom upstairs and help her clean up a bit. No one will bother you, we're closed for the night." Mattie put the other towel on her friend's shoulders. Laura's teeth chattered loud enough for her son to hear them grinding against each other. The sound made him think of teeth being furiously bashed with a baseball bat.

Mattie carefully took Laura's hand into her own and led the dazed woman to the apartment upstairs while Eddie dried off. The towel slowly drove his goosebumps away, but he continued shivering, his body unable to beat the chill deep in his bones. The fluffy cloth felt good, like a warm blanket on the coldest winter night. As he dried his hair the best he could, Eddie kept glancing at the rain through the bay window at the front of the store. The downpour was getting even heavier, and an explosion of purple lightning splintered the horizon. Thunder followed.

The phone next to the register began to vibrate and its shrill ring filled the store, but Eddie only heard it in the same way he sometimes heard his alarm clock as he came out of a deep sleep. He had been pulled into a waking dream, a living memory, and nothing was going to break his concentration. The sound was lost in the distance, beyond a wall of white noise.

Chapter Twenty-three

Now

As soon as Eddie arrived at his apartment, he hurried to the bedroom and opened the bottom drawer of the dresser. He grabbed the leather scrapbook he kept under a stack of old sweaters, next to his writing notebooks and his journal from his month in the hospital. If anyone ever found the scrapbook or his writings, Eddie would have all kinds of problems, so he kept them hidden, especially whenever he left for the day. He never knew when some of the more adventurous kids in town were going to break into his apartment on a dare to steal a possession of the infamous Eddie Farris. That was probably where his missing books had gone.

Eddie opened the scrapbook. Pasted to the pages were articles and editorials from the local newspaper, which until ten years ago had published daily, but now published weekly. He had found the articles after doing long hours of research in a poorly lit room in the basement of the newspaper's office on Main Street. They called that room The Morgue.

Every story he had collected dealt with his family in

some way, and Eddie flipped to the section about his father. As he had collected the articles, he had taken a black marker to the statements he considered to be inaccurate. Only after the editing could he stand to read the news clippings about The Showdown. None of the reporters had gotten the story right. They hadn't even tried. The events of that day were an instant legend, a tall tale, a myth. No one cared for the truth. The gossip and rumors were a more powerful fuel for the hurried and hushed discussions at the post office and the diner and the general store.

"Maybe I missed the key," Eddie said, flipping back through the sections, finally stopping on a random page. A headline screamed at him from the top of a slightly blurry photocopy of a news article: "Six Killed in Town's July 4th Celebration!"

Below, on half a sheet of lined paper, Eddie had written notes in a small, compacted script. As with many of the newspaper stories, even the ones dating back to the beginning of the century, he didn't accept the official histories as the gospel. Instead he conducted his own investigation. He read the diaries that had been donated to the town library (they were kept in the reference section and could not be loaned out) and he talked to the old-timers in town—the ones who would speak to him, at least. After finishing his research, he wrote his own version of the events. He often tied threads of past history together to explain *why* the event had taken place. Sometimes what he discovered had really occurred was quite different than the official story.

On the topic of July 4th, 1942, he had written the following:

George Farris was a drinking buddy with practically everyone who drank in Black Hills, but his wife Martha was painfully shy. She avoided the townspeople whenever she could. She had two children, a boy named Jonathan and a girl whose name was Hope.

George wasn't really a bad person until he lost his janitorial job at the asylum. This was early in the Great Depression, when there was no end in sight, and there was no other work for him, not even in the mines.

He and Martha had secretly committed their little girl to the asylum. He tried to stop people from finding out, but everyone heard the news soon enough. Secrets are impossible to keep in Black Hills.

The asylum had a rule forbidding their employees from working around their own families, so George was fired.

He became a mean drunk. He made wild accusations. Crazed outbursts. He was even banned from the bar, eventually. So instead he beat his wife and harassed the locals.

A few years later his daughter died in an unexplained fire at the asylum. Over eighty patients were killed.

And a few years after that, George cut his own throat with a broken beer bottle.

As far as anyone could tell it was a suicide.

After George's death, Martha's ties with the town were cut. People saw her and her son Jonathan when they ventured to the general store for supplies, but no one ever really got to talk to the two of them. Martha and her son simply weren't social people.

And then came the Fourth of July when the innocence of Black Hills was lost forever. Everyone was shocked to see Martha and Jonathan arrive for the annual festival, but not shocked in a bad way. This was two years after George killed himself, and no one blamed Martha for the type of person her husband had become before his death. Little did the townspeople know that the pies Martha and Jonathan brought with them had pieces of razors inserted into the apples. Not all the pies, but just the ones meant for the girls in the pie-eating contest. Somehow it was planned just right to only get the girls.

A few moments into the contest, the girls began spitting bright streams of blood onto the dry ground. One account said the blood glistened like shiny tin in the bright summer sunlight as it sprayed through the air. The girls fell onto the table, flipping it over. They all died.

The story of the pie-eating contest in the news article is correct as far as I can tell, but it doesn't mention how Martha was lynched by an angry mob later that night . . .

I have to wonder if Jonathan played more of a role in the killings than his mother.

Call it a hunch . . .

And according to the newspaper archive, Jonathan went to that same tree seven years later on the anniversary of the lynching to hang himself with some homemade rope. By then he had a wife and a little baby boy, and for reasons nobody actually knew (but enjoyed speculating about), he had decided to take his own life. But why?

"Why did he kill himself?" Eddie asked the empty room. "Was it guilt?"

Eddie's hands trembled as he flipped to the front of the scrapbook. A graying photocopy of another news article from the *Black Hills Herald* was pasted there. The story itself was seventy years old, and although the clipping was the first one in the collection, it had been one of the last ones Eddie found. He wasn't even sure why he had photocopied it, but he had a gut feeling there was something in the story he was missing.

The headline read, "Dozens Killed in Mysterious Asylum Fire!"

"They never caught the arsonist," Eddie murmured. He contemplated the story and what he knew about his town's history. He considered his family, his family's past, and then he read the story again.

A thought jumped to the front of Eddie's mind like a bolt from the blue. It was an idea he had never considered in all the years he had been investigating his town and his family's past. Something so obvious he couldn't imagine how it had escaped his grasp for so long. The idea would certainly explain his gut feeling, to say the least.

Eddie closed his eyes and pictured a roaring inferno rising into the night sky. As his imagination took control, drawing him deeper into the events highlighted in the article, he saw the fire engulfing one wing of an imposing building, part of the sprawling state mental hospital. He could hear shrill cries and screams coming from inside. The flames licked the beautiful mountain night sky, reaching to the moon that shone onto the land. Even from this distance, even though none of it was real, Eddie could feel the heat rolling off the building in waves.

On the west side of the complex he saw a group of horrified doctors and attendants staring in shock as the fire grew in intensity. The men were dressed in bleached white uniforms and they spoke rapidly while pointing at the inferno. Most of the doctors had graying hair and thick glasses. The attendants were younger with bulky muscles and broad chests. Eddie tried to hear what they were saying, but the blood-curdling screams from inside the building drowned them out.

"No, wait, this is too late," Eddie whispered. The images in his mind slowed to a halt. The clouds above, the billowing smoke, the towering flames, the wind through the trees, and the men froze like a snapshot. Then the fire reversed course as the amazed doctors scattered backward into the complex, like some old news footage of Babe Ruth hitting a homer and sailing around the bases at an impossible rate, only in reverse. The moon slid back down the sky to the horizon and the sun rose again in the west to create a brilliant sunset of reds, oranges, and purples that painted the mountains.

Eddie imagined a middle-aged man creeping out of the forest, carefully searching for any witnesses as he trespassed on the state's property. In one hand, he carried a whiskey bottle with a cork stuffed in the top. In the other hand, he held a heavy metal key ring. The man was dressed in grubby overalls and work boots. His hair and his eyes were wild, insane with hatred.

"Yes, this is right," Eddie said. George Farris—the man slinking toward the building—had never actually been linked to the tragic fire by anyone. But now that Eddie thought about it, he could see the clues coming together.

George—father to Jonathan and Hope, husband to Martha—quickly ran to a side entrance of the building. He checked once more to see if anyone had noticed him, and then he unlocked the double steel doors. He pushed them open.

The inside of the building was like the prison cell blocks Eddie had seen in the movies, but with solid doors instead of barred ones. The rooms were marked from one to eighty, with the odd numbers on the left and the even numbers on the right. Although the exterior of the building was made of stone, the inside walls were white cinder blocks. The hall was barren and clean. There were no chairs or tables or clutter.

"I'm here to do some long overdue business," George told the empty hallway as he walked, his heavy steps slapping the floor, the sound mysteriously loud, drowning out everything except the slow breathing of the drugged patients in their rooms, which also seemed to be amplified. George stopped near the end of the hallway by a door marked SEVENTY-FIVE in thick, black letters. He selected another, smaller, brass key, and unlocked the door, removing the cork from the neck of the bottle. It didn't smell like whiskey.

"Here for some long overdue family business," George whispered, gleefully pouring the kerosene onto a white mass lying in the far corner of the padded cell. The child twitched, coughed, and rolled, but didn't wake. Her tiny body was horribly deformed, and she was restrained by a small straitjacket. Her legs were too short, and repulsive red blotches spotted her high cheekbones and wrinkled forehead. She coughed some more, a stark wet cough that made Eddie retch.

"Family business, private business, spare the whip and chain," George muttered. He tossed the empty bottle onto the floor where it shattered into a dozen pieces. He pulled a long wooden match from his pocket. He struck the head of the match against the doorframe. Fire burst from the end of the stick. His eyes showed his disgust as he looked at the small body of his deformed daughter. He tossed the flaming match into the cell.

The flames devoured the kerosene on the little girl's straitjacket. Her blind eyes blinked open and a hoarse, primitive noise erupted from her mouth. She screamed in agony as the flames ate at her flesh. Patients through the building began moaning and howling and crying out.

Eddie opened his eyes and shook his head, the vision fading into nothingness. What he had imagined may not have been the complete truth, but it was close enough for him. He had a pretty good hunch what had pushed George over the edge, what had transformed George into a killer. In all the stories Eddie had ever heard about the man, there was one observation that was always repeated.

"George lost his job because everyone in town knew his daughter was a patient in the asylum," Eddie said, staring at the faded photocopy of the news story. He wondered why he had never thought of this before. It made so much sense. It was almost too obvious. Without knowing how, he understood the new nightmare had brought this realization to the front of his mind. The thing that called itself Lehcar and the horrible events on Main Street had told him what to search for. She had asked him who had started the fire. But why?

"Seven years later George killed himself. He cut his throat with a broken beer bottle."

Eddie closed the scrapbook.

Chapter Twenty-four

Then

The lights by the magazine rack cast long, twisted shadows across the store, but Eddie was no longer seeing row after row of bookshelves. He no longer heard Mattie and his mother moving about upstairs. Off in the distance, the phone was ringing, but that didn't make any sense. There were no phones where Eddie was now. In his memory, he was surrounded by low-lying bushes and trees ready for winter, yet still caught in the grasp of a chilly fall season. The slight warmth of sunlight beamed onto his face as it cut through the brown and gold and red leaves. He was in the woods with his father. And he was holding a rifle.

"This is the day you become a man," Michael proudly proclaimed as he and his twelve-year-old son, both dressed in camouflage pants and matching jackets (which, for the record, had none of the orange required by state law), sat in a tree far behind the Farris property, a dozen yards from a babbling brook and downwind from the trails the deer followed to the water.

"Dad, why do I have to do this? I don't want to." It was not the first time Eddie had tried to convey his loathing for what they were doing. He held a rifle in his hands, the barrel slanting toward the ground like a dead branch. He wanted to let go of it, to let the weapon fall into the forest underbrush, but he knew what his father would do then.

"This is no place to be scared, boy. You see anything move, you shoot it. Then you're a man."

Eddie could smell the harsh scent of sour mash whiskey on his father's breath, and he wanted to be anywhere but in the tree. He wanted to go home. He couldn't shake the ball of fear tearing into his gut like a burning fist. It was a beautiful day. Normally he'd be exploring the woods or playing football against an imaginary team in his backyard. Sometimes he'd go to the end of his family's driveway and watch the occasional traffic on RR #324. But not today.

Out of the corner of his eye, Eddie saw movement. Acting purely on instinct, he raised the rifle. Horror and fear punched him in the gut. He yanked the trigger as he jerked the rifle. A single bullet sliced through the forest, snapping off twigs and cutting through thin, termite-hollowed branches. It splashed harmlessly into the brook.

"Goddamn it!" Michael yelled. He quickly took aim at the deer leaping back through the woods from which it had ventured. The sound of his rifle firing exploded all around Eddie. The deer fell.

For as long as he lived, Eddie would never forget the long hike across the rugged terrain to where the deer lay waiting for them. Following a few steps behind his father, the minutes dragged on for a lifetime as Eddie walked. He dropped his rifle, not fearing the consequences any longer. He was numb with horror. He let go the rifle, but kept on moving, although slower now. His father didn't seem to notice.

Eddie and his father stepped past a fallen tree and into a small clearing where the sun spotlighted the trembling animal.

To Eddie's horror, the deer wasn't dead.

His father's bullet had ripped through the deer's neck, but its front hooves were scrapping at the ground, carving ragged little lines into the cold dirt. A river of blood was spilling from the side of the animal, and terror filled its small, black eyes. Its body shuddered. Blood trickled from its nose and small mouth, pooling in the leaves under its trembling head.

"This is where you finish the kill," Michael whispered as he retrieved a long knife from inside his boot. It slid out of the leather sheath with a smooth, slick hiss. He handed the knife to his son. Eddie reluctantly took the handle of the blade, but he didn't move. When he didn't proceed, Michael pointed at the deer's neck, then made a slashing motion across his own throat, illustrating his point.

"No." Eddie tried to run, but his father grabbed him by the arm.

The memory of the deer hunt sparked a quiet anger within Eddie. Rage was building inside of him, like the pressure inside a volcano waiting to erupt. He thought of the deer, of his mother, and of what his father had tried to do to him. His hatred was unrelenting. There was nothing he'd rather do than see his father die. He wanted his father's death to be horrible.

Eddie began to shake. He realized he didn't just want to see his father die. He wanted to kill him. He wanted to make sure the job was done right. He wished he had shot his father in the back on that fateful day when he was twelve. Or in the head. Shot him once, right in the head.

Then none of this mess would have happened.

Chapter Twenty-five

Now

Eddie awoke in a strange place, but for once he wasn't screaming or shaking in terror from a horrible nightmare. In fact, his sleep had been dreamless for the first time in years. He was wrapped in a blanket of darkness, his mouth pressed against the cold, sweating glass of a window. He blinked his eyes open. As his vision cleared, he saw the lights along the street below, but they were blurry, out of focus. He blinked and wiped the dry crust from the corners of his eyes. Falling snow filled the view from horizon to horizon, from ground to sky. Eddie rolled off the window ledge and onto the shabby carpet of the fifth-floor hallway.

I came like Rachel asked, but she wouldn't let me inside her apartment. She told me to stay here and wait for my dad to show—for someone to show, at least . . . But . . .

He had fallen asleep.

"Shit," Eddie muttered. He scrambled to his feet, stumbling to his right as a wave of dizziness rolled through his mind. He bumped into the cracked mirror set in the heavy, wooden frame, knocking it to the floor with a thud. Pieces of thin reflective glass scattered across the frayed carpet.

"Shit," he said again, steadying himself, moving toward the door marked FIFTY-SEVEN. He didn't remember nodding off, but it was obvious he must have done exactly that at some point in the long night. What could he actually remember from earlier in the night? Rachel telling him to be careful? The hours spent watching the street below? Watching the shadows for movement? Listening for the creak of the stairs as heavy feet trod upon them? He didn't know. Everything was a blur of images, thoughts, and memories.

Eddie stopped dead in his tracks, his legs growing weak under the weight of his body. His back contorted like a corkscrew had been shoved through his spine, the cold metal twisting around and around. There was a large, dark mark on the door to apartment fifty-seven. As he inched closer, a jolt of disbelief and terror rocked him.

"This can't be real," he whispered, his body twitching in disgust. His eyes were fixed on the burgundy puddle forming on the worn carpet at the base of the door. He could hear the blood dripping onto the carpet like a leaky faucet. His chest grew tight as he examined the fat black cat nailed to the door by its tail. The tiny skull had been ripped from the animal's head. The paws had been smashed flat with a hammer, and the cat's claws were ripped from its flesh. The fur was matted with blood. Someone had written on the door in a bloody, wild scrawl: *Ashes to ashes, dust to dust. You are your own fire!*

Eddie stared at the writing, fear bursting inside him

and consuming his rational thought. His heart stuttered, he stopped breathing. He saw the blood-covered metal hammer lying at the base of the doorway. Without thinking, he picked up the heavy tool. He knew the hammer. Not just the type or the brand, but the actual hammer and where it had come from. It had been his father's favorite. This hammer had always been proudly displayed on the tool rack in the garage when Eddie was a kid. But how could this be the same one? That wasn't right! It didn't make any sense. He kept expecting to wake up, but this wasn't a dream. This was all real. And very, very wrong.

In a bright flash, light washed over Eddie, and he saw the door to apartment fifty-seven opening, the cat swinging by its tail like a carnival horror house pendulum. The light flooded into the hallway. For a brief instant Eddie didn't recognize the woman standing there. She was surrounded by a blinding white aura.

"What are you doing, you filthy bastard?" Tabby Matthews demanded. She saw the crucified cat. She screamed, her chest rising and falling as the guttural screeches tore from her throat.

"No," Eddie said, holding the bloody hammer out like a crucifix. "You don't understand!"

"You damned monster! You god-awful monster! Haven't you done enough?"

"No, I was trying to help!" Eddie panicked, dropped the hammer, and ran away from the light and the biting accusations. He couldn't find a way to explain that this was all a misunderstanding, that he was the good guy. His lungs felt empty and he was suffocating on his own dread.

"I'm calling the police, you bastard!" Tabby yelled as Eddie sprinted for the stairs. His legs were plated with lead, almost too heavy to lift, but the hallway blurred and before he knew it, he was running down the steps two at a time.

Chapter Twenty-six

From the Handwritten Account

My Mental Reconstruction of Events Past
by Eddie Farris

This is really coming along nicely.

I don't usually write in such a fragmented style, but the memories are just flowing this way.

I want to get some more done before the nurses bring my dinner.

The meds make me so tired.

But I'm healing, I think.

I heard the doctors talking today. I could be discharged sometime in the next week.

I wonder when I'll see the bookstore.

Everyone I've left behind.

The world beyond these white walls, the white ceiling, the bright lights, the tests, the doctors, the nurses.

When will I really be able to leave?

Soon, I hope.

* * *

This is when Rachel comes and finds me: The bell above the front door of the bookstore rings.

I think *he* must be here.

I never bolted the lock.

Like Mattie, I didn't think of it. Never even occurred to me.

The memory of that horrible day deer-hunting with my father had me hypnotized.

Whoever is opening the door probably knocked just like I did, and then tried the doorknob when no one answered . . . just like I did.

Rachel runs into the bookstore.

Her wet blond hair lies loose on her shoulders.

Her jacket is soaked.

Her eyes are teeming with fear, but they're beautiful, too.

The door slams shut with a jarring clang, the orange sign swinging back and forth. The bell rings faintly.

I'm surprised and I ask, "What are you doing here?"

"You never called and I tried to call you and no one answered and I got a bad feeling," Rachel explains, the words rushing out in one long sentence. She hurries to me and wraps her arms around my neck.

I want to kick myself.

Worse.

I had promised to call. I had crossed my heart, hoped to die.

But after the horror of the run to my house and the relief of discovering my father wasn't home, I didn't think of it. Not once.

I can't imagine how worried Rachel must have been waiting for a phone call that was never going to come.

She knew what could happen if my father was pissed, which he would have been if he had been home.

So she waited and waited.

All alone.

The dread crawling through her.

The storm making the emotions more intense.

And for some strange reason a warmth fills me. I don't think I could love her more than I do at this very moment.

She says, "I was scared and I tried calling Mattie, but she didn't answer. I was too afraid to go to your house and check for you so I came here."

I hug her tighter.

I'm so grateful she didn't go to the house.

The very thought makes me want to die.

The thought of what could have happened.

Only God knows what my father would have done.

Maybe what he did to Mary?

I hold Rachel tighter. I love her. But . . .

I totally forgot my promise to her. How could I have been so stupid?

She asks, "It was your father, wasn't it?"

And I need to tell her.

Chapter Twenty-seven

Then

Eddie grinned as Rachel grasped his hands and they sat together next to the magazine rack, leaning their backs against it for support. He was still freezing, but he immediately warmed to her touch. Her skin was soft and warm, and he couldn't hold her hands tight enough. He saw a sparkle in her eyes, a glimmer of concern mixed with passion and love that could be overwhelming in a wonderful way.

"Things were bad. My dad finally lost it," Eddie said. "Mom's upstairs with Mattie. She's hurting. But I beat my old man! I really did!"

Pride resonated in his voice as he spilled all the details, omitting nothing except for the part about hitting his father with the bottle of cologne. He suspected that might be a little too much for Rachel to hear. When he finished, he was nearly breathless.

"Are you sure you're okay?" Rachel asked, pulling him closer.

"I'm fine." Eddie gently kissed her cheek. The horrible images from a few moments before had been overcome by her unexpected appearance. He loved her for it. "Really, I am."

Rachel leaned forward. Their lips pressed together. A spark surged through Eddie. It felt wonderful. He wanted to be in Rachel's bed, just the two of them, naked and together. He played with her wet blond hair, running his fingers through it. His hand slid under the back of her jacket, under her shirt as the kisses grew more intense. Rachel and her warmth, her scent, and the way she pressed against him was enough to push his most painful thoughts away.

Without warning, a burst of savage images popped into Eddie's mind. He violently broke off the embrace, nearly falling over in his hurry to release Rachel. Suddenly he was back in his bedroom, the bottle of cologne crumbling in his hand as he pushed the jagged glass into his father's eye, farther and farther until brains poured out in a pink stream. Brains and gray pulsating goop. Brains and blood. Eddie trembled in fear. He saw himself punching his father, kicking and beating, feeling no pain, no pity, no concern for the consequences of his actions.

"Eddie, what's wrong?" Rachel cried as she reached into the nightmare growing larger before his eyes. Her voice broke the spell weaving through his mind, and when her fingers wrapped around his hands again, the visions ended. They were replaced by a wave of desperation and depression. The emotions crashed down on Eddie, smothering him. He blinked and shook his head, staring wildly around the bookstore like he couldn't believe he wasn't in his bedroom beating his father to death. His gaze returned to Rachel's alarmed expression. He tried to regain his composure.

"I'm sorry," he whispered, not sure what else to say. So he lied, just a little. It came naturally enough. He was writing fiction on the fly. "I guess I was thinking about my parents. I don't want to be like my father. Not ever." He stalled, then admitted, "And I guess I'm afraid I might end up like him anyway."

"Oh, Eddie." Rachel put her warm hand on his cold cheek. "You're nothing like him. He's a monster, but you're sweet and kind and I love you. We'll make it through this. I'll do whatever it takes to help you."

They held each other while Eddie shoved the horrible images out of his head. He committed himself to deciding what he and his mother could do next, pushing everything else away. There weren't many options, and none of them particularly thrilled him.

To be honest, Eddie had already decided what he needed to do. He would call the cops, bring in the big guns, and confront his father once and for all.

Chapter Twenty-eight

Now

Eddie sat in the living room of his rundown apartment. The lights were off. He needed the darkness so he could try to think. The snow had ended a few hours earlier and a full moon shone onto the white valley. He couldn't open the shades. Even the dull winter moonlight was too harsh, too accusing, like a white hot spotlight in some old black-and-white police movie. He wanted to drag himself under his bed and die. There weren't many more appealing options. He was in a world of trouble.

By now Rachel and her mother would have called the cops. And what would they say? Well, that Eddie was stalking Rachel, of course. It all made sense when he tried to see recent events from her point of view. The calls, the crucified cat, the crazy message, all of it. If he hadn't been standing there holding the hammer when Tabby opened the door, maybe then he could have explained his presence, but not now.

"I was set up," Eddie whispered, the realization turning his flesh to ice. "Whoever is calling Rachel framed me. Jesus, what do I do? She knows my voice on the phone. She has to realize I haven't been the one calling her. But after tonight . . ."

He trailed off. Eddie raised his head and slowly examined the walls lined with hundreds of books. The stories always carried him away from Black Hills. In the years since he had been exiled within his own town and Rachel had left him, the books had made up for the loss of human companionship. He loved the written word.

His own writing had been good for killing time, at the very least. There were days when he still fantasized about seeing his name in print, but he knew a writer's life was more of a pipe dream than anything that could actually happen. The stories he wrote in his notebooks were scary enough—some were based on The Showdown and his recurring nightmare, after all—but he didn't even have a computer to prepare the manuscripts. No one in publishing read handwritten works in this age of laser printers. So he was pretty much shit out of luck, as his father would have said.

But his dreams of fancy silver laptops and umbrella drinks and hardcover books and hefty publishing contracts didn't matter today. He was losing Rachel all over again, and his mind was spinning in maddening circles. He couldn't believe the events of the last few hours. This was a nightmare, only a million times more terrible because it was real.

"She has to understand I didn't do it!" he cried in a weak and desperate attempt to convince himself that even this disaster could work out okay. He got up, slowly walking to the kitchen. He opened the refrigerator. The scent of spoiled food oozed out, causing his nose to twitch in disgust. Although the light inside the refrigerator was broken, he could see the rows of beer cans on the bottom shelf.

Eddie had never wanted the alcohol, but the free clinic wouldn't prescribe more of the sleeping pills he needed. After he built up a tolerance to Tylenol PM—the blue-and-white capsules actually kept him awake instead of knocking him out—he had been forced to find an alternative to bring an end to the more painful days. Beer was cheap and it did the job.

He grabbed a red can and closed the refrigerator. As he stood motionless, staring at the door to his apartment, an idea hit him from out of nowhere, making his head hurt. This spontaneous eruption of thoughts happened constantly when he was writing fiction—two random concepts came together at the exact same instant, forming the basis for a story—but this wasn't make-believe. This was serious. It was something he never would have considered even three days ago, but now . . .

"What if my dad *is* alive?" Eddie asked. Dread crept through him like a crawling shadow at sunset. No matter how insane the idea was, it would explain a lot—the mysterious man, the burning notebooks, the calls to Rachel, the cat on the door, all of it. Eddie pulled the tab on the can of beer and took a good, long gulp. The beer tasted terrible, like it always did, but it also warmed him, just a little. The beer made him feel better and think clearer. "What if my dad's trying to get his revenge for what I did to him?"

There was a hard knock at the door. Eddie's head snapped up and he dropped the can of beer. It hit the floor with a quiet thud, the brown liquid splashing out. He slowly made his way to the other side of his apartment, momentarily forgetting the spilled beer. He edged to the door, pressed his eye to the peephole. The hallway was too dark to see anything. His imagination kicked into overdrive.

What if it's my dad? the paranoid part of Eddie's mind asked. *It could be! What if he wants his revenge?*

Eddie was instantly convinced his father was standing in the shadows, waiting and biding his time. Whether or not his father was alive didn't matter. Eddie could picture him dressed in his prison guard uniform, his eye dripping blood as he prepared to pounce like a jungle cat when the door opened.

"No," Eddie said. "Not in real life. In movies and books and superhero comics, but not real life." His sweating hand tightened onto the doorknob in a death grip.

"Come on, boy," a booming voice called from the hallway. "Open this door so we can talk."

Eddie's mind screamed at him to run and hide, but he couldn't. He had no place to go. He was trapped. If his father was out there, Eddie would have to deal with him. There was no other way. He forced himself to unlock the deadbolt and open the door. The looming figure appeared larger than life, and Eddie thought: *He's going to kill me!*

"Eddie Farris," Sheriff Jason Breiner stated, stepping out of the shadows. He looked tired and haggard in his brown uniform. Dark, puffy bags hung under his eyes, like he had taken a couple of bad blows while breaking up a bar brawl. "We need to talk."

Eddie retreated into his apartment, his hands shaking. This was still bad. Very bad. There was only one reason the sheriff was calling on him so late at night. That damned cat.

Eddie turned on the light and said, "Come on in. We wouldn't want to bother my neighbors, would we?"

Sheriff Breiner stepped into the apartment, and Eddie closed the door behind him. There was an uncomfortable silence, as if both of them were secretly saying they really didn't want to be here. The sheriff gestured for Eddie to sit on the couch. Eddie did so without comment. His stomach cramped into a knot, the same way it always had in high school when he was sent to the principal's office. That old feeling, one of intense suspicion that tried to convince him that someone was out to get him in trouble no matter what, also returned. The mistrust crept through his body. It started in his stomach and spread from there, making him feverish with paranoia.

"I got a call from someone in the Richard Street Apartments. You know why?" The sheriff appeared to be calm as he studied the contents of the room, but Eddie knew cops could be tricky. That fact hadn't been lost on him in all the books he had read and movies he had watched.

"Can't say I do."

"Well, it seems a cat was nailed to the door of apartment fifty-seven, and a resident of the building is certain you were involved in some way," the sheriff said, still not paying any attention to Eddie. He appeared to be inspecting the books on the far wall. "She even offered to swear on a dozen Bibles."

"She must be mistaken." Sweat was forming on Eddie's brow. He quickly wiped it away. "I've been here all night."

"Can you prove it, son?" The sheriff finally turned so he could see the young man sitting on the dirty couch.

"Well, sure, all my friends were here, too," Eddie said, a bit too sarcastically for his own good.

"Curb your tongue," the sheriff snapped. "I want to help, no matter what you may think." He selected one of the hardcover books sitting on the coffee table. It was shrouded in a mylar wrapper. *Mental Health From The Inside Out: Controlling Your Dreams, Nightmares, and Fantasies.*

"You believe this stuff?" he asked, as if he had found a copy of the *Satanic Bible* sitting there.

"One of the counselors at the free clinic recommended it," Eddie carefully replied. No need to discuss his past any more than he needed to, right? They both knew well enough what Eddie had been through, but that didn't mean it needed to be discussed. "The author was featured on *Oprah*, I think."

"Well, I don't care what you're reading, but you've gotta keep your nose clean, boy," the sheriff said, shaking his head, the book hanging from his hand like he was on the verge of dropping it. "Is there any reason you'd be bothering Rachel's mother?"

"No, sir. I avoid her and her place. I'm not wanted there."

"Good," the Sheriff said. His tone changed. "Eddie, I'm sorry about what your father did, but you can't ever forget that some people hold you responsible for how it all went down. The deaths. I don't blame you for any of it. Not even . . ." He paused, touched his hat. "Not even what he did to me."

"I'm sorry," Eddie said.

"I'm not here for apologies," the sheriff replied. He continued holding the book as though he had totally forgotten it even existed. "I've been getting reports from people of you acting strange lately. A lot of people. This would be a good time to keep a low profile, you know what I mean?"

Eddie nodded to show he understood perfectly well what the sheriff meant.

"Good," the sheriff said, finally returning the self-help book to its original pile on the coffee table. He took off his peaked hat and ran his hand through his hair. What remained of his hair, at least. There were bald streaks on the side of his head, a result of the horrible scarring of his flesh. At least he wasn't dead, although he probably should have been considering what Michael had done to him. That was too horrible for Eddie to even imagine. His nightmares showed him the wounds too often as it was.

The sheriff said, "Sorry to stop in so late. I sure hope I never have to do it again."

"Same here," Eddie said, standing and opening the door for the sheriff, just as a good little host was supposed to for his special guest. The sheriff nodded, looked Eddie in the eyes—his stare was like broken glass under soft flesh—and left. The sound of his boots echoed down the hall like thunderclaps. He disappeared into the shadows from which he had appeared.

Eddie bolted the door. The room immediately felt cold and bleak, as if it was closing in to smother him. He was all alone. Tonight the loneliness bothered him, although it never had in the past.

The phone rang.

Oh, shit! Eddie thought. *Please, God, no!*

Were the calls starting again? The thought made him want to weep. Although it was the middle of the night, Black Hills was a small town. If word was already spreading that he had supposedly nailed a dead cat to Rachel's door, there were bound to be problems in the days to come. There would be hell to pay.

Eddie sat on the couch and reluctantly answered the phone. It had been ringing for nearly a minute when he picked up the receiver, and he was both relieved and horrified when he heard Rachel's voice.

"Eddie, I know you didn't do it. It wasn't your fault."

"Are you and Adam okay?"

"Yeah, but we need to talk. There was a note under my door tonight."

"What did it say?" A thousand replies ran through Eddie's mind, but he was so happy Rachel had called that he couldn't think straight. He didn't even contemplate why she might be so ready to believe he wasn't the one who had nailed the cat to her door. Could there be some other motive for her call? The paranoid part of his brain was already working hard on that question, searching for an answer.

"You should read the note for yourself."

"When can we meet?"

"Can you be here first thing in the morning?"

"Yeah, no problem."

"Okay," Rachel said. Now she was the one who sounded relieved. "But don't come inside the building. We'll meet out back, okay?"

"I'll be there."

"Thank you, Eddie," Rachel replied. "This means a lot to me."

"You can count on me." Eddie quickly made a judgment call. Should he say what he was really thinking, or just leave well enough alone? He decided to take the chance. He had to tell her the truth, to tell her what he was feeling. "I let you down years ago, but I won't now. I promise."

"I have to go." Rachel hesitated, but said nothing else. The line went dead.

Eddie hung up the phone, but he couldn't move. Rachel had understood he wasn't the one who had nailed the cat to her door, and that in itself was a miracle, but something felt wrong. He couldn't put a finger on what was bothering him, and the paranoid voice in the back of his mind was silent. It wouldn't remain that way for long.

"She knows me better than everyone else," he said, shaking his head.

The phone rang again, and Eddie almost jumped. He reached to answer it, expecting Rachel, but instead he heard a softer, childish voice.

"Hello?" the voice said.

"Who is this?"

"Are you Eddie Farris?"

Eddie grimaced. The thought of the chants and taunts consuming his days and nights was too terrible to consider.

He demanded, "Who are you?"

"It's Adam Matthews, Mr. Farris."

"Adam, what are you doing up?" Eddie asked, his voice instantly calmer, although wavering with faint surprise. This was his son. Not some random kid, but his *son.* Suddenly Eddie felt like he really was a father. He was a man who should be leading by example, who should be giving guidance and advice. He wanted to catch up on everything he had missed. The drives to and from school, the Christmas mornings, the birthdays, the trips to the park, the Disney and Pixar movies, visits to the Sea World in Ohio, the kiddy meals at the fast-food joints in Slade City. All of it. He wanted to be a father. He wanted a family.

"I heard Mom on the phone," Adam said. "She's upset. She gets upset a lot these days."

"Don't worry about anything, little guy. I'll take care of it."

"You're my daddy, aren't you?"

Eddie felt breathless. He wanted to say yes. He didn't understand where the strong yearning came from, but it struck with a tremendous blow. He wanted his son to know him. He wanted to know his son. But he also realized he couldn't tell the boy the truth. Not yet.

He asked, "Why do you think that, Adam?"

"Everyone at school says it. They say I'm going to be just like you. Gotta go."

The line went dead.

Eddie remained motionless, his mind a buzz of conflicting emotions. His son. His little boy. His son had called.

Eddie reached for the pile of books. As he retrieved an old leather-bound text called *Sources of Demon Manifestations and Earthly Hauntings,* a thousand thoughts ran through his mind. He was almost blinded by the insanity of the events of the last few days, but he had to figure out what was happening before it was too late.

"Just in case," Eddie whispered, holding the tattered book like a family Bible. He opened it and read passage after passage he had underlined while doing research for a short story he had wanted to write. A story about a dead man returning to avenge his death.

"A demon can take human form in a number of circumstances," Eddie read aloud. He flipped through a few more pages to the section on ghosts and the afterlife: "Ghosts can return to the plane of the living, especially if their death was traumatic, and to any humans they might pass during this period of flux, they could appear to be a living, breathing person. . . ."

Chapter Twenty-nine

From the Handwritten Account

My Mental Reconstruction of Events Past
by Eddie Farris

While Mattie was in her apartment upstairs and Rachel was in the bathroom, I spoke to Sheriff Breiner.

I called the operator and she put me through to his cabin outside of town.

The Slade City side of town.

Now I'm ready to leave, but I haven't told anyone yet.

When Rachel and Mattie step out from the office area, I know I have to go.

I say, "I'm going back to my house."

They are bewildered by this declaration, as if I have proclaimed I am an alien from outer space. I can see the fear and confusion on their faces.

"No, Eddie," Mattie says. "You can't. It's too dangerous!"

"I have to."

"Eddie, please don't," Rachel says.

I hear the panic in her voice.

She thinks I'll die if I go there.

She shouldn't even be here. If I had remembered to call her, she'd be in bed, or watching TV and waiting for her mother to get home, or doing some homework.

I wish she wasn't here.

I don't want her to be scared, but I have to go back.

If I don't, I'll never escape my father.

No matter what happens with the sheriff and the law and the courts, I'll never really escape him. Never.

"I have to."

Before they can fight me about my decision, I kiss Rachel on the cheek and hurry into the rain.

The sheriff is probably already on the road, but he'll be coming from the other side of town, so I have a head start.

I drive quickly, only slowing when I finally reach our gravel driveway, the truck splashing down hard where the shoulder dips, sending icy water flying in all directions.

Soon I'm sitting at the top of the hill, hoping my father doesn't come out of the house.

I sit and wait.

Rain pounds the truck; thunder and lightning batter the valley.

The sheriff skids his patrol car to a stop at the top of the gravel driveway.

I can't help but imagine what's going on inside his mind.

He studies the scene.

The brick ranch home hasn't changed much over the years. Neither has my family.

He sees me sitting behind the wheel of my father's pickup truck.

"Jesus Christ, what's he doing here?" the sheriff mutters as he opens the door. He unstraps the twelve-gauge shotgun from the dashboard where it rests day after day. He has an extra box of shells in his breast pocket, but he has never needed them.

"Just in case," the sheriff says. Black Hills is not the type of community where a cop requires a lot of firepower, but sometimes dangerous situations do arise.

The sheriff has fired his revolver once against real criminals, four years ago when two out-of-towners made the mistake of trying to rob the bank.

The sheriff was cashing a check on his lunch break.

The out-of-towners shot at him when he identified himself.

He returned fire. He had no other choice.

The town crowned him a hero for the human life he took.

He gets out of the patrol car and, almost as an afterthought, grabs his black Mag-Lite flashlight. It's the big kind that takes five or six D-cell batteries and is nearly a foot and a half in length. It weighs as much as a small dumbbell.

He walks around the back of the pickup truck.

The blinding beam of light from his flashlight cuts through the night and the storm.

He knocks on my window.

Rain drips off his hat and splashes at his feet.

"Thanks for getting here so fast," I say, opening the door, swinging my legs out.

The sheriff stops me with a gentle shove to the chest, pushing me back into my seat.

"Eddie, you can't go in. You shouldn't even be here. Why don't you go back to Mattie's and wait for me?"

"No," I say. "I need to see this done."

"If you really have to stay, stay in the truck. I can handle this."

He pushes me again so he can close the door.

When he's certain I won't follow, the sheriff walks toward the front of the house.

All the lights are off and the screen door is hanging open, swinging in the wind like a dead man at the gallows, slapping against the wall with a dull metallic thud.

Lightning crashes as the sheriff peers through the pouring rain. There is some sleet now.

His hands tighten on the shotgun and the flashlight.

The wind gusts, blowing icy rain at him.

"Michael?" the sheriff calls. He holds the shotgun level at his waist.

"Let's have ourselves a talk."

There is no movement outside the house, and none inside that he can see.

"Listen up, Michael. Let's not do this the hard way."

The sheriff plods through the puddles in the front yard.

Keeping the shotgun level and pointed forward, he steps up on the porch and cautiously studies the living room through the wide picture window.

The lights are off, but he can see the house has been trashed.

The coffee table has been tossed upside-down, beer

cans are strewn about, and glass from the TV screen litters the floor.

There is no one in the room.

The sheriff must be worried.

He knows what my father did to Mary.

Seven years ago.

Even if he couldn't prove the crime, he knows the truth. He knows the monster my father has become.

The sheriff moves to the open door, steps into the living room where the floor is wet from the blowing rain cutting under the roof of the porch. His black shoes sink a little on the drenched carpet.

He circles by the dead television and into the dining room and then the kitchen.

His flashlight cuts through the darkness, showing him everything in a wide, bright circle.

Nothing appears to be out of place in the kitchen, other than the overturned trash can and the burned Hamburger Helper on the stove. He turns the stove off. He glances through the back window at the woods beyond the house, but all he sees is rain and mud and trees and the night.

The sheriff returns to the living room. His stomach tightens into a tiny ball.

The door at the end of the hall, the one to my room, remains wide open, as does the door to the master bedroom.

But the doors to the bathroom and the spare bedroom are shut.

"Ah, hell," the sheriff says, his stomach tightening more, like a snake coiling and constricting.

He hears a loud thump from somewhere in the rear of the house.

He stops, his eyes wide and his head cocked. His flashlight sweeps the hallway.

He sees the overhead light has been smashed. It lies in pieces on the floor. Streaks of dried blood are barely visible on the broken glass.

He creeps to the first door on the right and holds his breath.

A dull hum fills his ears.

The tightness grows worse inside of him.

Now he feels the scorching need to take a good, long piss.

His left hand trembles as he rests it on the cold metal doorknob.

He holds the shotgun ready.

The flashlight is pointed at his feet.

Sweat drips off his forehead as the fear builds inside him.

His heart races, and he pushes the fake brass knob on the bathroom door.

The door creaks open. His flashlight's fixed beam bursts through the narrow space.

For a brief instant he sees someone leaping out of the darkness! He can't think! He has to react or he'll die! He knows this, and he almost tugs the shotgun's trigger.

But the movement is only the green shower curtain.

When he shoved the door open, the curtain gave a little wave. That's all. A little ruffle of plastic before it settled back into its routine of hanging at the edge of the tub.

Otherwise, the bathroom is empty.

The yellow tiles show the age of the house, and water drips from under the bottom of the chipped sink. But no one is there.

The sheriff sighs.

He proceeds down the hallway, the flashlight leading the way.

The door to the master bedroom remains wide open, but the door to the spare bedroom is shut tight.

"Ah, hell," the sheriff says again.

Over the storm he hears a sputtering, like an engine fighting to start. Someone is crying in the master bedroom.

He edges closer, moving sideways, his back to the wall. He stops a few feet short of his destination.

Out of the corner of his eye he catches a flash of movement.

The sheriff spins toward the living room, the shotgun rising level with his waist.

Chapter Thirty

Then

The hallway was dark, as if the home had been abandoned for years, but Eddie could see the shotgun barrel swinging up toward his chest, followed by the blinding light from the Mag-Lite. He threw his hands in the air, stumbling backward and trying to keep silent. He didn't want to yell, couldn't yell. That would probably bring his father running.

"Jesus H. Christ," the sheriff whispered, lowering the shotgun and waving the teenager out of the house. Eddie didn't move. He had vowed to see his father taken care of, and he wasn't going to leave until that was done, no matter what the sheriff or his own instincts were telling him. Fear and desperation were twisting his guts into knots, but it was too late to go back. Instead, he listened to the noises coming from the master bedroom. The muttering was growing louder.

"I didn't want to be like you!" Michael cried. "I remember the day my mother died."

There was a long pause. Eddie almost expected someone to reply.

"Yeah, but it's your fault," Michael said, answering a question only he had heard. "I started drinking after Mary died. I wanted to escape the shit-talking in town!"

Michael's voice was rising in anger.

"We got hitched after Laura found out she was pregnant with Eddie. I loved her. I loved our babies. I still love them! I really do!"

There was another pause from Michael, although his sobbing continued. In response to another unheard question he said, "Yeah, but I came home drunk and Laura was waiting for me. This was a few months after Mary died and I had been drinking a lot and I had promised Laura I wouldn't, but I was lying . . . I came home shit-faced and Laura really tore into me and I don't remember much else, but I know I clubbed her upside the head and she went flying onto the wooden chair we used to have in here. It was a nice chair. The kind you get at Pier One in the city. I had saved my paychecks for a month to buy her the chair . . ."

The sheriff waved Eddie away again.

"I can't," Eddie whispered. "I have to stay here. I have to see this through."

"I'm going in. Get the hell out of here," the sheriff ordered, pointing his flashlight toward the living room.

Eddie did as he was told. He stepped over the glass on the hallway floor and around the corner into the living room, stopping by the shattered television. He refused to go any farther. This was a side of his father he had never heard before, and he just couldn't leave.

Holding his breath, Eddie edged back toward the hallway, glancing around the corner. He could see the outline of the sheriff at the end of the hall, his body silhouetted by the flashlight. For some reason, Eddie thought it was like watching a man approaching the doorway to heaven.

In one quick move, the sheriff stepped through the open door, raising his Mag-Lite and shotgun.

Chapter Thirty-one

Now: The Second Nightmare

Eddie immediately recognized where he was standing as the dream defined itself within the blank void of his mind. The interior of his family's home hadn't changed much in the last forty years, but he couldn't quite believe what he saw. A young boy sat on the couch facing the television. The television's curved screen gave off a white, flickering glow. The boy wore blue overalls and a black-and-yellow Pittsburgh Pirates T-shirt, and his dirty brown hair was wild and uncombed. Tears were running down his pale face. It only took an instant for Eddie to understand.

Oh, man, this is fucked up. The little boy had to be his father. There was no doubt in Eddie's mind. In some twisted way the conclusion made perfect sense. The boy's eyes were wide with terror, but he was obviously trying to stay glued to the images flashing on the TV. If Eddie had learned anything the last few years he lived with his father, he understood why little Michael couldn't look away. The boy had discovered a long time ago what would happen if he interrupted his mother and father fighting.

Near the fireplace a thin woman lay on the floor. Long, dingy hair fanned out behind her head. She was wearing a faded pink dress with a torn strap. Her legs and arms were pitted by a sea of tiny white scars from past assaults. Her right eye was swollen and her face was covered with black-and-blue marks.

A heavyset man loomed over the woman, his huge fists raised in anger. His thick brown hair was knotted, dirt was ground into his exposed flesh, and even the Salvation Army would have rejected his clothes. The blue jeans were ripped and dirty. The white T-shirt had caked food stains on the front, sweat stains under the arms. Strips of duct tape held his tennis shoes together.

The man had to be Eddie's grandfather. The woman was his grandmother. A front page article in the *Black Hills Herald* had reported her death in a rifle-cleaning accident, and although Eddie had read the article with his own eyes, almost everyone in Black Hills said the official report probably wasn't the truth. He had to agree.

Piled in the fireplace was a pyramid of split logs. They crackled and popped in the billowing red flames. The roaring fire lit the front of the room, and shadows stretched into the dining room, to the badly painted green table covered with dirty plates, empty whiskey and beer bottles, and an old rifle. The house reeked of spilled alcohol, spoiling food, and the unwashed bedding of people who had no hope.

"No, Kurt!" Dana Farris whimpered, raising her arms to block a blow. It did no good. Her husband kicked her in the ribs again and again. Each gut-wrenching impact brought forth a pained gasp from her cracked lips.

"Shut up, you bitch!" Kurt savagely kicked her in the face. Dana's nose popped and she wailed in pain. Blood trickled to her chin.

Kurt turned and staggered to the table in the middle of the dining room where he grabbed the bottle of Jack Daniel's. He took a swig, letting the burn flow from his chest to the rest of his body. Then he grabbed the rifle and returned his full attention to his wife. He stood like some hulking giant ready to stomp on his prey. Dana's tear-filled eyes were fixed on the floor and the blood pouring from her nose.

"Are you sorry, bitch?" Kurt asked, pointing the rifle at her head. "Are you sorry, Dana? You should have known not to betray me, woman. I'm your man and you should have known I'd find out!"

Terror dawned on Dana's face as she raised her head.

"Kurt, you've been drinking. I didn't do nothing. Put the gun away. You're scaring little Mikey and you're scaring me."

"You shouldn't of done what you did, you stupid bitch, you stupid, stupid bitch." Kurt pulled the trigger, sending a single bullet into Dana's nose. She flipped like a beached fish. A ribbon of blood splashed onto Kurt's face, but he didn't even blink. The flames from the fire were reflected in his hate-filled eyes.

Eddie remained frozen by shock, his heart racing, his eyes wide. The corpse was no longer Dana Farris. Lehcar twitched, moaned. Her eyes opened and she sat up, stiffly, as if she was a puppet being controlled by heavy cables. She yawned and grinned. Her right hand mindlessly twirled her blood-soaked hair.

"Why did this have to happen, Eddie?" Lehcar asked in a tone of voice more appropriate for some kind of lover's joke. Half of her face was dotted with blood. There was a tiny mark where the bullet had pierced her flesh. A rush of blood, bone chips, and slimy gray matter spilled out through the opening in the side of her head. Eddie thought the carnage was far too melodramatic, that the bullet wouldn't have destroyed her skull like that in real life, but this was how he always pictured it when he heard the stories. This was how *everyone* imagined Dana's death.

"I don't understand!"

"Haven't you been reading the articles in your scrapbook?" she replied. "Remember the black fire of the soul! Some men are consumed by a black fire and they can be nothing but evil. They burn everyone they love, they burn their spirit and their mind! Eddie, those who ignore the past are doomed to repeat it."

Little Michael crawled across the dirty floor to his dead mother. He moved slowly, like he was lost in a dream of his own. His eyes were wide, though, as if he was burning the image into his mind so he'd never forget it. Kurt had fallen to his knees, his giant frame suddenly stooped over. He held the limp body in his arms, as though he could fix his atrocious act of violence.

"Daddy?" the child sobbed. "What's wrong with Mommy?"

"She's sleeping, and you should be, too," Kurt stuttered, tears streaming from his eyes. He gently put his wife back on the floor, laid the rifle by her hand, and got to his feet. His voice trembled with fear as he swept his son into his arms. "But first we've gotta go into town and take care of some business. It'll be okay, I promise you. I'll get you an orange soda pop."

Kurt carried little Michael out of the house, tenderly wiping the tears from the boy's face with a hand that was spotted with blood. The roar of his truck starting reverberated through the surrounding hills, and Eddie heard the squeal of tires as Kurt floored the gas pedal and sped away. Then there was silence, interrupted by the occasional crackle of the fire.

Eddie hoped Lehcar was gone too, but she wasn't. She was waiting patiently for him. She grinned, showing her chipped teeth, but her eyes remained dead and glazed.

"You'll kill," she said. "You can't help it. Remember? A man is his own fire. That is all he can be. A man cannot change the color of his fire, Eddie. You can't change your destiny."

Eddie was confused and horrified. "I'm not going to kill anyone! Never again!"

Lehcar laughed. She abruptly sat straight up, grabbed Eddie with one bony hand, and planted a bloody kiss on his lips. Her flesh was cold, and her snakelike tongue darted into his mouth, straight back to his tonsils. Her tongue was like ice smacking into the soft, warm lining of his throat. She grinned as Eddie frantically tried to escape her grasp.

She said, "Oh, but you will. Maybe you should kill yourself and save us all a lot of trouble. You are your father. Ashes to ashes, dust to dust, and all that jazz."

Chapter Thirty-two

Now

Eddie awoke in the darkened bedroom of his apartment, gagging, as if a piece of cold, hard fruit had been shoved into his throat. The blockage cleared, and he sucked the air in and out, over and over, fighting the urge to vomit. Terror slammed through his body, but he managed to hold down the contents of his stomach. It was a task made easier since the last two horrifying dreams had caused him to lose his appetite. He wasn't even sure when he had last eaten a meal, let alone a snack, other than the swig of beer earlier in the night.

Eddie felt the dampness under his mouth, but it was too heavy, too sticky to be tears. He rushed to the tiny bathroom with the green tiles and the moldy shower curtain inside the metal tub. He flicked on the light, stared into the dirty mirror.

"Dammit," he whispered. His bottom lip was bleeding. He grabbed a towel and turned on the faucet. At first there was nothing, but then the pipes groaned and the water squirted out in irregular intervals. He wet the towel and cleaned his face.

You are your father. Ashes to ashes, dust to dust, and all that jazz.

He shuddered, studying his reflection in the mirror. Lines had formed under his eyes and the bottom of his nose was red, as if he had been fighting the flu for weeks. His hair was wild and it definitely had more gray streaks now. His skin was pasty colored and blotted with dark spots.

"Jesus, no wonder everyone says I'm crazy," he said, turning off the faucet and light. He returned to bed. Lehcar and the reality of his dreams had left him badly shaken, especially now that Rachel was part of his life. Against his own best judgment Eddie continued to secretly hope she might fall in love with him like the old days, but these nightmares scared him. He didn't want to hurt her. He didn't want to see the blood on her hands again. Her fingers were so thin and delicate, and the blood had covered them completely.

"Oh, fuck, don't think about any of that," Eddie said, dragging the sweat-soaked covers off the bed and tossing them to the floor. He flopped backward, resting his head on the damp pillow. In the blue glow from his alarm clock, he could make out shapes on the other side of the small room—the chair in the corner, a pile of dirty clothes, and his tennis shoes on the floor. He examined the ceiling and bathed in the silence.

His thoughts returned to Rachel and the phone calls.

Someone keeps calling and saying things. Horrible things. He says he's coming for me. He says he's finishing what he started. He sounds like your father, Eddie. I don't know how that's possible, but I think it is your father.

The words echoed inside of Eddie's confused mind.

His father was dead. There had been no doubt that one of them wouldn't leave The Showdown alive, and Eddie had seen his father fall, his heavy body hitting the floor hard. He remembered holding Rachel, waiting to see if his father moved. He hadn't.

Eddie didn't believe in the supernatural, although he enjoyed reading and writing about it. Ghosts weren't real, and neither were zombies or vampires. Eddie knew that, no matter what some occult books tried to peddle as scientific fact. Eddie couldn't believe any of the books' claims. Even as a child he had eventually realized that the strange noises he had heard in the old Godwin Estate were nothing more than the wind and the rats, and the overactive imaginations of him and his friends, of course. And what had happened to his friends who had disappeared? He didn't know, but it couldn't have had anything to do with ghosts. Maybe they just decided to run away. Or maybe they returned to Black Rock Lake after midnight and drowned while swimming. That happened every couple of years and often the bodies were never found. Any of those things could have happened.

Intellectually, Eddie understood that the supernatural was make-believe, but sometimes the understanding dwelled in the same dark place where he hid the belief that he could have saved his mother's life if he had moved a little bit faster the day of The Showdown. But no matter how much of a possibility it seemed to be, no matter how well it explained the events of the last few days, the dead simply didn't rise from their graves. So where did that leave him? He was so frustrated his hands curled into fists. He wanted to run off into the night, to leave all the misery behind, but his inner voice took control.

"Oh, no," Eddie whispered as another idea popped into his head. Although he didn't want to believe it, there was an alternate explanation for what Rachel had been telling him. A horrible and strangely comforting theory.

"What if *she's* crazy?" Eddie bolted upright and stared at the tattered Dali poster on the wall behind his dresser. Slowly all the pieces came together, forming a larger picture.

"The man on the street was a prison guard going home from work. The strange phrase I heard in my head was just my imagination. I was all worked up because of the movie. I always get caught up in the movies. And the notebooks could have been some kids playing with gasoline, wanting to see how fast the paper would burn. The nightmares—"

Eddie realized he could even explain the increasing level of horror in his dreams.

"It's all because of Rachel. I'm stressed. Lehcar is a figment of my imagination. She looks like Rachel because Rachel is the one who has brought all this stress into my life. And she's in these dreams based on events that really took place here in Black Hills because I've been focusing on the stories in my scrapbook. Right?"

Eddie thought of the book the counselor at the clinic had recommended to him. The one that had been showcased on *Oprah: Mental Health From The Inside Out: Controlling Your Dreams, Nightmares, and Fantasies.* He had read of this sort of phenomena in a chapter devoted to the psychology of repetitive terror. Everything finally made perfect sense.

"Yeah, she's in my dreams to try to explain the mess of emotions I'm being bombarded with. She's a symbol or something."

The explanation was logical enough. His mind had been thrown into a frenzy because he was so overwhelmed by the very notion of having Rachel in his life again and by the bizarre things she was telling him. The absurd things. He had often worried he was losing his mind, but what if Rachel was the crazy one?

"I could be right. She might be the problem here, not my . . . my dad."

After everything the two of them had been through, what had been going on inside Rachel's head ever since she left? He had no clue, but she had been to the free clinic, and that had to mean something, didn't it? Then again, he had visited the free clinic and he wasn't crazy, no matter what the people in town said about him and his family. Yet Rachel had actually taken an extended stay at the *asylum*. He wondered how insane a person would have to be to get incarcerated there, away from humanity, away from reality.

"Jesus, this is all fucked up," Eddie told the empty room, his head drooping slightly, his eyes blinking open and shut. His thoughts were becoming slow and muffled, like frantic shouts heard from under deep water. He had two more hours until he needed to be across town for his meeting with Rachel, and although he didn't want to go back to sleep, he didn't have a choice. He was exhausted, as if the two new nightmares had been secretly draining him of energy. He couldn't stay awake for the next twenty minutes, let alone the rest of the day. His body ached like it sometimes did when he went too long without sleep. He could feel the muscles and tissue under his skin shifting, dancing in some perpetual state of flux.

I can be a man about anything, he thought, knowing he'd have to fall asleep and deal with his dreams sooner or later. He was certain he could handle whatever Lehcar threw at him now that he understand where she was coming from. She wasn't real. She was simply a projection of his emotions, a symbol of his current troubles.

Eddie studied the ceiling above his bed. His eyes grew heavy, and he heard Lehcar laughing in the distance. He trembled as her grating voice grew louder. The darkness consumed him.

Chapter Thirty-three

From the Handwritten Account

My Mental Reconstruction of Events Past
by Eddie Farris

The sheriff takes one step into the master bedroom, but then he holds his ground.

To move any closer to someone as unhinged as my father obviously is . . . well, it's not the best career move a person can make.

My father is dressed in his prison guard uniform. He is sitting on the edge of the bed.

Crushed beer cans litter the floor.

The room stinks of alcohol and misery.

The full-length mirror in the corner is damaged; a jagged crack stretches from the top to the bottom.

My father's hunting rifles are secured high on the wall behind the bed, nestled in a heavy oak rack.

The sheriff keeps his shotgun and the Mag-Lite level as he searches the room for whomever my father might have been talking to.

The sheriff sees no one else.

I didn't think he would.

He says, "Michael, why don't we discuss this little problem like decent folk?"

My father turns his head.

The sheriff sees my father's empty, bloody eye socket.

A black, blood-crusted gash is all that remains.

Dried blood-red tears dot his face.

The wound is probably the most horrible thing the sheriff has ever seen, I think. At least since John Mills fell into his mechanical thresher. From what I understand, there had been a lot of blood and chunks of flesh splattered on the walls of the barn.

I've written stories based on that incident, although I saw none of it.

I'm certain this is worse.

My father's other eye is bloodshot.

He can probably see out of it well enough, although I can easily imagine his vision growing fuzzy, like there is soft gauze in the corners of his eye.

"I've been sitting here," he says. "You hear the voice? I always wondered if that was what my father meant when he said he talked to the shadows. After my mother died. I've been hearing the voice a lot lately."

"Michael?"

My father's head wobbles a bit, like he can't hold up all the weight.

He stares at the sheriff's shotgun, as if he doesn't quite comprehend what it is.

My father is as wide as an oak tree across his chest and he can bench-press his own weight, but suddenly he has the lost and confused expression of a small boy searching for his mother.

He doesn't seem to be on the same planet as the rest of us.

He opens his mouth, and through the sobbing and slurred speech, he whispers, "I'm sorry."

He drops to his knees, pitching forward and landing on his chest, his arms out in front on him.

He grabs his head, squeezing it, like he's trying to crush his skull, trying to drive the anger and pain out of his mind, like he's having demons exorcised from his body. He's writhing in agony and crying.

The sheriff stands his ground.

"Michael? You gotta relax and let me take you to a hospital. You hear me, Michael?"

The sheriff is standing at the edge of the room, the shotgun and the light carefully trained on the twitching man on the floor.

"Michael!"

My father stares at the sheriff.

Tears are running down my father's face, even from the hollow socket where his right eye used to be.

He's suddenly a child of eight instead of a man who beats his wife and son and works at a prison bossing the cons.

The sheriff says, "How 'bout you sit up and take some deep breaths?"

My father does as he is told, slowly sitting up, tilting to the side but then regaining his balance, his long legs stretched out.

With a heavy hand, he gingerly touches his bloody socket.

He says, "My boy did this."

I cringe, thinking about what I've done. But I had no other choice.

The sheriff asks, "Does it hurt?"

"Not really. Seems like it should, but it doesn't. It did at first, but not anymore."

The sheriff nods. "Who were you talking to, Michael? I heard you talking to someone in here."

"My old man," he replies, as if that's the most logical answer possible. "He says he killed my mother and he's sorry and he wants me to kill myself so I don't hurt anyone. I think he's right."

The sheriff shakes his head. This is not a good sign.

"I love my wife and kid," my father adds.

I almost laugh, but I manage to bite my tongue.

How could a man inflict so much pain and then claim love is involved? I love Rachel. Does that mean I have to beat her? He's drunk. He's insane.

He goes on, though, and says, "I really do."

"So why aren't you treating them right?"

"Just because you hurt someone doesn't mean you don't love them," my father says. "I never meant to hurt them."

"You could have gotten help, Michael. It wasn't too late. It isn't too late."

My father shakes his head.

"Oh, it's much too late. I was born to be like this, I think. I'm a monster, haven't you heard? Haven't you heard what people say about me and my father and my family? They think we're all monsters, and maybe they're right."

Sheriff Breiner pulls the silver metal handcuffs off his belt.

"We need to go to the hospital, okay? We can discuss this some more when we get there. Stand up. Slowly. Very slowly."

My father does as he is told.

He gets to his feet, pushing up with his arms, his muscles flexing.

Blood drips from the hollowed-out socket in his head.

"Now put your hands behind your head."

Again, my father does as he is told.

The sheriff takes a cautious step forward, reaches out with the handcuffs in his hand.

His shotgun and the Mag-Lite dip a bit.

Now they're pointed more toward the floor and not the man he is taking into custody.

I see this. This is a problem. This is a huge problem. I want to warn him, but I can't speak. I take a step forward, almost into the room, my mouth open, but nothing comes out.

A board squeaks under my weight.

My father looks right at me.

"What the fuck is he doing here?" he demands. His voice is a dull, grating knife.

His muscles contract with an adrenaline surge.

His eyes cut into me.

I am in a world of shit.

Chapter Thirty-four

Then

It was a moment that would be etched into his mind forever, and Eddie instantly wished he had fled the house when the sheriff told him to leave. The same part of him that had understood what was going to happen when he spilled the glass of milk that morning was now telling him to run like hell. Maybe it wasn't too late!

"Eddie, I told you to wait outside," the sheriff shouted, swinging the flashlight's wide beam to the other side of the room. He glared at the rain-drenched teenager standing in the doorway. "Get out of here. I have this situation under control."

The sheriff held the handcuffs in his left hand. He moved to grab Michael's arm, but it was already too late. Michael's fist flew forward in one fluid motion, landing a swift blow between the sheriff's eyes. There was a loud crack as the sheriff hit the door frame. The flashlight fell from his limp fingers, landing on the carpet with a heavy thump, rolling, the light spinning around and around until it came to a stop by Michael's booted foot. He bent over, grabbed the heavy flashlight, and then he stood, growing to his full height like an angry grizzly bear.

"Dad, no!" Eddie cried.

Michael stepped forward, growling. He hauled back and shoved the metal Mag-Lite into his son's stomach, the beam of light flashing wildly across the walls and the ceiling. Fire surged through Eddie's upper body. He gasped as he fell into the hallway, hitting the wall hard, landing on the floor. Without thinking, he started crawling toward the living room, pieces of broken glass brushing his hands but not cutting into him. He could barely breathe and his chest spasmed. He reached the living room and headed for the front door.

In the master bedroom came the sounds of a fight: the dull crack of a skull being struck by a blunt object, the shrill cry of a man falling out of control, and the crash of a nightstand being crushed.

"No, no, no," Eddie whispered, stumbling to his feet and into the storm, his right arm slung across his stomach. Rain and sleet pelted the dark land as he hurried to the pickup truck and jumped inside. He jammed the key in the ignition, but he didn't move.

God, I screwed up bad! He shook his head. *I can't leave the sheriff!*

Eddie watched and waited, but there was no sign of life from the house, only the storm and the night. No lights, no movement, nothing. He desperately wanted to see the sheriff appear in the doorway, but his gut told him that wouldn't happen. The sheriff probably wasn't going to leave the house alive.

And Eddie knew it was all his fault.

He shifted the truck into gear.

Chapter Thirty-five

Now: The Final Nightmare

Eddie was dreaming, but this was very different from the previous two dreams, and it certainly wasn't his standard Showdown nightmare. He was sitting in a living room adorned with plush furniture, a coffee table made of glass, and a big-screen television. The TV was on, although the volume was muted. It was summer and a ball game was being shown on one of the Pittsburgh stations. The Dodgers were visiting Steel Country and kicking the collective asses of the Pirates. Eddie sighed. Some aspects of reality never changed, even in his dreams.

The room was as large as the house he had lived in as a child. He realized he was rich, at least in this dreamland, and that seemed very logical and matter-of-fact, despite the nagging voice in the back of his mind telling him this wasn't right.

A dozen copies of the same hardcover book were piled on the coffee table, but Eddie didn't really notice them. A thunderstorm was rolling through the valley. There was a large window behind the couch and the curtains were pulled open. Rain tapped on the glass. Blue lightning split the sky, filling the yard and the wilderness that extended for miles beyond it with a fractured light. Eddie was completely relaxed. But then—

"My God," he whispered, bolting straight up. His spine grew rigid, locking in place. If he hadn't glanced at the television, he might never have seen the breaking news interrupt the ball game, but he had looked and now he wished he hadn't. What he saw couldn't be true. It just couldn't be.

Even without the sound, the graphic displayed above the shoulder of Flora Williams, the anchorwoman for the hourly news breaks, said it all. BREAKING NEWS: RIOT AT MENTAL HEALTH FACILITY was superimposed onto an aerial photograph of the state hospital located a few miles down the road from Eddie's house.

He grabbed the remote off the coffee table, his hand striking the pile of books, knocking them to the floor. Eventually his mind might have registered that his name was on the cover, that his goal of becoming a best-selling writer had come true, at least in this dreamland, but for now that recognition was beyond him. He fumbled with the buttons on the remote, as if his hand wasn't fully under the control of his body. He finally found the volume button.

". . . sources within the hospital report at least three people are dead. Dozens have been injured since the riot began two hours ago. There has been no confirmation of whether the dead and injured are employees or patients at the Pennsylvania State Psychiatric Hospital, and State Police officials on the scene are not releasing the names of the victims. Several patients have reportedly escaped the facility and may be somewhere on the grounds or in the woods nearby . . ."

Hands shaking, Eddie turned the television off.

He didn't need to hear whatever might be coming next. *She* was out, and she would be coming for him. There was no doubt in his mind.

For Eddie, it was no longer a dream. He was living in a different reality, one created in his REM state and as real as anything he had ever lived through in his entire life. The horror was a mirror image of the previous nightmares, only magnified a thousand times. In this strange new reality, Rachel was after him. If he had been awake, the thoughts wouldn't have made any sense, but that didn't matter. He was reacting based on the rules of this dream. Those rules said Rachel was coming for him, and when she arrived she would kill him.

Acting purely on instinct, Eddie reached down beside the couch and grabbed the cane waiting there. He used the ornate wooden rod as leverage, carefully putting most of his weight on his left leg. In this dreamland, his right leg would never be normal again. Not after what Rachel had done to him. He knew without wondering why, without questioning the situation.

"She said she'd get out, she said she'd come back," Eddie muttered as he hurried to the front door, his cane striking the wooden floor like a hammer. The rubber tip came loose and skidded away, but he didn't stop. He felt like a rat in a maze, scurrying around dark corners, aware of large, unseen eyes analyzing his every movement. He couldn't walk fast enough. His mind blistered with images of Rachel and the things she had said and done in the days prior to when *they* took her away.

As Eddie entered the two-story, open foyer with its marble tiling and crystal chandelier, he focused on the front door. Both the deadbolt and the regular lock were secured. There was no sign of forced entry anywhere. He looked out through the tall, thin, vertical windows next to the door, flipping on the outside light with one quick movement of his hand. The porch was empty, except for the wooden bench and some potted flowers, and the front lawn was drowning in two expanding pools of rainwater.

"I have to stay calm," he said, moving back through the wide French arches and into the dining area. The centerpiece of silk flowers on the immaculate white tablecloth sat untouched. Lightning crashed, sending icy shivers up Eddie's spine to rattle his brain. The thunder rolled through the valley. He moved to the window. He grabbed the drawstring to the curtains and started to pull them shut. Then his heart jumped.

In the time it took him to blink and for another splinter of blinding lightning to explode from the sky, Eddie was certain he saw someone standing at the edge of the woods bordering his yard. The air left his lungs. No one else lived out there. In fact, there wasn't anything or anyone for miles . . . except for the asylum. It lurked in the pitch-black realm of night, in the heart of the storm. Through the heavy rain he couldn't see anything, not even the woods, until lightning split the night again, and the yard was lit up for barely a second.

Eddie saw no one. In the brief instant of clarity caused by the spiderweb of blinding light consuming the sky, all Eddie could see were the tree branches bending in the wind as the rain beat on the window. He couldn't see past the tree line, and anyone or anything could be in the woods, of course.

Off to his right, Eddie heard glass shattering in the basement.

"It can't be," he said, understanding full well what the noise had been. A window. A window had been broken. "Oh, shit, oh, shit! She's back. She's back!" A wave of panic rose inside of him. His hands shook. "Jesus Christ, I have to get hold of myself!"

The lights died without warning. No drama. No warning. Just electric death. He was enveloped by the darkness.

Muttering under his breath, Eddie put all the weight he could on his left leg and the cane. He quickly hobbled to the kitchen. He was holding his breath and involuntarily clenching his hand into a fist. He approached the phone mounted on the wall next to a white board with phone numbers he frequently needed. Somehow he knew the phone wouldn't work, the line would be dead, but he tried it anyway. He was right. There was no dial tone, no prerecorded message. Nothing. He dropped the receiver, letting it dangle from the cord.

Eddie limped to the cabinet where he kept some miscellaneous supplies. Somewhere in the garage he had a flashlight, maybe even two, but he didn't have time to search for them. The rules of the dream told him so, like there was a secret narrator whispering in his ear. He realized the voice was the same paranoid friend who lurked in the darkest corners of his mind.

He opened the cabinet over the microwave and quickly swatted inside the black, empty space until he found what he was searching for. He grabbed the cardboard box containing candles and hundreds of matches. The contents were heavier than he expected, and the box slipped out of his hands, landing on the counter with a loud clap. He cringed and blindly dug through the contents of the box, finally finding a long, thin candle lodged in a flat, metal base. He grabbed it and a few loose matches.

Eddie wiped the sweat off his forehead. His eyes were slowly adjusting to the dark, but he could barely see the outlines of the objects he held. He struck the match on the countertop. Nothing. He tried again. Still nothing. He reached into the box, dug around, and found an empty matchbox. He felt for the rough strip on the side and tried swiping the match there. The tip flared to life, giving off a harsh sulfate smell. He quickly lit the candle.

What I am going to do? Eddie thought, standing motionless. *I have to do something! I have to stop her!*

He reached for the largest carving knife in the wooden block on the counter. The knife was all he had to defend himself. He might have a chance to stop Rachel if he made the first move, but if she surprised him, he was dead.

Holding the candle and the knife in the same hand, and putting most of his weight on his good leg, Eddie limped to the foyer. He tried his best to keep his footsteps soft, and he carefully avoided the two squeaky boards in the hallway.

He stopped by the basement door. He thought twice about his next move, and backed a few steps to the side. The door opened toward him, and he wanted to be out of the way, just in case. He put his hand on the doorknob, balancing all his weight on his left leg while the cane leaned uselessly against his hip. He listened for any indication of movement in the basement. He watched the light from the candle reflecting off the polished blade of the knife. His heart was a jackhammer in his chest, causing his entire body to shake. The little voice in the back of his mind told him to run and flee into the storm, but he knew that was insane. He couldn't go out there. Not into the dark. The night would eat him alive.

Shoving down his fear, Eddie turned the knob. He slowly pulled the door toward him and, after a short hesitation, he threw it open with one heavy tug.

His eyes widened, his heart erupted, and in his panic he dropped the knife.

Rachel was waiting for him on the top step, nude, her blond hair trimmed significantly shorter than he had ever seen it. She was painfully thin, like a full-size human skeleton propped at the front of a college biology classroom. She was dripping wet from the rain, her sickly flesh glistening in the candlelight. She had streaks of mud on her legs, and cuts and bruises from her daring escape marked her flesh. Drops of water trickled from her shoulders, dripping off her erect nipples. Her ribs stuck out. Her right hand was bloody. The standard-issue gown every patient at the hospital wore was nowhere to be seen. She grinned, showing her white, nearly perfect teeth.

"No," Eddie whispered, losing his balance, putting too much weight onto his bad leg. His cane fell toward Rachel and she swatted it into the darkness awaiting them in the basement. It disappeared like a stick tossed into a bottomless well.

The candle dropped from Eddie's hand, landing with

a thud at the top of the steps, the flame flickering, but staying lit.

Rachel reached out with her bony fingers, grabbed Eddie by the shirt, and pulled him forward, letting gravity take hold of his weight and drag him down the steps. The dark washed over him. A series of white-hot stabbing pains ripped through Eddie, and light flashed inside his eyelids. Then there was nothing.

The agony Eddie felt was intense. He didn't know if he was asleep or awake, but he knew he was badly hurt. He winced, resisting the urge to call for help. If Rachel had remained nearby, which he was absolutely convinced she had, he didn't want to lose any slight advantage he might have.

He was lying on the basement floor at the bottom of the steps, his flesh freezing cold, like he had been placed on a slab of ice. The basement was almost completely dark, the only exception being the dancing light coming from his candle at the top of the steps. The light wasn't enough to show him more than a few feet of the basement, but it was better than nothing.

She's around here somewhere, Eddie thought. *I can smell her hate.* Whatever the hell that meant.

The rain tapped on the basement windows set level with the ground. He could hear running water. In a flash of lightning he saw a broken window in the wall farthest from where he lay. A river of rainwater was running into the basement, destroying all the cardboard boxes stacked there for safekeeping. The secret narrator of the dream told Eddie there were hundreds of green, spiral-bound notebooks in the boxes. Thousands of stories.

Tens of thousands of dream fragments. Now they were being destroyed. Nearby was the funhouse mirror from the movie theater. It had a long, wild crack running from top to bottom.

The light faded away, and Eddie finally realized why he felt so cold. He was completely naked. Naked and bleeding. Not a lot, but enough. His cuts were not from the fall. In the dim light from the candle, he could see the pattern of tiny crosses Rachel had carved into his flesh with the knife. There were hundreds of them. Blood trickled off his brow and he wearily wiped it from his eyes. He lay naked on the cold concrete, his mind racing in a thousand directions while his flesh leaked his blood. He tried to roll over, but pain ripped through his nerves and every cell in his body cursed at him.

"You awake, Eddie?" Rachel asked, emerging from behind the stairs. She was still wet and naked, and she walked with her hands behind her back, taking slow steps, circling the room. Each action was deliberate and planned. She moved farther into the dull, twinkling light. She kept her hands hidden. Eddie knew she was holding something, and he had a pretty good idea what it was. He had to escape soon or he was going to die.

Rachel asked, "Why'd you have to do what you did? Why? Why'd you have to make me go to that vulgar place?"

His voice trembled as he whispered, "I did what I had to do. What I thought I needed to do. What was best for both of us."

Rachel waved her hand, as if to say Eddie was the insane one. "Why'd you try to stop me from doing what God was telling me to do?"

"You're not hearing God in your head." Eddie's mind spun. *What the hell? She's never been religious in her entire life and now this? It doesn't make any sense.* He stated, "Those voices aren't real."

"It is our Lord!" she roared, the rage and indignation flaring in her cold eyes. "It is! He says I have to take your dirty parts. You and your filthy name and your filthy parts! You can't be allowed to populate the earth with your demon seed!"

While she ranted, the muscles on her arms twitched. She whipped one hand from behind her back, bringing an object into the candlelight. It wasn't what Eddie had been expecting.

"I see you kept this garbage," she said, holding the hardcover book like it was some horrible work of pornography and she was a preacher. Eddie recognized the cover immediately. *A Tear and a Smile* by Kahlil Gibran. How could he ever forget?

Rachel recited what Eddie had written on the front page, although her tone showed no affection, only sarcasm. "I love you with all my heart! No matter what, I will be with you until the end of time. That is a promise I could never break. Love is the blood of life and I'll always love you."

"Rachel . . ."

"Don't Rachel me! You have to spill some of the blood carrying your love, making me sick, making you sick."

Lightning punctured the sky. Behind Rachel's back the blood-crusted blade of the knife reflected the splintered light, and Eddie saw the gleam flashing on the wall. He didn't have much time. He had to keep her talking.

"We don't have to be like this, Rachel. We're better than this. We can still love each other—"

She laughed and threw the hardcover book. It flipped end over end, disappearing into the darkness, smacking the wall and falling to the concrete floor. Eddie had a fleeting thought, although he didn't grasp what it really meant: *The book landed open to a piece called "Have Mercy, My Soul."*

Rachel yelled, "Don't try to confuse me!"

She dropped to her knees, landing across Eddie's hips. He screamed and his body buckled in pain. Rachel brought her other hand out from behind her back, the knife coming within inches of Eddie's chest. She laughed and lowered the blood-crusted blade closer and closer to his already carved flesh. She grinned like some crazed, wild beast in the jungle, as if the smell of his blood were exciting her. As if she could taste death in the air.

"Listen, Rachel, this isn't right." Eddie's lungs heaved and sputtered like they were sucking lead. He coughed, a stream of blood spitting through his clenched teeth. A hot, metallic flavor spilled into his mouth. His chest squeezed even tighter and he understood he would probably drown in his own blood if Rachel didn't kill him with the knife first.

"After what you did, your death needs to take as long as possible. You have to pay for your crimes."

"Rachel, I didn't mean to hurt you!" Eddie cried as Rachel lowered the blade. She ran the tip of the knife across his chest, slicing more of his flesh ever so gently. She quickly slid backward, her weight pressing onto his bloody thighs and then onto his knees. Eddie screamed again. His body jumped. The involuntarily sit-up ended quickly, and his head smashed against the concrete, but during the surge of agony he saw something to his right. Something that could save his life if he were quick enough.

In the blink of an eye, Rachel raised the knife and stabbed it into Eddie's right side, just above his hip, digging the blade in as deep as she could and tearing open a hole in his flesh. Fire burst through him, like razors were being swiped across his nerves. The exquisite pain above his waist overwhelmed the throbbing inside his head. Rachel reached into him and broke off one of his ribs. There was a slight twinge and his entire body went numb. The rib dripped raw meat and blood, and Rachel raised it to her mouth.

"I am the mirror of your soul," she growled. She chewed on the rib, his blood splattering across her lips. "I am your dream lover!"

"Rachel, I'm sorry—" Eddie never finished the sentence. He focused his energy on his right hand as it groped blindly for the cane. His fingers found the rubber grip.

He raised the cane like a sword, pulled his arm back as far as he could until his elbow hit the floor.

Rachel stared fiercely at Eddie, and he drove the impromptu spear forward with all his might, shoving the ornate wooden rod into her abdomen. There was a sickening snap and her flesh ripped open. Her ribs cracked. Her body shook as the cane tore through her flesh. Eddie twisted the cane around and around, breaking apart Rachel's flaking skin, like she was a papier-mâché doll. She dropped his rib. Her chest cavity collapsed and dust was propelled outward in a burst of air, reminding Eddie of the time he had forgotten to check the vacuum cleaner's bag for several weeks until it popped, covering one corner of his apartment with a layer of gritty gray powder.

Eddie gagged as thousands of maggots streamed out of Rachel's chest. They poured onto him: little white scurrying creatures that looked like rice. They wiggled as they searched for a new place to live, and he felt a million tiny fingers caressing him. He gasped, let go of the cane, and swatted at the maggots.

Rachel spit blood and fell forward, landing across Eddie's chest, her head hitting the floor by his shoulder with a loud crack. He was trapped holding her body. It had become very heavy. As a rule dead bodies were heavier than the living person, at least in his experience. He tried to scream again, but no air escaped his lungs. They were soaking in his blood.

Then, except for the rain and the thunder, there was nothing.

Eddie's mind kept asking, *Will the nightmares stop or will they get worse? Will they get so bad they drive me insane, too?*

When Eddie finally opened his eyes, he got his answer.

Chapter Thirty-six

Now

Eddie studied the rear facade of the Richard Street Apartments, his head pounding with a headache too wicked for even the strongest aspirin to beat. A light snow was falling and the air was cold, but not as biting as it had been in recent days. There wasn't as much wind. Real winter hadn't hit the valley yet, although with all the snow lately that seemed hard to believe. Soon the heavy storms would roll in, some of them closing most of RR #324 this side of Slade City for hours or even days, if a nor'easter came from the south.

As Eddie waited for Rachel, he tried to focus on anything but the headache. The pain made him want to scream. He fought the urge. He didn't need people to see him standing behind the Richard Street Apartments, screaming at the top of his lungs. That could feed the gossip mill for months, maybe years. Who knew how far the story would go. Eventually it might become so twisted that even Eddie himself wouldn't be able to figure out how the townspeople had misconstrued the reality of his situation so badly.

This is going to be okay, Eddie thought. *We're going to talk and everything will be all right and we'll find a solution to this whole mess.*

Eddie studied the building, starting with the rusted fire escape, carefully examining each level until he reached the flat roof. The bricks were dirty, the mortar blackened, and some of the windows were boarded up. The icy fire escape shook in the slightest breeze.

The window to the Matthews' apartment slid open, and Eddie heard the raw squeal of metal on metal. The window had been replaced a few years before, but the person who did the repair had been careless. Rachel stuck her head out and gave a little wave in Eddie's direction. Legs first, she swung herself onto the rickety metal platform. She was wearing a heavy winter jacket, faded blue jeans, and her old, battered tennis shoes.

"I can't believe she's doing this," Eddie muttered as Rachel walked across the fire escape, the metal frame groaning. She climbed to the fourth floor, and then the third, and so on until she reached the lowest level where a metal ladder hung from one end of the platform. The bottom of the ladder was supposed to be suspended eight feet off the ground to keep intruders from waltzing right into the apartments, but someone had lowered it decades ago.

Rachel reached the ground without incident, and Eddie breathed a sigh of relief, although he really wasn't relieved. He had a bad feeling the newest dream was an omen of some kind. If Rachel was losing her grip on reality, that could explain her belief that his dead father was alive. And only a crazy person would dare use the damned fire escape, right? She could have used the back door.

Eddie's right side began to ache. He realized there was a much more horrible explanation for what had been occurring the last few days. The last dream could have meant something else entirely. Something more sinister and appalling. Maybe Rachel was out to get him. Maybe the nightmare had been a warning . . .

Stop it! Eddie screamed silently. *She isn't crazy. I'm going to help her! I am!*

"It's getting worse," Rachel said. She looked at Eddie, stopped dead in her tracks. "What's wrong?"

Eddie was going to wave a little wave to say nothing was wrong, but then he noticed Rachel seemed a bit younger somehow, as though some of the stress lines around her eyes had melted off in the last twenty-four hours. How could that be? Maybe she had gotten a good night's sleep. Why did that seem so wrong? He shoved the question away.

"You okay?" she asked.

"I have a bit of a headache. Had a bad dream," Eddie muttered.

"About what?"

"Nothing important. Same old shit."

Rachel handed Eddie a folded piece of lined paper. He examined what was written on the outside. FOREVER, the jagged letters proclaimed. The handwriting appeared familiar, but he knew that could have been coincidence. He unfolded the paper and read what was written there in a blotchy red ink.

You'll pay for what you did to me! Tonight!

"It has to be your father," Rachel urged as she and

Eddie walked together toward Copper Street. The wind kicked up, blowing rogue flakes of snow at them.

"But how, Rachel? How? He's dead. Even crazy old me knows that."

"You're not crazy," Rachel said. "You're not. You're no crazier than I am."

"Rachel, we watched him die." Eddie glanced back at the apartment building. He saw Adam sitting in the living room window of apartment fifty-seven. The boy waved.

"We must have been wrong. You didn't kill the cat and nail it to my door, did you?"

Eddie couldn't tell if Rachel was accusing him or confirming what she already believed. He said, "Of course not."

"You haven't been calling me, have you?"

"No."

"Or following me?"

"No."

Eddie found himself lost in her sad eyes. Even with the pure terror of the nightmare, he wanted to help her. He wanted to be her white knight and save the day. Even if she was crazy, did that mean she had nailed the cat to her own front door? That wasn't right. The Rachel he knew couldn't be so cruel and twisted. Someone else must have done it, and that person *could* be after her for reasons neither of them understood.

Rachel replied, "I don't have the car anymore, so I walk home from work and sometimes it's pretty late at night. He's been following me. I can feel him watching me."

My dad is dead! Eddie thought. *But Rachel can't be imagining this. I saw the damned cat!*

The thought trailed off as the more dreadful speculation that had been plaguing him as of late spoke again. The nightmare might have been a warning, his subconscious mind trying to create a big red light. Rachel *could* be insane. Or she could be setting him up. Maybe both. How would he possibly know? Until a few days ago, he hadn't spoken to her in years.

Could she be doing this to get back at me for what I did to her? But why this? Why the notes and the story and the pleas for help? Unless she really is—

"Please don't look at me like that," Rachel whispered. "I knew you didn't believe me! You think I'm crazy."

"This whole thing is a little hard to accept, Rachel," Eddie replied. He took a deep breath. She obviously needed help. Some kind of help. So much had changed in a matter of days, but he still wanted to be the one to protect her, to save her, to love her. No matter what. "But we'll get to the bottom of this. We will. I promise. I'll do whatever it takes."

Eddie was about to say more, but Sheriff Breiner's car pulled to a stop on Copper Street, the tires screeching. The red-and-blue lights on top were a frozen block of slush. Mud was splashed across the doors.

Oh, shit, Eddie thought, his heart sinking.

"What the hell are you doing here?" the sheriff called as the passenger side window rolled down. His face was red, like he had been running recently, or maybe drinking, or maybe on the verge of stroke. The top three buttons of his uniform were unbuttoned, showing off his white undershirt.

"I was just—"

"Jesus Christ!" the sheriff said, getting out of the car, leaving the engine running. "Damn it, boy, I thought you and I had reached an understanding."

"I had to try to figure out what happened."

"People are creating a firestorm because of that damned cat on her door!" the sheriff said. "They think you did it, Eddie, and you being here is gonna make them think they're right."

"I'm sorry."

"Eddie, get your dumb ass away from here! It's for your own good, boy. I can't deal with this shit." The sheriff got back into the car. He slammed his door shut. A layer of ice and snow slid off the roof, crashing to the street with the thudding sound of slush landing on slush. A moment later the car roared off into the distance, skidding left at the next intersection.

Rachel whispered, "I'm sorry I got you in trouble."

"It's not a problem," Eddie replied, staring at her pale skin, sad eyes, shivering hands. He wanted to save her so badly he hurt. "I can handle it. What do you want me to do?"

"I work the late shift today." Her sad eyes glimmered, just a little. She was getting excited. "Can you watch me leave and see if he follows?"

Eddie hated her request. It was a bad idea, the worst idea. But he couldn't tell her that. All he could say was, "Yeah, I'll be there."

"Thank you." Rachel headed back to the apartment building. As she slowly walked across the vacant lot littered with junk, Eddie kept glancing at the rusted fire escape and the towering building. The structure returned his gaze with cold, dead eyes. He shivered. A bad thing had taken place here seven years before. He believed something even more terrible was going to happen. Soon.

Chapter Thirty-seven

Then

As he fled his father for the second time, Eddie didn't bother to stop at the bottom of the gravel driveway. He slammed on the brakes long enough to make the turn—the truck groaning and sliding sideways, threatening to smash into the embankment on the other side of RR #324—and then he floored the gas. The storm bombarded the truck with blasts of freezing rain and sleet, and the windshield wipers labored back and forth as fast as possible, never really clearing the glass of the white, wet sludge. Ice was gathering at the edges, on the side mirrors, and on the hood of the truck. The headlights barely showed Eddie fifteen feet of road, yet he drove on. He could hear and feel the water spraying behind the front tires, striking the undercarriage of the truck like liquid gravel. He didn't slow. Nothing would stop him.

"Oh man, this is not happening," Eddie whispered. He drove crouched behind the wheel, his eyes darting between the mirror and the road stretching out in front of him. The sheriff was probably dead. The night was becoming a horrible, never-ending nightmare, and he kept waiting to wake up. He had experienced that kind of bad dream in the past, the kind that felt so real that everything he saw and touched and tasted became his reality. Then he would awaken in a cold sweat, certain everyone he loved was dead or spiders were crawling into his mouth or his mother had hanged herself in the garage or Rachel was threatening to jump off the apartment building—any number of terrible things, and for the first few minutes after he awoke, the false reality was still horribly true. The dread would flood his heart and drown his mind. Sometimes not even the gentle morning sunlight could convince him he had only been dreaming.

Eddie saw the sign announcing WELCOME TO BLACK HILLS, THE FRIENDLIEST MINING TOWN THIS SIDE OF PITTSBURGH! POP 667 appear in the distance. He pushed the accelerator to the floor as he passed the place where the town's sidewalks and streetlights began. He was going too fast for the slick roads, but he didn't care. He had to get back to Mattie's bookstore.

Instead of accelerating, the engine sputtered. Eddie stared with disbelief at the dashboard. The truck was running on empty. He hadn't bothered to check the gas gauge during the frantic drives to and from town. He had never even thought of it. The engine died and the truck began to coast. Eddie pounded on the steering wheel, as if the futile act would keep the truck going.

"Dammit!" he cried, steering toward the side of the road. Although the truck was useless now, he had made it into town. Through the pouring rain he could see Rachel's car sitting by the bookstore a few blocks up the road. He was close enough for government work, as his father was fond of saying.

Eddie jumped out into the rain, not bothering to shut the door. Then he ran. The urge to look over his shoulder was uncontrollable, the primitive part of his mind convinced that his father was hot on his heels. He kept expecting a hand to fall on his shoulder and drag him to the ground. Or even worse, for a hand to catch his legs and trip him, sending him face first into the rough concrete, his teeth chipping on impact, his jaw snapping like a twig, his nose rubbing raw on the sidewalk, his face smashing into the cold, wet concrete again and again, his blood splattering everywhere until the world was a cold, dark place and he died.

Eddie reached the bookstore unscathed, his lungs burning, his muscles cramping. His body wanted to let go, to collapse and sleep for a million years. He put his hand on the doorknob, turned it and shoved, but the door wouldn't budge. This time Mattie had remembered to bolt the lock.

After a moment, the door slowly opened, creaking like an old piece of machinery. Eddie quickly jumped inside, nearly knocking Mattie to the floor in his hurry. With one urgent, violent movement he closed and relocked the door.

Mattie lurched toward the register and cried, "Eddie! What's wrong?"

"My dad was killing the sheriff!" Eddie stated, not bothering to explain more. He ran for the rear of the store. He didn't stop, not even when he clipped the books on an end-cap display, sending them flying. He sprinted into the office area and up the wooden stairs, the steps bowing a little under his feet. He threw open the door at the top.

His mother was sitting in the kitchen, staring at the television. A blurring, twisting, distorted advertisement for VISA flashed on the screen. She had dried her hair, and she was wearing a pair of Mattie's blue jeans and a red sweater. She seemed calm, although her mouth and chin were swollen and bruised.

Rachel was pouring a can of Diet Pepsi into a Hardee's All-Star racing team cup. The soda was fizzing and bubbling, causing the ice cubes to crackle. The cup nearly dropped from her hand when Eddie rushed into the room.

She asked, "Eddie, are you all right?"

Between heavy breathes, he replied, "I think Dad killed the sheriff . . ."

"Oh, God!" Laura grimaced. She tried to stand, and Eddie could see her legs grow weak. She fell back into her chair. She whispered, "That's horrible."

"We have to go," Eddie said, panting. "We have to get out of—"

"This has gotta stop!" Laura suddenly screamed, cutting her son off in mid-sentence. She struck the kitchen table in a burst of anger. "Why won't he just leave us alone?"

"What can we do?" Rachel asked.

"I know what we have to do," Laura stated, her voice full of anger and darkness. Eddie took a step back. He had never seen or heard his mother so angry before. "We have to stop him, once and for all. We have to kill him."

Eddie recoiled, but didn't say anything. They both remembered when his father began the long, painful road to becoming the man he was now. It was like some kind of evil spirit had been living behind his eyes. A wizard behind a curtain. An evil wizard who had grown tired of working in the shadows where no one could see him. He wanted out and nothing would stop him.

Maybe that was why Mary had died. Maybe she had somehow gotten in the way of the monster behind the man. Everyone had wanted to believe her death was an accident, even with the strange things Eddie's father was doing and saying. Everyone desperately wanted to write it off as God having a bad day, God taking a little one from his flock and bringing her home earlier than expected, but Mary's death had gotten people in town thinking. Old gossip that had almost been forgotten was being whispered again. The whispering became talking. Everyone had a Farris family story they were eager to tell, and the gossiping made Michael angrier. Meaner.

Before Eddie could reply to his mother's suggestion, a sharp knock rattled the front of the store. He froze, a knot forming in his stomach. Somehow, deep down, he knew his father was out on Main Street, just waiting for him. He didn't need the voice in the back of his head to tell him that.

But how could it be my dad? Eddie wondered. He tried to compose himself, but it did little good.

The new voice, the one that told him what he didn't want to hear, now spoke: *He probably took the sheriff's car. Those workhorses are unstoppable, a battering ram powered with an engine. It's him!*

"No," Eddie muttered, forcing the relentless voice back into the murky cave where it lay in wait for its next chance to cast doubt into his thoughts. Laura and Rachel looked at him, but said nothing.

The silence was broken by the sound of wood snapping, glass shattering, and a single piercing scream. There was a loud crash followed by another scream.

"Mattie!" Eddie called, instinctively grabbing a dirty frying pan from the kitchen sink, knowing he'd be a dead man if he went to confront his father without some kind of protection. Not that the frying pan was much of a weapon, but it was better than being totally unprepared. He sprinted to the doorway, down the stairs, and past Mattie's desk where paperback books and piles of invoices waited patiently.

Michael had stormed through the shattered front door at the front of the store. The door was hanging from a single hinge, and the beaten and battered man was beyond pissed. He was homicidal. The utter fury rushing through him couldn't be hidden, even if he had wanted to conceal it. The inner storm was on display in his twitchy hands, his angry eyes, and the way he half-crouched next to the register, like a tiger stalking his prey. The butt of the sheriff's service revolver was sticking out of Michael's pocket, and he held the shotgun level with his waist. The barrel was pointed at Mattie. She pushed back against the magazine rack, pure terror washing across her face.

"Get away from her!" Eddie yelled. Rachel and his mother cried in surprise upstairs, and he hoped they were calling the cops. Then he realized they couldn't call anyone. The lone phone in the building was sitting by the cash register, and Michael held his ground mere feet from the counter, as though he was daring his son to make a try for it. Michael looked at Eddie and let out a savage laugh.

"Well, hello son," Michael said in an eerily calm voice as he reached up and touched the bloody socket. "I'm feeling a little . . . blind today."

"How the hell did you find us?" The frying pan was clenched tightly in Eddie's hand, but he didn't move.

"You think I'm dumb? I knew right where you'd be." Michael smiled. "Son, do you remember when I took you to the ball game in Pittsburgh?"

His father's tone was so calm Eddie couldn't reply. At first, he didn't recall the baseball game, but then the images formed in his mind, as if a mental wall had crumbled. He had forgotten all about the beautiful spring day when he was seven years old. Now he didn't just remember that the Pirates had played the Mets, in his mind he experienced it in an instant: the crack of the bat, the announcer on the PA system, the hard plastic seats, the foot-long hot dogs, the pretzels, the syrupy taste of the root beer, the green outfield, the cheers of the crowd, and the stench of the alcohol on the noisy guys next to them.

"Yeah," Eddie replied. "I guess I do."

"Remember how Jay Bell hit a homer in the bottom of the ninth to win it?"

Eddie nodded.

"It was a hell of a game. We had us a lot of fun," Michael said, as if he had momentarily forgotten his reason for being in the bookstore. Suddenly he pivoted, took three large steps forward, and belted his son upside the head with a clenched fist. Eddie flew into a rack of books, sending the wooden shelving crashing to the floor. Dozens of paperback romances rained on top of him. Pictures of Fabio danced before his eyes and pain shot through him, but he held the frying pan in a death grip. He got to his feet.

As Eddie steadied himself, his fear changed into another emotion. Fiery anger streamed from his belly and fought for control of his mind. He felt nothing but hate, nothing but an unstoppable demand for blood, for revenge, for justice. If his father hadn't been holding the shotgun, Eddie would have been at his throat. The blinding rage was overpowering his common sense, but he no longer cared. Regrets and reservations and principles meant nothing.

Fueled by the fury coursing through him, Eddie said, "Either you leave us alone or I'll kill you."

"Wow, when did you grow a set of balls?" Michael asked, pointing the shotgun at his son's feet and pulling the trigger. The room was splintered with quicksilver thunder as the floorboards in front of Eddie exploded, sending shards of wood in every direction, leaving a gaping, smoking hole in the floor. The teenager jumped to the side to avoid falling into the empty, pitch-black void below the store.

The anger and hatred inside of Eddie boiled over. It was too much to take. He was no longer in control of his thoughts or his body. A primitive, more savage side of him had taken command. With the frying pan clenched tightly in his hand like a club, he screamed a battle cry and ran at his father, leaping over the smoking hole in the floor.

Michael Farris raised the shotgun and pulled the trigger. There was a click. He pulled the trigger again. Nothing.

What occurred next took mere seconds, but for Eddie it lasted a lifetime. Lightning flashed, filling the room with slivers of blinding light. He saw his father waiting for him, daring him to keep on coming, to bring it on. Michael's stance said it didn't matter if the shotgun was empty. He didn't need a gun. He could take on twenty teenagers with his bare hands.

There was another flash of purple lightning and a shrill crash of thunder, followed by an explosion that rocked every building on the block. The lights flickered, the phone rang a single ring, and the security mirror in the corner shattered as if it had been struck by a heavy blow. The power died. Michael stumbled, almost tripping and falling, and his son didn't miss the opportunity. Eddie raised the frying pan over his head.

Michael looked up in stunned surprise as the hard, metal edge smashed into his face. He dropped to his knees, teeth and a spray of blood erupting from his mouth. Eddie brought the improvised weapon down again. And again. And again. The impacts sounded like knotted pine logs popping in a fireplace. Michael grunted as he collapsed to the floor, his arms and legs spreading wide like they did when he fell unconscious from drinking too much.

Mattie gasped in horror, her back pushing so hard against the magazine rack that copies of *Time* and *Sports Illustrated* fell to the floor.

"Is everyone all right?" Laura asked as she and Rachel timidly appeared at the rear of the store. They shouted in surprise when they saw Michael lying on his chest, a pool of blood running from his head to the jagged hole in the floor. Although Rachel and Laura appeared to be horrified, Eddie could also see the deep sense of relief, an almost gut-wrenching emotion. With a tremor in her voice, Laura added, "Good. I hope he's dead. He looks dead."

"We should call the cops," Rachel said, her hand pressed tightly to her mouth. Eddie dropped the bloody frying pan and went to hold her. Together they watched his father's body. He did indeed appear to be dead. The four of them stood motionless in the darkened room. They were depending on each other for support, waiting for someone to take charge.

Finally Mattie pried herself away from the magazine rack, crossed the room—being careful to keep as much distance between herself and Michael as she could—and checked the phone next to the register. She promptly placed the receiver back on the cradle.

"It isn't working," she said.

Eddie let go of Rachel and slowly approached his father. He inched forward a step at a time. Lightning roared in the storm, sending scattered light across the floor. A puddle of blood was forming next to his father's head. Eddie stopped just short of his destination. He squatted down and reached out for his father's wrist. Eddie's heart hammered his chest, and the sound of his beating heart throbbed in his head, blocking out the storm. Before his eyes, he saw his father grabbing him, raising his broken face and grinning. That thought caused Eddie to shudder, quickly jump, and retreat back to Rachel.

Mattie glanced around the darkened room, her eyes

showing her anger and fear and determination not to panic. Eddie had a pretty good idea what she was thinking. They'd better get the hell out of Dodge. She said, "So let's drive to the police station, what do you say?"

"Yeah, let's go," Eddie replied, his eyes again locking on the puddle of blood forming at the top of his father's head. The stream had become a gentle trickle, and it was slowing to almost nothing as they left the room.

Chapter Thirty-eight

Now

Eddie spent the rest of the day pacing around the bookstore while Mattie completed her daily paperwork. Dark thoughts void of logic assaulted him. He replayed the final altercation with his father over and over again. The confusing images and blurring recollections swirled around his mind. Occasionally he glanced out the bay window, as if he didn't believe the world would be waiting there for him when he left the store. Night had fallen, the streetlights had automatically turned on, and the dense fog was rolling in right on schedule.

"Eddie, you're marching a path into the floor," Mattie called, leaning back in her chair to stretch the kinks in her spine. Today she was wearing a red, white, and blue patch over her empty eye socket. She glanced at Eddie through the doorway. The curtain that normally divided the office from the sales floor was tied to one side so she could see any customers in need of help. "You feeling all right?"

Eddie shrugged. The store was empty and probably would be until they closed. It was nearly eight o'clock and business was terrible. Had there even been one customer today? He didn't think so. How could Mattie keep the place running like this?

"Not really," he finally replied.

"Well, for the love of God, you gotta talk to me," Mattie said and laughed. "It's getting lonely back here without my favorite assistant to keep me company."

Eddie reluctantly crossed the sales floor. He stopped twice to straighten some books, to delay their conversation as long as possible. What would he tell her? What *could* he tell her? When he entered the office, goosebumps dotted his flesh. He sat on the folding chair next to Mattie's desk. The metal was freezing. He rubbed his hands together. He wished Mattie would turn on the heat. It was getting too cold to be frugal. His bones were like ice.

Mattie asked, "So what's wrong?"

Eddie opened his mouth, then closed it. He wasn't sure what to say. He had promised Rachel he wouldn't talk to anyone about what was happening, but Mattie wasn't just anyone. She had saved his life. She was closer than family.

"Eddie," Mattie stated as she sat straight up, her tone quiet but serious. "We've been through a lot together. You can tell me anything. Is it about the cat?"

"I didn't do that."

"Of course you didn't! Talk to me. Is it someone in town? Are they making trouble for you?"

"It's just," he said, "I have this friend who has a problem."

Mattie raised an eyebrow in feigned surprise, but Eddie barely noticed. He was too busy figuring out how to convey the gravity of the situation without breaking his promise not to tell anyone Rachel's theory about what was happening. He was also reluctant to tell Mattie about Adam. The boy had to be a secret. At least for now. He couldn't go against Rachel's wishes.

"And?" Mattie prodded.

"Well, this friend is being bothered by someone," Eddie explained. "Bothered a lot. This guy keeps calling her and saying stuff and leaving threatening notes under her door and he might be following her."

"That's awful! Has she gone to the police?"

"No, she doesn't want to. She thinks they'll say she's crazy."

"But she believes she's in danger?"

"Yeah," Eddie said.

"Well, she really needs to contact the sheriff then. At least give him a chance to help her."

"I don't think she will." Eddie composed himself and added, "She wants me to watch her tonight to make sure this person isn't following her."

"Oh, Eddie, that's too dangerous." Mattie shook her head. "You really should call the cops."

"I can't. I can't fail her again," Eddie stated, his gaze dropping to the floor. "I can't."

Eddie knew Mattie was staring at him. Tension filled the air, but he didn't know what to say. He had probably already said too much. How hard would it be for Mattie to figure out who he was talking about? What if she mentioned this conversation to Tabby? To anyone? Yet Eddie was certain Mattie wouldn't say a word. She minded her own business when it came to this sort of thing, no matter how concerned she was. She was too private a person to step into someone else's affairs, unless they asked her for help.

She sighed and said, "Well, please consider calling the police for her. I'm going to be worried."

"Don't worry about anything." Eddie was relieved Mattie hadn't decided to lecture him further, but he saw the tremors of anxiety on her face. She obviously hadn't wanted to give in, yet she must have known he wouldn't change his mind. He could see that simple understanding in her good eye where the wariness remained. "I'll be all right. I promise."

"You'd better be. I couldn't live with myself if you got hurt." Mattie checked the clock, did a double-take, and got to her feet. She grabbed her keys and coat. "I need to get to the general store before Dolores closes for the night. Lock up the shop for me and then go do whatever you have to do, but be careful, okay?"

"Don't worry, I'll watch my back," Eddie said, flashing Mattie a quick smile.

"Please, please be careful. I mean it!"

"I will. I promise." As he stood, a stray thought occurred to Eddie. It was a question he had never asked Mattie, but had always wanted to. Why hadn't he asked her before? He didn't know. "Mattie, why'd you make yourself a decoy that night? Why didn't you run with the rest of us?"

"Because you guys were family to me," Mattie replied without hesitating. She put her hand on the doorknob, her fingers trembled. She didn't move. "Can you help me with this?"

"Of course." Eddie crossed the room and opened the

door. The hinges cried for oil. The night air was chilly, and a wisp of fog seeped in at floor level.

"Good-bye," Mattie said, shivering. Her statement sounded final and her brittle tone confused Eddie, but she was gone into the night before he could ask her what was wrong. She limped, and she looked tired and crippled as she moved through the shadows, past the green Dumpster the town's garbage truck never emptied anymore.

Eddie closed and locked the door. He was about to head to the sales floor when he abruptly changed his mind.

"Could it still be there?" he asked, returning to the desk and getting on his knees. He reached for the black safe hidden in the shadows. After three failed attempts, he correctly entered the combination on the white dial and opened the heavy door. Mattie hadn't changed the settings after all. He reached inside, moved some papers and envelopes to the side, and discovered what he had been hoping to find: the silver and black revolver. He caressed the barrel. He knew the gun could have altered the outcome of the day his father attacked them. He often wished he had known about the revolver's existence before his father had arrived at the bookstore on the cold, rainy night seven years before. He knew how the chain of events could have ended differently.

"I might need this." Eddie shoved the gun under his belt and untucked his shirt. If anyone saw him with a weapon, his ass would be grass, to use the expression he had relished so much as a kid, but he had to take the risk. He reached inside the safe, grabbed a small, white box of ammunition, and slipped it into his pocket.

The bell above the front door rang, surprising Eddie, causing his leg muscles to jerk. He jumped. He expected to see the door swinging shut, but it had already closed when he spun around. That seemed wrong for some reason Eddie wasn't able to explain.

Someone by the register sang in a sweet voice: "Down by the river, down by the sea . . ."

"Can I help you?" Eddie called, stepping out of the office, pulling the red curtain closed with one quick motion. The store appeared to be empty.

Did the person already leave? But the bell had only rung once.

Shelves of books crashed to the floor off to Eddie's left, and he instantly thought of the fight with his father and how he had been thrown like a rag doll.

Oh shit! My dad really is alive! Rachel was right all along!

But that didn't seem right. Why did books falling make him think his father was alive? Still, Eddie wasn't taking any chances. He knelt and crept along the bookcases like a secret agent hard at work behind enemy lines. He shuddered and his breathing grew faster. He reached the last row and peeked around the corner. Then he stood and stepped into the aisle.

"Hello, Eddie, I've been waiting for you." Gene Varley stood there in his red usher's uniform, grinning and holding a copy of *A Tear and a Smile.* Other books were scattered across the floor.

"Gene, did you hear someone singing?" Eddie asked, a potent jolt of fear striking him. A rotten odor from the old man relieving himself in his pants washed across the room. Next came a wave of popcorn butter flavoring, carried on a current of air that appeared out of nowhere.

"I sing good, don't I?" the old man asked. He smiled, and two dark teeth fell out of his mouth. Eddie's gaze slowly lowered to the floor until he found where each tooth had landed. Then he saw the red high-heeled shoes Gene was wearing. Why the hell was the old man in women's shoes? And what had happened to his teeth? Eddie looked back at Gene's face.

Only Gene was gone. He had been replaced by Lehcar. Her slim body was raw and decaying, her eyes dead. The foul stench of death flowed to Eddie.

"What the hell?" he yelled as he stumbled behind the cash register like it was a sanctuary. He pulled the gun from his belt. "You can't be here! I'm not dreaming! I'm awake!"

Lehcar smiled the same smile she had given Eddie when he saw her in the first nightmare, the one at the scene of Kurt Farris's pickup truck accident in the middle of town. She dropped the book to the floor. It landed with a cold, hollow thump.

"Oh, silly Eddie," she said, her dead eyes gleaming. "I can be anywhere I want to be. Anytime I want. I'm a part of you. Why won't you accept your fate? Why don't you enjoy it? Death really isn't so bad, and you'll murder again if you don't kill yourself."

"I'm not going to kill anyone!" Eddie yelled, pointing the revolver at Lehcar. "I won't let myself."

Lehcar laughed. "Don't you understand? You really don't have any choice!"

An intense pressure was building inside Eddie's head. This wasn't right! His mind felt like it would implode from the very thought of Lehcar being here. He had to be asleep. No, not asleep. Awake. He had to be awake. This was all too real!

"You won't be able to stop yourself."

"Yes, I will!" Eddie yelled, tugging the trigger. The lead-jacketed bullet ripped a hole in Lehcar's rotting body. A trickle of blood trickled from the gap in the middle of her abdomen. She glanced down at the wound, back up at Eddie. She grinned and began shaking wildly, like she was having some kind of seizure.

"You can kill, Eddie, you can kill!" She laughed like a banshee. Then she vanished. Her cackle lingered behind her, but she was gone. What she had said echoed in Eddie's mind.

You can kill, Eddie, you can kill!

Eddie heard a police siren off in the distance. He bolted the lock on the front door. He had to hurry. The cops would be searching for him. Firing the gun had not been a particularly bright idea.

Chapter Thirty-nine

Then

Mattie led the way to the alley and into the pouring rain. Lightning crashed in the distance, followed by rolling claps of thunder that rocked the four of them. Rachel tripped, but Eddie grabbed her arm before she could fall. She nodded that she was okay and they continued toward the little blue Chevette parked next to a giant, green Dumpster that stank of wet cardboard. Mattie jumped inside the car, put the key in the ignition and turned it with a little too much force. The engine started with an angry growl. Mattie shifted the passenger seat forward so Rachel and Laura could crawl in the back.

"He broke my front door and shot my beautiful floor," Mattie stated with utter disbelief as Eddie got into the car.

"Don't worry," Eddie said. "We can get everything fixed, no problem. A little hard work never killed anyone, right? You guys okay?" He looked into the backseat. His mother and Rachel were more than ready to go. They stared with wide eyes at the rear of the bookstore as if they expected to see Michael stumbling after them like the antagonist in some cheaply made slasher flick.

Mattie said nothing more as she drove to the end of the alley. The short, dirty buildings seemed to tower on both sides of the car. The alley had never felt so dark and ominous before, and Eddie held his breath until they reached Elm Street.

Rainwater was running along the curb like a raging river. Heavy gusts of wind pounded the car. The windshield wipers struggled, the rubber blades sliding across the slick glass, the waves of rain and sleet too much for the small motors to handle. The rain tapped on the roof like a million fingers. This was becoming a storm of the century for Black Hills. It was like driving through a solid wall of water.

As Mattie approached Main Street, she hit a deep pothole hidden under an inch of running water. The car bounced hard and Rachel let out a panic-filled cry.

"Sorry," she whispered.

"It's okay, baby," Eddie said, reaching back to hold her hands. Her skin was as cold as ice. He rubbed her flesh, trying his best to get her warm.

"Do you think he's dead?" Laura's voice trembled. "I didn't really mean it when I said we should kill him. Really. But if he's dead, he can't hurt us. Right?"

"I don't know if he's dead, but he's not going to touch you guys ever again," Mattie answered. She let her foot off the gas as they approached the town's single stoplight. It hung over a deserted intersection. The light was not working, just like everything else in Black Hills that fed on electricity, and the yellow box was twisting around in the strong wind. There was no one else on the road, but Mattie stopped just to be safe.

Headlights flashed on behind the Chevette. A police siren wailed, and the red-and-blue lights on the top of the cruiser blazed to life.

"Is that the sheriff?" Rachel asked as she tried to wipe a layer of fog off the rear windshield. The police cruiser was gaining speed and coming right at them, like a missile homing in on its target. Eddie could see the car was coming too fast, but he didn't want to believe what he knew that meant. The cruiser was getting closer, and closer, until it was less than a block away.

"I have a bad feeling," Mattie said, glancing in the mirror and pressing on the accelerator. "A real bad feeling."

The little Chevette began to move. Mattie pushed harder on the gas pedal, making the rear tires spin, the smell of burning rubber filling the interior of the car. The frame vibrated, rattled, but then the tires gripped the road and the car accelerated. A moment later, they were passing thirty miles an hour.

The sheriff's cruiser screamed through the intersection behind them, the headlights growing larger and brighter. The sight brought a biting memory of a real police video television show to the front of Eddie's mind. It was seven seconds of footage that had given him nightmares for weeks. The program had shown a young woman hurrying across a double set of railroad tracks. The film slowed to a crawl as the woman turned her head and was cut down in mid-stride by a passenger train. Every night for weeks after that, as he lay in the dark, Eddie had wondered what the engineer had thought when he saw the yellow blur of the woman's dress as she was sucked under the train and mangled, or what emotions had surged through the woman when she saw the huge, black engine and realized it was too late to escape her destiny. What had she been thinking in the last split second of her life?

"Oh shit! Hold on!" Eddie was almost hypnotized by the blur of red-and-blue lights on top of the cruiser roaring toward them. The headlights were blinding, and far too close. The two cars collided. There was the shriek of crushing metal. Mattie fought the wheel, trying desperately to stay on the road. She clipped a blue mailbox, sending it flying off into the night with a scream. The police cruiser retreated from their bumper, but not very far.

Lightning hit a metal sign on the roof of the old Black Hills Hotel and Restaurant, sending sparks raining down on the street. In the flash of light, Eddie could see his father at the wheel of the car chasing them. Michael was grinning at him through the rain-streaked windshield. Blood poured from the wound on his head and his busted eye socket, but he didn't seem to mind. He raised one hand in a casual wave.

Michael floored the gas, striking the little car, pushing it toward the edge of the road. The Chevette shook and rattled, veering at the sidewalk, barely missing a row of trees and streetlights by inches. Mattie nearly lost control, fighting the wheel with all her might. They didn't have much longer given how things were going. The police cruiser was too heavy and too fast.

"Hold on," Mattie called as she neared another intersection. She slammed on the brakes and cut the wheel hard, sending the car skidding across the wet pavement. Her passengers flew to the left, grunting as their seat belts locked. Rachel's head hit the side window with a loud crack and she barked a sharp cry. She tried to brace herself the best she could as Mattie put all her weight on the accelerator, sending the car speeding down Carmike Avenue.

"Rachel, is your mom home?" Mattie asked, her voice rippling with panic. She made another quick turn onto Copper Street, sending her passengers flying again.

"No, she's working late at the diner today." Rachel held her hand to her head, wiping the trickle of blood away. She glanced at Eddie. "She's the closer tonight."

"But you have a good set of locks on your doors, right?"

"Yeah, I guess so, but why?"

Mattie didn't respond. At the speed she was going, they were at the abandoned lot behind the Richard Street Apartment Building in less than a minute. The Chevette squealed to a halt, the rear of the car fishtailing on the slick road. Mattie didn't bother to finesse the car any closer to the curb. She obviously wasn't planning to stay very long.

"What now?" Eddie asked, glancing up at the towering structure highlighted by the flashing lightning. He looked over his shoulder. The police cruiser was nowhere to be seen, but the chase couldn't be finished. His father wouldn't stop without a fight. Not in a million years. He was out for blood.

"You guys go and hide," Mattie explained. "I'll head for the State Police barracks at Slade City."

Eddie asked, "But why didn't you drive straight there?"

"He was too close to us, but now I can get some help."

She was lying and Eddie knew it. She looked in the backseat. "You guys okay?"

Laura was applying pressure to the scratch on Rachel's forehead. "I think so."

"Okay, then get going. The phone lines are probably still down, but try to call the cops anyway."

"But why, Mattie?" Eddie asked. "Why don't we all go with you?

"I can't be tearing across town like a NASCAR driver with you all in the car. Now get going!" Mattie ordered, quickly reaching over and opening Eddie's door. He was puzzled, but then he nodded in understanding. He got out, feeling like he had jumped into a waterfall. The rain pounded on him like God's fists. He shielded his face and pulled the passenger side seat forward to help his mother and Rachel exit the battered Chevette.

A few small chunks of hail whizzed by Eddie's ear, walloping the car's roof and leaving dings and dents in their wake. The trunk and rear bumper were smashed, like the lone survivor of a demolition derby. Steam rose from under the hood, releasing a long steady hiss. Eddie was amazed Mattie had managed to stay on the road, let alone keep driving.

The three of them ran past the piles of rubble, junk, and rusted car frames to the rear of the brick building, holding their arms up to block the rain and hail, keeping their eyes on the muddy ground so they wouldn't trip. The world was grimy and wet and cold, and the rain and wind battered them. A piece of hail struck Eddie's arm, another hit his leg, and then three more smacked his back. He screamed, like someone had driven white hot rods into his body. He pushed on, covering his face.

Eddie and his mother came to a stop under the rusted fire escape, the *thunk-thunk-thunk* surrounding them as hail bombarded the metal structure above their heads while Rachel frantically opened the door.

After they were inside, Eddie looked back at the road. Mattie was already gone. He heard the roar of an engine in the distance. A minute later, the police cruiser sped by.

Chapter Forty

Now

Eddie studied the Black Hills Diner from the shadowy alley on the other side of Main Street, his eyes narrowing. He tried to see inside the restaurant. No luck. It had closed earlier than normal for the night, but he didn't know why. He hadn't seen Rachel leave and that worried him. There was a glare on the windows. The squeegeed glass reflected the streetlights through the fog. Near where Eddie waited was an old-fashioned phone booth painted a dull red color. He wondered if the phone inside actually worked.

The alley was dirty and smelled of old piss and spoiled food. Darkness wrapped around Eddie. The dim streetlights were nearly hidden in the fog, but he didn't dare cross the road to gaze inside the diner's windows or knock on the front door. The sheriff had driven past twice in the last ten minutes, and Eddie knew the entire police department was probably searching for him. The three deputies and both patrol cars had most likely been sent out into the foggy night. So he waited in the dark and carefully reloaded the gun.

Down by the river, down by the sea, Eddie killed his family and blamed it on me!

"Stop it!" Eddie cried, pressing his hands against his head and squeezing. The rhymes and taunts of the town's children had been echoing inside his mind ever since he shot Lehcar. He couldn't make the words stop.

"Children can smell a bad man. Bad men have a stench," Lehcar said, appearing behind him and putting a dead hand on his shoulder.

Eddie jumped and turned in one quick motion, nearly stumbling into the street. He hit the phone booth first, breaking a small pane of glass with his elbow. Pain ripped through his arm. He pulled away and checked the large gash in his jacket. Blood gushed from his elbow to his wrist. He clamped his hand onto the wound, squeezing as hard as he could to stop the bleeding.

"Why are you doing this to me?" Eddie pleaded. He stepped back into the shadows where the monster waited. He knew Lehcar wasn't really there. She couldn't be real. He had seen a lot of strange things in the days after The Showdown, but the doctors and counselors had taught him that the visions were nothing more than the ugly products of his overworked imagination and the pain-killing drugs. So no matter how fast his heart was pounding in his chest or how tight his throat was constricting, Lehcar wasn't real. But the cops were. And they would find him sooner or later if he wasn't careful.

"Because you're the monster," she replied, her hand rubbing her stomach, the gesture of a small child signaling she was hungry. Eddie found himself hypnotized by the movement. Around and around her hand went. Around and around. The bullet wound in her stomach was breathing, like a tiny mouth. It might have been growing larger, too. Little bubbles of blood poured from the hole. "You're as bad as your father."

"No, I'm not."

"You have killed, just like your father. You will kill again. You will beat anyone who gets close to you until they break and crumble under your fingers." She paused, grinned. "Just like your father."

"I don't want to be like him," Eddie said. He pulled the gun out of his belt. He moved without thinking, without questioning why. He was running purely on terror and primitive instincts. "I won't!"

"Do what you must, Eddie, but I'll be with you forever, until the day you die," Lehcar replied. "Remember, I am your guardian angel. I am your curse."

She made a sound in her chest like she was sucking phlegm from her lungs. The noise was raw and horrible. She smiled and spit out the bullet Eddie had fired into her at the bookstore. It hit him on the chin with a quick, hard slap. The fragmented piece of lead fell to the ground.

Lehcar blinked into nothingness, but her last statement echoed behind her: "Remember, I am your guardian angel. I am your curse."

Eddie put the gun into his belt and kicked the bullet against the brick wall before returning his attention to the diner. No one had come out or gone in the half hour since the lights inside the restaurant had been turned off. The street was usually a pretty lonely place after dark, but tonight Black Hills was even more quiet than normal. Perhaps it was because of the denser than normal fog. The town seemed completely deserted.

Eddie decided he had to take the risk of leaving the safety of the dark alley. If Rachel wasn't in there, the stalker might have gotten to her already. She could be in serious danger. The crazed caller might be torturing her. Or worse.

Eddie stepped out from the alley. He didn't see either of the town's police cruisers, but then again, the world was a wall of white mist, of shameless ghosts dancing in the dark. He could scarcely make out more than two or three buildings up the road, and like those astronauts behind the far side of the moon, he felt cold and alone and helpless, lost forever in the mystery of the night.

He hurried to the phone booth and opened the door, which whined as if it hadn't been used in years. Broken bottles littered the floor, their shards popping and cracking under his shoes. One of the town winos had pissed in the corner and profane messages were carved anywhere someone could scratch a few letters or numbers with a pocket knife.

Eddie picked up the receiver and dropped some change in the slot. He dialed the diner's phone number.

When Rachel finally answered, her voice was hesitant, strained. "Hello?"

"Are you okay?"

"Eddie, where are you?" She sounded scared and relieved.

"I'm in the phone booth across the street," Eddie explained. "What happened? Why are the lights off?"

"I was the closer tonight," Rachel said. "We closed early when we heard the news. I told everyone I could handle it myself so they could go home. They didn't want to leave me, but I told them to go, and then after they left, I got a really bad feeling. I was afraid your father was waiting out there for me. I didn't see you." After a brief pause, she added, "Jesus, Eddie, what did you do?"

"I can't explain. I'm sorry, it wouldn't make any sense. You wouldn't understand."

"They say you killed her," Rachel said quietly.

"What?" A block of ice had formed in Eddie's gut. He felt the coldness, like his intestines were frozen. The cold was dragging him down. It burrowed into him, burying itself into his flesh and bones. He managed to ask, "Who said that?"

"Everyone," she replied. "The police say you shot her. Someone saw you running from the bookstore. They found her body inside."

Eddie shook his head, unable to believe what he was hearing. Had they found Lehcar? That wasn't possible, was it? Even if she was somehow real, he had just seen her. Lehcar couldn't be dead in the store.

He asked, "What are you talking about?"

"They found Mattie," Rachel whispered. "They say you killed her."

Eddie shuddered. The block of ice inside him was growing larger, swallowing his heart and chilling him to his core. He stared at the rectangular windows on the front of the diner. The streetlights were a blur across the glass. He heard an animal howling in the distance, briefly breaking the sleep seizing Black Hills, but he was paralyzed by the coldness seeping through him.

Mattie can't be dead! She just can't be! That isn't right at all!

Eddie's emotions jumped wildly between rage and

fear and heartache. He didn't want to hear what Rachel was saying. It couldn't be true. Mattie had been fine the last time he saw her. A little shaken, but in no harm. Yet the way she had said goodbye had chilled him. He remembered her final words too well. Had she known what was going to happen to her? How?

"Do you believe it?" he finally asked.

"Of course not," Rachel said. "It was your father, wasn't it?"

"I . . ." Eddie stopped. He couldn't believe his father was alive. That wasn't possible. But then again, Eddie hadn't killed Mattie.

What if Rachel killed her? part of his mind asked. The paranoid little voice of insane reason always picked the worst occasions to speak. *What if this is part of her plan to get you, just like in the nightmare?*

Rachel didn't kill anyone! She couldn't have!

You want to jump her bones, the paranoid voice said. *That's why you want to help her, but just because you love her doesn't mean she can't be a bad person. Maybe she changed. Maybe she* is *out to get you. Maybe she killed—*

No! Eddie silently screamed at the nagging voice.

"Eddie?" Rachel asked. "You there?"

"Yeah, sorry."

"It was your father, wasn't it?"

"Rachel, he's dead!"

"I think it must have been your father." She sounded more confident than ever, as if she hadn't heard Eddie's reply. "I'm heading home. You watch and see. He'll follow me. I'm sure of it."

Eddie's stomach knotted with fear and he put one hand across his gut. The block of ice was melting, the coldness spreading into his veins, chilling the blood rushing through his body. Perhaps his father *was* alive. Was that the explanation for everything? If his father was after Rachel, Eddie knew he had to protect her.

"What should I do if he shows up?"

"What you should have done right the last time," Rachel whispered. A darkness had entered her voice. She didn't sound like the scared young woman who had been terrified by her own shadow the previous day. She sounded like a hardened woman who had been beaten one too many times and was finally fighting back, her teeth like rusty nails and her fists like slabs of concrete.

"What?" Eddie understood exactly what she meant, but he couldn't believe it.

"Kill him," she said with an appalling coldness. "You have to kill your father, just like your mother wanted you to."

Eddie was still holding the phone to his ear, the dial tone changing to a prerecorded message about hanging up and trying again, when he realized Rachel had already hurried down the steps in front of the diner. She was walking toward the east side of town, rapidly vanishing into the fog.

Eddie fought the urge to call to her as he exited the phone booth, leaving the receiver dangling off the hook. The night chill pierced him. He walked quickly, crunching salt and cinders beneath his feet, staying as close to the buildings and as far from the streetlights as he could. Not that the lights were of much use. The fog was thick. The air was bitterly cold and his eyes were watering. He blinked the tears away and tried his best to keep Rachel within his line of sight, but she had disappeared into the heart of the fog. Fear wrapped its cold, callused hands around Eddie's throat.

I'll never see Rachel again! She'll vanish into the night and it won't let her go! The night will eat her alive!

He started to jog. He could barely see the lights on the other side of Main Street, let alone a person. He wanted to call to Rachel, but he couldn't. Alerting anyone to his presence would ruin her plans.

She's leading you somewhere, you fool! She'll kill you! the paranoid part of his mind shouted. *Why are you letting her do this to us? She's setting you up!*

"No," Eddie whispered, moving closer to the road and gazing into the fog. He fought the doubting voice, pushing it into the darkest corner of his mind. He thought he could make out the shape of someone on the other side of the street. He squinted, staring into the blanket of white, his legs carrying him forward.

And that was when Rachel screamed.

Chapter Forty-one

From the Handwritten Account

My Mental Reconstruction of Events Past
by Eddie Farris

Remember those shadows on my wall?

Remember how I thought I was chained to this bed?

I was in a cave and all I had for entertainment were the dancing bits of darkness.

I once wondered what would happen if I broke free and found the source of the shadows.

I asked, what would I find? How would my perception of the universe change?

Now I think I understand.

I think I'm breaking free of the chains binding my mind.

I still can't remember much more than what I'm writing at any given moment, but as the words flow onto the page, more and more comes back to me.

I'm breaking the chains, walking toward the source of the light.

I'm rebuilding my world. Searching for the source of the shadows.

I hope I find good news.

This is what I see out the window of the apartment: perpetual wind-driven rain, sleet, and hail beating on the glass.

It's almost midnight.

The power is still out.

"Someone try the phone," I say.

Little specks of light dot the glass.

Rachel has lit tiny, white candles, and their flickering glow fills the room.

She says, "It still isn't working."

She quietly hangs up the dead phone on the end table. Next to it is *A Tear and a Smile.*

She tried to read earlier to calm her nerves, but when she opened it to the piece entitled "Have Mercy, My Soul," she immediately closed the book, as if the story was the most horrific thing she had ever seen.

Now Rachel quietly sits in the tiny living room, facing the dead television, the kitchen dark behind her.

My mother sits next to Rachel. Mom's smoking again.

Hanging between her fingers, pressed against her lips, is a cigarette from the pack Rachel's mother left in the kitchen. I don't say anything.

"Why are the phones dead? They usually work when the power is out," Rachel states.

"I really don't know."

I think of the explosion I heard when I was fighting my father in the bookstore.

The explosion in the distance, right before the electricity went out.

I say, "Maybe the power and the phone lines were knocked out by the storm."

That seems to make sense.

Perhaps there was an accident.

"It's been too long," my mother says. "What are we going to do?"

She's right.

I stand there by the window, my mind playing a hundred terrible versions of what might be happening to Mattie.

We have to do something.

If we don't, someone's going to die.

Chapter Forty-two

Then

Eddie studied his mother in the twinkling candlelight. They hadn't seen or heard anything from the police, and the streets were deserted, their black surfaces now raging rivers. Eddie didn't know what to do, but he knew they couldn't just wait in the safety of the apartment if Mattie was in trouble.

"We could take my car," Rachel said. Then she sighed, a frown twisting her lips. "Except it's sitting in front of the bookstore."

Eddie saw the tears forming in the corner of Rachel's eyes. They sparkled in the candlelight. He went and sat with her on the couch. She said nothing, but instead threw her arms around him.

"Everything's going to be fine," Eddie whispered. He wanted to make a run for the police station on his own, to get a deputy or anyone who could help, but he was terrified of leaving Rachel and his mother alone. "I won't let him hurt you. I won't let anything happen to us. Do you believe me?"

"Yes, I believe you," she said, wiping away the tears. "I love you."

"I love you, too."

"Are you okay?"

"Yes," Rachel said, whispering in his ear so his mother couldn't hear her. "But we're going to get married someday, right? Get married and have a kid and be a family, right?"

Eddie pulled back and stared at his girlfriend, trying to change the confused expression locked on his face and finding he couldn't move a muscle.

Where the hell did that come from? he wondered. He loved her, but marriage? A family? Kids? They had talked about running away together before—many times, in fact—but never any of that. Yet he didn't find the ideas to be revolting at all. In fact, although he had never really thought about it before, marriage and family and a nice little house with a white picket fence was a comforting thought for Eddie. He liked the idea. He liked it a lot.

Rachel wiped at some more tears. Her skin was red and there was a darkness under her eyes.

"Not now, but someday," she added, sounding ashamed.

"Yes, I think so," Eddie finally replied, pulling her tight, kissing the top of her head.

A moment passed, and silence filled the room.

"Goddamn! I wish Mattie had remembered her gun!" Laura declared, almost jumping to her feet. "That damned thing. I knew we should have killed the bastard. I knew it!"

"What do you mean?" Eddie asked, stunned, and not just because his mother never swore. *Never*. He hadn't heard about Mattie having any kind of weapon, let alone a firearm. And although he could understand why his mother was so angry—he felt the anger, too, felt consumed by it, in fact—he was surprised by her aggressiveness. She really wanted to see her husband dead. She had always been so passive, so restrained. This was an entirely different side of her, like a darkness was clouding her judgment. Or maybe she had finally seen the light. "A gun? Where?"

"In the safe under her desk." With a weak, pitiful laugh Laura explained, "She was afraid of your father, Eddie. She bought a cheap revolver for me from some store in Slade City, but I wouldn't take it. Couldn't. He would have found it."

"I understand," Eddie said quietly, thinking of how different the day's events could have been with the gun in his hand. Hell, this would all be over if he had run straight to the master bedroom and grabbed one of his father's hunting rifles. He hadn't thought of that until now, and he wanted to kick himself. How could he have forgotten them? The same way Mattie and his mother had forgotten the gun in the safe, he supposed. It was hard to think clearly when you were certain you were going to die.

"She made the combination on the safe my birthday, in case I ever needed it, but I forgot. I forgot. I was so scared . . ." Her voice trailed off.

Eddie was about to reply, but then he heard a noise. He wasn't sure what it had been. He stood. "Do you hear that?"

"What?" Laura asked. She and Rachel cocked their heads to the side, like curious puppies in the candlelight.

An odd expression appeared on their faces. Laura held the cigarette in her trembling hand, but she had obviously forgotten it. There was the noise again. And again. Hidden under the rain and the nearly constant thunder, there was a creaking like old box springs.

"What is it?" Rachel asked.

"Not sure," Eddie muttered. He approached the window. The valley was a sea of darkness, and the freezing rain and sleet pounded the window. It was like trying to look under the surface of a dark, muddy lake, but Eddie peered through the glass anyway, trying to make some sense of what he was hearing. He saw the rain and the sleet and the endless gloom of night.

Lightning flashed and Eddie found himself nose to nose with his father's scowling face. Michael gazed in at him through the window. His flesh was badly beaten and bloody. He had become a patchwork monster, scarred like he had been stitched together from a dozen different donors. Eddie could see the untamed madness in his father's one good eye, and he backed away in terror.

The lightning faded and the world became dark. Then the window shattered and a body flew into the room.

Chapter Forty-three

Now

Eddie sprinted through the fog in the direction of Rachel's screams. Terror had him by the throat. He ran forward like a soldier charging an enemy hill, but when he reached the sidewalk directly in front of the All-American Deli, Rachel was gone.

"Rachel!" he cried into the chilly night air. Two blocks up the street, Rachel screamed his name. He turned toward the sound. She called again, her voice filled with terror and desperation. That got him running. His legs burned and his heart pumped pure acid through his sizzling veins. He fought for breath, but didn't slow his pace. The little voice that believed he was being set up, that Rachel was out to get him, had fallen silent. She was in trouble! He could hear the dread in her voice. And he was the only one who could save her.

"Rachel?" Eddie called as he came to the lone stoplight in town. The red dot beamed at him like the eye of a vengeful God through the swirling banks of fog.

Eddie heard a noise to his right, some sort of loud crack. He moved in that direction, each step slow and deliberate as he searched the foggy road. He came to Richard Street and stopped. He had a bad feeling about where the chase was headed.

"Shit," Eddie whispered. He listened, but heard nothing. The entire town seemed to be deserted. He hadn't seen anyone in a long time, but he did see a small puddle of red at his feet. He knelt, touched it. It was blood.

Rachel screamed again, and Eddie knew where she was: right outside the Richard Street Apartments.

He sprinted for the tall, shadowy building wrapped in a vast cocoon of fog. A few lights were on in the windows, but most of the residents had gone to bed. The lights made the building look like a hulking prehistoric monster with burning eyes.

Go slow, be alert, Rachel needs me, Eddie thought. With the gun in his right hand, he approached the concrete steps resting beneath the sign that announced RICHARD STREET APARTMENTS in big, scripted letters. The front door was hanging open, and he carefully edged closer to where he could glance into the lobby without stepping through the doorway. He saw no one. He leaned in, searching the area near the wall of mailboxes. Neither Rachel nor her attacker was there. A single light sent shadows dancing and darting into the corners. The shattered mirror from the fifth floor hallway was now sitting on the far side of the lobby.

Keep calm, go slow. Eddie took a step inside, wisps of fog trailing him. He held the gun up in front of his face the way the cops in movies held their firearms. He crept forward through the empty lobby, stopping short of the door to the stairwell. He tried to hear if anyone was on the other side. The building was eerily silent. There was nothing, not even the scratching of a rat crawling in the walls or the creaking of a single floorboard. He prayed for a footstep, for Rachel to call out, for any kind of noise, but still, there was silence. He slowly opened the door.

Be calm. Then, without warning, Eddie's right side erupted with a powerful blast of pain. He fell, the gun flying from his hand, hitting the floor and skidding to the mailboxes. Fiery bolts spread from the old wound, as if his flesh was the home to millions of hungry fire ants. He lay on the cold floor, unable to move. He braced his hand on his hip and grimaced as the ache spread.

The door to the stairwell had remained open, and someone was standing there. Someone he knew all too well.

"No," Eddie cried. "It isn't possible!"

Michael Farris walked into the lobby—he limped, as if a mass of muscle and bone had been hollowed out of his left leg—and he gazed at his son with his one good eye. The other eye was covered by a black cloth patch, but little else had changed about the man since the last time Eddie had seen him. His chin was crossed with white scars and he was dressed in his old blue prison guard uniform, although the clothing showed its age. His father wearing the uniform should have seemed ludicrous, yet to Eddie it made some kind of insane sense.

"Oh, yes, it's quite possible," Michael stated. "You betrayed me, son. You and your mother both did. You tried to kill me, but the dead never stay dead forever. Not when they're Farris men. We live on."

Someone else entered the room through the front door. It was Lehcar. She sneered at the two men, her eyes bulging. Her skin was ripped open and bloody.

"Eddie, Eddie, Eddie," she said. Michael seemed oblivious to her presence. "Didn't I say you are your old man?"

"I'm not!"

"But don't you see?" Lehcar calmly asked. "You never had any choice, Eddie. You're him, all over again. Here and now. You are your father's son."

"No, I'm not!"

"You're a crazy fuck," Michael said. "Must be from your mother's side of the family. You prove what everyone says. We're all as crazy as they think we are. Don't worry, I'll finish you off real soon, but I have some business to take care of first. You can't save your girlfriend, Eddie. You never could." He grinned. "Ashes to ashes, dust to dust, and all that jazz."

Eddie remained motionless, unable to think or move. His body refused to respond, like he was trapped in one of his nightmares. He watched his father casually walk to the stairs, his limp less pronounced now. Michael was headed for the fifth floor, but his words lingered behind him.

Ashes to ashes, dust to dust, and all that jazz.

Lehcar towered over Eddie like an angry Greek goddess. At first he thought she was surrounded by a wide aura, but then he realized it was only the overhead light burning through the threads of fog drifting into the lobby. Anger and fear flooded through his body, and his hands shook under his weight as he pushed himself to his feet and past the demon haunting him. He staggered to where Mattie's revolver had landed. He groaned, grabbing the gun before he fell again. Another hot lightning bolt of pain shot through Eddie, striking his nerves and setting them on fire.

"Don't do it! If you love anything or anyone, kill yourself! It's your last chance!"

"Shut up!" Eddie yelled, crossing the lobby, stumbling a little. "Leave me alone!"

"More people are going to die," Lehcar said, her voice like the whine of a sick baby. "Kill yourself!"

"Leave me alone," Eddie whispered. "Please leave me alone."

He regained his balance and took a few steps toward the open door to the stairwell. His head throbbed like a beating heart and he could hear the blood rushing through his veins, but he didn't have a moment to waste.

Chapter Forty-four

Then

Mattie St. Claire's body flew through the window, smashing the glass and snapping the wooden frame. Her body seemed to be folded in half, and she landed face-down on the floor with a thud. Drops of blood and shattered glass showered the carpet around her, splashing like a bucket of rainwater tipping off a roof. Her right leg was twisted awkwardly under her body. She didn't move.

"Mattie!" Laura screamed, dropping her forgotten cigarette. For an instant she looked like she was going to run, but then she simply fell to her knees and put her hands on the limp body. She began rolling her friend over, and everyone in the room saw Mattie's right eye. Or her lack thereof. The eye was gone. Blood dripped from the empty socket. Rachel screamed and jumped to her feet, nearly tripping. She pitched to the side, like a boat in heavy waves. She tried to make a run for the door. Now she *did* trip. She fell behind the couch, landing near the edge of the kitchen's linoleum floor.

Michael crawled through the broken window, the

glass cutting bloody streaks along his arms. He was soaked to the bone and his blue prison guard uniform was spotted with burgundy stains. His empty eye socket was blackened, although white bone showed at the edges. He held the sheriff's revolver in his blood-soaked hands.

"An eye for an eye," Michael said and laughed. His mouth opened to show a bloody, toothless smile. "I always said the Bible was right about that. It's my kind of attitude adjustment."

In the flickering candlelight, Eddie saw Mattie's fingernails had been savagely ripped out, leaving behind twisted fingertips. He couldn't help but imagine the pain, the screams of terror, the infinite horror Mattie had experienced. Laura must have seen the damage too, because she bent over, the sour contents of her stomach heaving out of her mouth and onto the motionless body of her friend.

"I had to pull them all," Michael explained. He held out a handful of blood-flaked fingernails, letting them fall to the floor. "I drove her right off the road! She never saw it coming! Good thing I found those pliers in her trunk. What would I have done without 'em? Lord, did she scream! I think she went mad! She screamed! Lord, did she ever."

"Why are you doing this?" Eddie demanded.

"Because I have to. Do you remember the ball game? Remember when you were crying in the eighth inning?"

Eddie did remember the incident. *I didn't earlier, though . . . Why?* Of course he knew why. He had blocked it out. He had forced the bad memories to disappear so he didn't have to deal with them. Like a lot of abused people, he was prone to fits of denial and suppression of memories, but he had been absolutely certain his father's mean streak hadn't begun until Mary's death. What the hell could this mean?

Eddie finally replied, "You smacked me."

"Because you were crying for a hot dog."

"Yeah," Eddie said.

"You were crying when you shouldn't have been," Michael said. "I had to fix you right then. You have to understand, Eddie. I have to fix you right now."

"Our family doesn't have to be like this," Eddie said, fear oozing through his veins. He watched his father's finger tighten on the trigger. His mind spun uncontrollably, and his life flashed before his eyes, blinding him.

"You can't be allowed to live, Eddie. I understand now. The shadows told me so, and they're never wrong." Michael pointed the revolver at Eddie's head, looked down at Laura, and said to his wife, "Say good-bye to your son."

"No!" Laura cried, vomit dripping out of her mouth and onto her shirt. She crawled past Mattie and reached up to her husband. She screamed, "Go away you bastard! Leave us alone or I'll kill you!"

Michael jammed the gun barrel into Laura's mouth with a quick shove. She gagged, her teeth breaking and flying into her throat. She began to choke, the sound raw and horrible. Michael slapped his wife, knocking the teeth loose. She fell backward, the gun slipping out of her mouth, the barrel covered in blood and the yellow, bubbling contents of her stomach. She put her hands up, reaching for her husband, like she was determined to strangle him even if it was the last thing she ever did.

Eddie screamed and lunged at his father. Michael cocked his fist and smashed it against his son's head. The teenager spun, collapsed next to where Mattie lay motionless. His vision faded as the world kept on spinning past him. He was blacking out.

I'm in hell, Eddie decided. He rolled, fighting the urge to let the darkness overtake him. He was sure death would be a lot less painful in the dark. Blood ran from his nose and his vision blurred. Above his head there was a loud explosion, but everything was slowly coming back into focus. He heard the crazed laughing of a madman in the distance, like he was at the far end of a tunnel. The sound surged at Eddie as his hearing returned. The laughs were deep, primitive, and savage. His vision was still fuzzy but no longer shaking. He pushed himself to his knees, and then to his feet, tipping a bit to the left, putting his arms out to keep his balance at the last second. He stared at his father with bitter confusion.

Eddie asked, "Why are you doing this to us?"

"Because you betrayed me," Michael said, his eye gleaming in the candlelight. He pointed at his dead wife. "You tried to kill me."

"Mom," Eddie whispered hoarsely. His mother's hair was a mess of blood and gray matter and he could see the fear frozen on her face. The rage boiling inside Eddie's gut spread throughout his entire body. "You killed her!"

"Shit happens, son. Ashes to ashes, dust to dust, and

all that jazz," Michael replied. He took a step forward. "Now I have to kill you."

"You're proving them all right!"

Michael stopped dead in his tracks. "What the fuck are you talking about?"

"Everyone in town. Everything they say about our family being crazy. They say we should be locked away in the asylum and you're proving them right."

"Well," Michael said, "I guess I am my father's son. And so are you."

Eddie held his ground. He knew one of them would not leave the apartment alive. Their conflict would end here. His entire life had been preparing him for this moment, and there was only one way he could escape the apartment to live another day. He and Rachel were probably as good as dead already, but he wasn't going to die on his knees like his mother had. He wouldn't give his father that satisfaction.

Don't go out like a coward, the voice in the back of Eddie's mind screamed. *If you're going to die, die like a man! Die fighting!* Eddie planned on doing exactly that.

"Dad, you can go to hell," Eddie said as he tensed his legs, took a deep breath, and dove forward, catching his father in the middle of his thick waist. Michael gasped. The revolver twisted upward and he pulled the trigger, sending a bullet through the ceiling.

They landed together on the blood-stained carpet and savagely fought for control of the gun. Michael kicked and punched in a vain attempt to gain the upper hand. Eddie's adrenaline rush quickened his thinking, strengthened his muscles, like he was a superhero no mortal could harm. Michael's finger slipped onto the trigger, and he squeezed it as hard as he could.

There was a loud noise under Eddie, similar to an engine backfiring. The bullet ripped through his right side and into the ceiling, adding another mark next to the first one, and his angry and surprised shriek cut through the apartment. He snatched at the gun, wrapped his hands onto the barrel, forcing his fingers through the trigger guard. He pushed into his father's flesh, and the bones in his fingers strained. He shoved his other hand onto his father's face and drove his index finger into the goo of the hollow eye socket.

"Goddamned muthafucker!" Michael screamed. He threw a hard punch into his son's right side, striking the bullet wound and knocking Eddie and the gun toward the broken window before the teenager could finish stabbing his finger into his father's brain.

Eddie roared, pain slashing through his side. He landed hard on the carpet. He rolled over, glass and pieces of the shattered wooden window frame cracking under his weight. Shards of glass sliced his hands as he pushed himself to his feet, grabbing the gun in the process. A warmth spread throughout his flesh directly above his hip. Eddie raised the gun.

Michael let out another barbaric laugh as he lay on the floor. He pushed himself to his feet in one motion. He smiled and said, "You're quick! Just like me! You'll always be just like me!"

"No," Eddie whispered, pointing the weapon at his father's heaving chest. Michael stood next to the bodies of his wife and her best friend. Behind him was the couch and the kitchen, and to the left of the kitchen was the door to the fifth-floor hallway, but the nightmare was going to end here. "I'll never be like you."

"Oh, but don't you understand, Eddie? I think you already are." Michael was running before his son had a chance to respond. Eddie quickly squeezed the trigger. The gun roared, kicking in his hand. The first shot missed wide to the right, the second missed to the left, but the third hit his father's right leg, sending a small spray of blood out behind the charging man. Michael staggered, growled, but he didn't stop.

Eddie squeezed the trigger, and everything moved in slow motion. He could see the last bullet exploding out of the barrel of the revolver. He heard the boom of the gun, but the sound was a million miles away.

Chapter Forty-five

Now

Eddie stood outside the door marked FIFTY-SEVEN, his chest rising and falling. He sucked in the stale air. He checked the hallway again. There was no one to be seen, although the fog pushed against the window at the end of the hall like it was alive and trying to get in. He put his hand on his right side in an attempt to smother the pain. He felt like one of his ribs was on fire.

"Why are you doing this?" Lehcar asked as she stepped out from the stairwell. "Why do you want to kill again? Do you really want more people to die?"

"I'll never hurt Rachel!" Eddie yelled, his voice cracking. He held the gun tightly, his arm shaking. Sweat dripped from his forehead and his eyes were wide with fear. *What the hell is going on? Why am I wasting my time talking to a hallucination? Why am I wasting Rachel's time? Adam's time?*

He knew why. He feared what he would discover when he opened the door. What if he wasn't able to save Rachel? Or Adam? How could Rachel love him if he didn't save their son? If she didn't love him, what would he do? Kill himself and get it over with?

Lehcar replied, "Oh, but you will. If you don't want to hurt anyone, I suggest you go ahead and put the gun to your head. You have plenty of bullets, but you only need one. Do it right!"

Eddie hesitated, and the voice of paranoia spoke: *Don't go in there! Rachel's gonna kill you because of what you did! If you open the door, you* will *die!*

"I have to help them!" Eddie yelled as he checked the doorknob. It was locked. There was no quiet method for doing what he needed to do, and even if there were, he didn't have the time it would take. He lifted his foot and kicked next to the doorknob. The door shook and his leg quivered in pain, but the lock held. He stumbled to the far wall.

"Fuck it," he muttered, raising the gun and firing two shots into the lock. Then he kicked again, and again, and the door flew open.

Eddie ran into the darkened apartment and called Rachel's name. His mind instantly flashed back to when he was fighting his father in this candlelit room, and the images overlapped before his eyes. He remembered the screams and the blood and the smell of death.

There was a flash of light to his right. Somebody was charging out of the bedroom, coming straight at him, arms outstretched. Eddie swung the gun in the direction of the movement, his mind reacting on pure, animalistic instinct. Sweat poured into his eyes and his vision blurred, but he knew it was his father. It had to be! The beast of a man was leaping at him, holding a gun the size of a brick in his right hand.

Eddie pulled the trigger, firing as rapidly as he could until the gun in his hand was clicking metal over and over. He saw his father reel, the rounds slamming into his massive chest. The gun was empty, but Eddie knew he had been in time. He had saved Rachel!

A moment later, a heavy body hit the floor.

Chapter Forty-six

From the Handwritten Account

My Mental Reconstruction of Events Past
by Eddie Farris

The doctors are pleased with my progress.

This has taken me almost a month to write, but they say I'm healing.

I might be able to leave tomorrow.

We'll see.

I feel the sharp pains in my side, like the bullet is still in there, searching for my heart.

I wrote a poem last night.

It's the first piece, other than this journal, I've worked on since I got here.

It was supposed to be an allegory about love.

It was supposed to be about how love can drive us all a little mad.

But it's really about something else.

"Black Fire of the Soul"
by Eddie Farris

James Kidman

A man's heart and soul are
filled with a fire that
burns in his words
and his actions and in his love.
Some men are
consumed by a white fire
and they do good for the world
and
they love life with a passion
that burns to and from everyone they meet.
Other men are consumed
by a black fire
and
they can be nothing
but evil.
They burn everyone they love,
they burn their spirit
and their mind.
A man is his own fire.
That is all he can be.
He has no say in what he becomes;
it is decided
long before
he ever steps forth
onto the earth.
A man cannot
change
the color of his fire.

It's rough, but it rings true for me.

My father had a black fire in his soul.

Yet for some reason, even with everything he did,

even with all the pain and misery of the past few years, I can't quite make myself hate him.

I don't think he had any control over his actions.

I don't think he wanted to be a bad person.

I love him, I think. I love my father.

He just had a black fire in his soul.

I don't know about mine.

Maybe the doctors can tell me when I leave.

This is how I killed my father: In the wavering light of the candles, I can see the smallest detail on the bullet. It moves in slow motion.

I watch the tiny piece of killing metal diligently rotating clockwise as it passes right below my father's heart.

As I wait for him to scream, I think of seven years ago, when I was eleven and my little sister landed face down in a stopped-up sink.

Kicking and screaming, the soapy water filling her mouth.

The soapy water sloshing inside her ears.

Her lungs.

Mary tries to scream, but her mouth is full of water.

And soap.

Her lungs begin to choke.

How did she get on the kitchen countertop? Why was she all alone? Where was my father?

I was in my room, writing and reading, and listening to the radio.

They played a bunch of my favorite songs. I sang along. I often do.

That's probably why I didn't hear Mary's cries.

Or the sound of her little legs kicking.

Kicking the air.

My mom was asleep in her bed. The previous night had been a long one for her.

Mary had been screaming, terrified by some nightmare.

My father had screamed even louder.

He never screamed at us until Mary came along.

But after she was born, my father began acting differently.

I've never understood why.

He began to work double shifts to get away from us. He began to drink. To yell. To hit. To kick.

He never left marks on my face, or my mother's.

He hit where no one would see the bruises.

He was very good at his job.

And on the day Mary drowned in six inches of water, my father claimed he was working in the garage.

Working on what, Dad?

Working on what?

He hadn't used his tools in forever, not since Mary was born.

One night, maybe a year later, he tried to explain her death to me. He was drunk, but this was a drinking binge to combat his depression instead of one fueled by rage. He didn't always get angry.

He burst into my room, woke me. His speech was slurred and none of what he said made much sense.

He said the voice in the shadows made him do it.

The voice in the shadows showed him the truth of his life. His destiny. He couldn't escape his fate.

The whole experience was like a dream, a very bizarre

dream, and sometimes I wonder if maybe his little talk about death and the shadows and destiny never really happened. Maybe it *was* just a dream.

The whole rant was drunken bullshit, but these days I consider the things he said.

Was the voice the creation of my dad's own insanity? An insanity controlling him? Or did the voice drive him insane?

Today none of that matters.

Today I am my father's judge.

I am his son.

And I have judged him guilty.

Guilty of murder.

There will be no plea bargain. There is no option of life without parole.

Poor Mary.

My poor mother.

Now I'm back in the living room of Rachel's apartment.

Gone is the past, gone is my sister.

For one-millionth of a second, my father looks surprised.

A tiny part of his chest opens up, and the bullet pierces his heart.

He smiles, but it is cold and demented.

Does he think of Mary? My mother?

I do. I think of them both.

And from the fear in his eyes, I think my father does too.

His heavy body falls forward, landing on the already bloody carpet.

He doesn't try to get up.

He doesn't move.

The scene is like the climax of every action movie I've ever seen, but this is real.

I feel my stomach churn.

Chapter Forty-seven

Then

Eddie's eyes shifted between the gun in his hand and the unmoving body of his father. There was no sign of life. Not even a flicker. He looked at Mattie and his mother, and he knew he had done the right thing. There had been no other way. He and Rachel wouldn't have left the room alive if his father had lived. They would have been carried out in black body bags by the sheriff's deputies for transportation to the morgue in Slade City. Their stories would have become a permanent source of town gossip. They'd spend eternity in cheap coffins in the ground, buried in the unmarked paupers' section of the Black Rock Cemetery. The paupers' section, where the unloved and unwanted rotted. Down the hill from the pet cemetery. Buried in the rocky earth with those who had no names.

Eddie studied the frozen expression of horror in his mother's eyes. A puddle of her brains and blood was spread across the floor.

"Rachel?" he whispered, his hand slipping to his right side, holding his throbbing wound. The gun dangled from his fingertips like some kind of alien appendage. "Are you okay? You can get up, Rachel, but . . ." He hesitated. "But face the kitchen. I don't want you to see any of this."

There was no response. He examined the blood-stained floor, the couch, and beyond. Finally he heard the rustle of clothes shifting and Rachel's voice.

"Eddie?" she whispered. She slowly stood, emerging from behind the couch like a flower blooming. Eddie watched her, but at first he didn't understand what he was seeing. She rose like a ghost. There was something wrong with the way she moved. "Eddie?"

In Rachel's abdomen, there was a small, dark hole leaking a trickle of blood.

She stared at him with strangely calm eyes. Her hands slid over the bullet wound. She glanced at the blood staining her fingers, then at her boyfriend. The revolver hung limply in Eddie's trembling hand. A whiff of smoke curled in the air between them from the cigarette still burning on the carpet.

"Eddie?" Rachel whispered again.

"Oh, oh God no!" he cried, dropping the gun and jumping over the bodies, forgetting his own wound. He vaulted the couch, his foot colliding with the end table. The phone rang as it slammed on the carpet and the receiver went flying onto the kitchen floor. Rachel's copy of *A Tear and a Smile* landed and flipped open to the page she had been trying to read shortly after they had entered the apartment.

Eddie caught Rachel's thin body in his arms as she stepped out from behind the couch and fell to her knees.

She gazed into his brown eyes, sad confusion washing across her pretty face.

"I love you," she said, a thin line of blood seeping from her lips. She coughed, blinked sleepily. She put a bloody hand onto Eddie's cheek and tenderly stroked his skin. "I'm sorry."

Chapter Forty-eight

Now

Eddie stepped past the body lying by his feet, not bothering to double-check whether his father was dead. He couldn't make out any features in the dark anyway, and he didn't want to see death ever again. His father wasn't coming back. The bullets had shredded his chest. Some had missed, ripping holes in the wall between the living room and the bedrooms, sending splinters flying in all directions, but at least two had struck Michael. He had hit the floor like a sack of cement, and he was finally as dead as dead could be.

"Rachel? Adam?" Eddie called. He headed to the open door to the larger of the two bedrooms. Biting his lips, he ignored the pain cutting through his right side. He walked into the room. The small black-and-white TV was flashing images of *The Tonight Show*, and the heavy green covers for the bed had been tossed on the floor. He called Rachel's name again, but she wasn't anywhere to be seen. He examined the three bullet holes dotting the open door behind him. Panic dragged Eddie back into the short hallway.

Oh fuck, what could he have done to her? No! Fuck no! I didn't move fast enough!

Eddie pushed open the door to the other bedroom. It was where he and Rachel had made love for the first time.

"Rachel? Are you okay?" Eddie flicked on the light. And then he froze. The bed was neatly made, and Rachel's teddy bears and childhood dolls were tucked under the covers. Candles lined the floor.

Eddie clutched the revolver to his chest and whispered, "What in the name of God?"

(A man's heart and soul are filled with a fire that burns in his words and his actions and in his love. A man cannot change the color of his fire.)

Wallpapering the room were dozens of tiny, cross-shaped mirrors surrounded by newspaper clippings and photographs from every stage of Rachel's life. Some of the photos were faded near the edges, a result of her mother's ancient Polaroid camera.

Why didn't you call her that night? Why'd you break your promise? a menacing voice in Eddie's mind asked, but he barely heard. He couldn't pull his eyes away from the photos. *If you had called . . .*

Some of the pictures were dotted with spots from the blazing sunlight, but many of them were pretty good. They all featured Rachel—playing at the beach when she was five years old, dressed up for her first day of kindergarten, hiking with the Girl Scouts in middle school, and standing in her costume as the Cowardly Lion for the class play sophomore year. There were several photos from when Eddie and Rachel went to the senior prom. Tabby had used up an entire roll of film before they managed to leave the apartment. The images had conveyed a love so inexpressible as to be absurd.

But now someone had cut Eddie out of every single picture hanging on the wall, as if he had never been a part of Rachel's life.

Chapter Forty-nine

Then

"It'll be okay," Eddie said, pressing his hands against the wound. Was he saying that to comfort her or himself? He didn't know. She was so warm, and the blood was hot and sticky. His own lifeblood mixed with hers. Terror rocked him. He desperately tried to think of something to say or do. He wanted to run to the door, to scream for help, but he couldn't leave her. She needed him. She was depending on him.

"I love you," Rachel whispered, running her fingertips across his face, leaving a line of blood on his flesh.

"I love you, Rachel. It'll be okay." Eddie put his hand on her chest. He could feel the beating of her heart slowing.

"Please don't let me go."

"I won't," Eddie whispered. "Never. I'll never let you go." His life flashing before his eyes, like *he* was the one leaving his earthbound body behind. He opened his mouth to say more, but then Rachel gasped and the rhythm under his hand stopped, and his mind lost sense of all rhyme and reason. The living, breathing human being in his arms was gone. And it was all his fault.

Eddie stared into Rachel's glassy eyes, her fingers on his face. Her body slipped to the floor. Her shoes pushed across the carpet, leaving tiny indentations in their wake. Eddie pulled the limp body against his. He repeatedly cried her name. It was all he could do. There was no more rational thought for him. Game over. Everything he had ever loved was gone.

When the police arrived, Eddie's vocal cords were rubbed raw, but his mouth was still open wide and trying to scream.

Chapter Fifty

Now

Eddie was lost and confused, his right side burning and his mind screaming as he searched for some sign of Rachel. Then he got a good look at the newspaper clippings, and his eyes widened. His flesh became very cold. Taped neatly on the wall, the articles told the story of the worst month of his life.

FARRIS MEN KILL FOUR IN ALL-DAY RAMPAGE

FARRIS VICTIMS LAID TO REST

EDWARD FARRIS NOT CHARGED IN MURDERS

SCHOLARSHIP IN RACHEL MATTHEWS'S NAME DEDICATED

BOOKS & NEWS TO REMAIN CLOSED AFTER NO BUYER FOUND

EDWARD FARRIS RELEASED FROM ASYLUM; PUBLIC PROTESTS PLANNED

"No! That's not right!" Eddie stepped out of the room. Fingers trembling, he turned on the light in the kitchen. When his eyes focused, he wanted to scream, but the air had rushed from his lungs. Terror overwhelmed him.

(Other men are consumed by a black fire, and they can be nothing but evil. They burn everyone they love; they burn their spirit and their mind.)

Tabby Matthews lay face down by the open front door. Eddie had forgotten how much heavier she had gotten during the last seven years. Her hair was rolled in curlers and her green-and-white nightgown was splotched with blood.

(. . . like I'm all alone in the store . . .)

"What the hell?" Eddie knelt and rolled the body over. Tabby's large breasts were perched on rolls of flab. Her skin had been stretched to its limits like she was bursting at the seams. A cracked hair dryer lay under her. She clenched it in a death grip, and her expression was a mask of fear.

(. . . like Rachel wasn't sitting there with me . . .)

Eddie touched the holes in Tabby's nightgown, as if he couldn't believe she was real. He put his hand on the floor where her blood was pooling, and then he held his trembling fingers in front of his eyes.

"No," he whispered, stumbling out of the apartment and into the hallway. Somewhere in the distance he heard doors opening, people gasping and screaming, and those same doors slamming shut as locks were hastily fastened, but he blocked the sounds out.

(. . . like I'll never see her again . . .)

"Where's Rachel? Adam? Where's my father? I don't understand!" Eddie dropped to his knees, the gun hanging limply from his hand. He stared through the open doorway at the body, a strange giddiness growing within him. Bloody footprints led from the apartment, and Tabby Matthews watched him with cold, dead eyes.

"Oh, Eddie, what don't you understand?" Lehcar emerged from the shadows. She sounded genuinely upset. She put a cold hand on his shoulder. "Have you completely missed the point of what I tried to show you?"

"What point?" Tears streamed down Eddie's face.

"You've known for a long time, but you couldn't stand the truth," Lehcar replied quietly. "You blocked the memories and I failed to bring them to the surface. I'm sorry I couldn't help you more, but now you'll do what you have to do. A man cannot change the color of his fire."

She disappeared, and Eddie screamed into the depths of the darkened hallway. He demanded she return and explain what the hell was going on. What had she had done to him? To Rachel? To Adam? To his father?

But there were no more answers coming from Lehcar. Eddie was all alone in the hallway. He started crawling blindly for the stairs.

Lost memories of the last seven years flooded his mind. He remembered his extended stay at the asylum after the killings, the sessions with the counselors, the struggle to write in the makeshift journal while the drugs caused his mind to become foggy, the way the doctors had taught him to be normal again. With crystal clarity he saw how the people in Black Hills had reacted when he was finally released. The protests. The chants.

Often, in the middle of the night, he had taken long walks to the edge of town. Sometimes he stopped at the Richard Street Apartments, just to be there. Eventually he began visiting Mattie's abandoned bookstore. He remembered sitting on the concrete steps and gazing in through the dirty windows. Someone had taken the bookstore's stock and given it to the library, and no one ever bought the building. The front door had been put back on its hinges and boarded up, but Eddie soon learned they hadn't secured the back door very well. He had been able to pry it open without much effort.

"How long was I going there?" Eddie whispered as he crawled, the gun clutched in his hand. He vaguely remembered breaking into the office area and exploring the dusty, cobweb-covered store. He had marched back and forth inside the shop for hours on end, imagining how life would be different if Mattie and Rachel had lived. In the middle of the night he took books from his apartment and arranged them on the shelves in the bookstore, as if Mattie were alive and her shop was open for business. He did this in secret. No one could see him or it would ruin the fantasy. He had moved in the shadows and fog, watching for suspicious eyes following him.

When did I lose it? He didn't know, but he finally understood. At some point he had snapped. The lines between reality and his fantasy world had blended together. Everything after The Showdown with his father had blurred. The memories and the nightmares and Lehcar and all the daydreams had become his reality. *No Rachel. No Mattie. No father. No Adam . . . no son.*

In the distance a siren wailed through the night. Eddie reached the door to the stairs. He stopped. He didn't want to leave the building. This was where the horror had ended the last time, and it seemed right that he stay here now.

Ashes to ashes, dust to dust.

"I am my father's son," Eddie whispered, pulling himself up onto the window ledge.

His right side no longer ached. The pain had faded away.

He considered the nightmares and the stories he had photocopied at the newspaper's office. In the funny, poorly lit room in the basement. The one they call The Morgue. He had spent so much time reading those articles and recreating the events in his mind. Now he understood why he had used a black marker to edit the stories and the letters to the editor about his father and the shooting. Without his corrections, they would have stopped him from believing in the fantasy he had created for himself. They were the same articles Tabby kept framed on her dead daughter's wall as a memorial. As a shrine.

(They burn everyone they love; they burn their spirit and their mind. A man is his own fire. That is all he can be.)

Eddie's mother had once said he had a vivid imagination, and she had been right. After he did his research into his family's history, he had spent weeks contemplating the horrible things the men in his family had done. Some days he imagined the murders from the victim's point of view, and other days he saw it from the eyes of the killer.

"We get away with our crimes, us Farris men," Eddie said. He tried to remember the conclusions he had drawn from his research, the events he had seen in the dreams. George Farris murdered his daughter and dozens of innocent patients at the asylum. Jonathan Farris released his inner rage by putting razor blades in the pies. He got his revenge on the town he blamed for his father's death by killing six of their girls. Kurt Farris killed his wife and told everyone it had been an accident. Michael Farris killed his daughter. He held her down in the sink until she stopped kicking, until the bubbles stopped dotting the water around her tiny waist that stuck out like a ship disappearing into the depths of the ocean forever. Then he killed Eddie's mother. And Mattie. And although Michael got what was coming to him in the end, the carnage of his last rampage would never be forgotten.

Yet Eddie realized his conclusions hadn't gone far enough. Although none of the men had ever gone to jail, they had all paid for their crimes.

George cut his own throat a few years after he burned the part of the asylum where his deformed daughter slept. On the seventh anniversary of Martha Farris's death, Jonathan hanged himself from the same tree that was used to lynch his mother. Kurt died when he flipped his truck on Main Street, and Eddie was almost certain it hadn't really been an accident. Most likely Kurt had spent the years consumed by guilt, then he awarded himself one last wild night with a hooker from Pittsburgh before killing himself, taking the streetwalker with him. Taking two lives for the price of one was somehow in keeping with the family spirit, wasn't it?

And Michael . . . well, Michael had gotten what he asked for, hadn't he? Murder by son.

But, no, that wasn't right.

Michael had probably planned to kill Eddie first, and then take his own life. Maybe he had a good reason. Maybe he had understood the truth his son would need years to discover. Death was the only escape. The shadows had told him that was how it had to be, after all.

As Eddie sat quietly by himself, alone with his thoughts, he wondered if all the Farris men had been haunted by their own versions of Lehcar. He couldn't be certain, but part of him was pretty sure he was on the right track. Maybe nothing quite like Lehcar, but there must have been some inner voice warning them they would never stop killing the ones they loved. The voice in the shadows.

Now Eddie was the last man left on the Farris family tree.

"It's gonna end here," he said. The paranoid voice inside his head was gone, just like Lehcar. He wondered if they had been one and the same. Not that it mattered anymore.

Eddie stroked the gun and watched the fog dance within the lights lining the streets of Black Hills. There was something very comforting about the sight. He remembered all the times he and Rachel had sat on the ledge and discussed running away to Pittsburgh. Between them they had shared so many plans and dreams, but he had killed their hopes. He had killed her.

Ashes to ashes, dust to dust.

Soon the flashing mosaic of red-and-blue lights bathed the street below, and Eddie saw the dark figures moving through the fog. He caressed the dull-colored barrel of Mattie's revolver again. He had become his father. No matter how hard he had tried to prevent it, he had failed.

At least the pain would end soon.

Somewhere in the back of Eddie's mind children chanted, *Down by the river, down by the sea . . .* And, if he listened closely enough, he was convinced he could hear Lehcar's voice too. Maybe she wasn't actually gone for good, but merely hiding in the shadows. Maybe she was waiting for the right occasion to reappear. Eddie tried to block the words, but it did no good. They were etched into his mind, engraved on his soul. He couldn't escape the taunts and the accusations and the truth of who and what he was.

"I am my father's son, but I'll be the last," he whispered. He put his hand in his pocket, removing the box of ammo waiting there. He carefully selected six more bullets. He loaded the revolver. "I can't change my fire, but I can kill it, I think. I hope."

(A man cannot change the color of his fire.)

"I can make my fire die." Eddie slowly returned his gaze to the flashing lights below. There was a lot of movement down there now, but he couldn't distinguish many details through the fog. He heard someone shouting orders. He saw police officers ducking behind the two patrol cars blocking the road. People were standing on the street, gathering with a sense of morbid curiosity. Eddie suspected they were already gossiping. Soon they would have even more to talk about over their morning coffee, while picking up their mail, and at the town council meeting at the beginning of next month. They would always remember his name. He was going to be famous.

The fog devoured everything. The people became the shadows of shadows, disappearing into the night. They were slipping into the quiet grip of the fog that danced and swayed in the street. Although Eddie was only five stories up, everyone seemed small and powerless. He wondered what they would do when they found him with the gun, when they found the body in the apartment. What would the townspeople say? Would they be relieved the horror was over? Would they ask each other what sort of horrible mental illness could drive a person to do what he had done? Eddie didn't know for sure, but he knew what he had to do.

Not just yet, though. He had a few more minutes before he had to go. So he sat and looked out at the fog. He loved the way it flowed through the town, like a quiet stream in the woods, gentle and peaceful. There was something so natural and perfect about the motions. He sat and he watched. And then Eddie smiled.

At times the fog moved like it was alive.